WING AND A MISS

Deadlights Cove
Book 3

B. PERKINS

AIMEE VANCE

Revel Books

Revel Books
ISBN: 979-8-9863649-6-4

To anyone who needs the reminder that sometimes the most courageous act is knowing when to accept help.

SELENE

Prologue

Three Months Ago

"So glad you came with me," Petra yelled in my ear, her voice barely audible over the loud bass as she pulled a piece of cotton candy off a stick. Lysander and his band, The Lost Talisman, had just retaken the stage at Blaze's annual Halloween party, and I looked over the crowded beach.

Nudging her with my shoulder, I smiled at my best friend. Her red hair was held back by a black ribbon bow, the blue dress with white pinafore making her the perfect Alice in Wonderland. We'd picked out costumes a few days ago in Boston, and my cape lifted in the breeze. Devanna had spelled my normally dark hair platinum blonde for tonight, and a small, stuffed black dragon perched on my shoulder, making sure everyone knew exactly who I was.

Khaleesi.

The Mother of Dragons.

Daenerys Targaryen.

Was I late to the Game of Thrones obsession? Yes.

Did I know how it ended? Also yes.

Did I care? Nope. Not one bit. That bitch rode a dragon, and nothing was cooler than that.

Petra pinched off another piece of cotton candy, holding it out for me, but I shook my head no, sipping at my empty drink in hopes it would magically refill itself. Considering everyone at this party but Petra was some sort of supernatural, it wasn't a total impossibility. It was strange to see my two very separate worlds collide like this, but the ever-present itchy feeling I'd had every other time I'd returned home since my mom had passed away wasn't there tonight.

Nothing was the same without her, but Deadlights Cove was changing. In my mind, everything here should have been frozen in time, a fragile picture of what life used to be like and never would again. But now, seeing my human best friend mingling among the supernaturals I'd grown up with… it was different.

I was different.

Maybe I was ready for new memories. To find a way to blend my former life with my current one.

Staring into my empty cup, I tried to think of the words to a spell that might refill it, but my mind was blank. Any spells I'd once known had been replaced by the medical jargon I'd spent the last 10 years focusing on as I ran from my past.

"Having fun, ladies?" Blaze shouted as he worked his way towards us through the crowd, two cups held aloft. Tiny white angel wings fluttered in the breeze behind him, his normally chaotic dark hair brushed into a severe combover. I bit my cheeks to keep myself from laughing at his costume, dressed like the overbearing mayor of our town, Orion.

"You look ridiculous," Petra snorted, taking the cups from Blaze's outstretched hands and giving one to me.

Blaze grinned, teeth flashing as he waggled his brows before wiping the expression off his face and adopting a far more serious look. "Sorry. I forgot I'm not supposed to smile. And I've only sighed twice tonight. Need to up that count if I want to be believable. Maybe I should shine my boat shoes. Whip out an iron and fix some tablecloths. Go annoy Devanna. Something."

I laughed, stacking my new cup over the empty one still in my hand, giving up on the idea of magically refilling it. "Is Orion still here or did he leave early?"

"He's here somewhere." Blaze waved vaguely towards the crowded beach, lit by the low moon hanging over the ocean to our right. "I saw him at the bar with Ryker earlier, about to start a grump-off."

"Sounds fun." I tried to sound disinterested as my brain picked up on the name he'd mentioned. I'd met the reclusive dragon shifter at Morgaine's house a few weeks ago, and he and his bike were hard to forget. Standing on my tiptoes, I scanned the beach, looking for a blond head above the crowd, knowing of only one male in Deadlights Cove who wore his hair tied up in a man bun like that.

Petra shivered and Blaze dropped an arm around her shoulders, pulling her away from me. "Gonna get my girl settled in front of a fire. You coming, Selene?" Blaze asked, but I waved them off, not feeling the third-wheel role tonight.

"I'll find you later," Petra said over her shoulder, and I smiled.

Blaze and Petra were an odd pair, but I loved the way he

doted on her. Petra's friendship over the last decade had been unexpected and exactly what I'd needed. I was thrilled to see her happy, even if it left me feeling the weight of my loneliness. We'd lived together for years, and I missed my best friend.

"Snap out of it, Selene," I scolded myself, looking around the crowd for Nimue and Devanna, my two childhood friends who were both here somewhere. I took a gulp of the drink from Blaze, ready for a buzz to kick in. The fruity taste washed over my taste buds as I swallowed, looking down into the cup. "Damn, that's good."

Without a thought, I headed towards the bar, hoping Maia or whoever was working tonight could make another one of whatever this was. Not watching where I was going, I slammed right into a wall, my drink splashing out of the cup and down the front of my costume.

I jumped back, hands held wide as I looked down at the red liquid on my tunic, then noticed the motorcycle boots in front of me. Frowning, I studied the boots — not a wall — before my eyes trailed up a pair of long legs, then over a giant torso, all the way up to a tattooed neck, and a severe face, topped with a blond man-bun.

Holy hell, why was Ryker so unbelievably attractive? Imagine if Chris Hemsworth and Charlie Hunnam had a baby, then tattooed every square inch of his pale skin and topped it with the sexiest haircut only a handful of men could pull off. It was unfair how beautiful this male was, and my buzz lent me just the hint of a fiery temper at the injustice.

"Watch where you're going," Ryker's deep voice rumbled, his blazing green eyes focused on me as he took a napkin from the bar and wiped the liquid from his leather jacket.

"How about you not be so huge and in the way?" I shot back, not sure whether I was annoyed that he'd blamed me, or that my body wanted to hurl itself at him. "Surely your view from way up there is better than mine."

Ryker's jaw worked, forcing me to focus on his trim beard, and I wondered what it would feel like against my skin before he did me a favor by reminding me of his personality when he grunted, "You are unusually short, even for a woman."

I sighed, gulping back the last of my drink because yep, I was annoyed with how attracted I was to this man. Watching my friends fall in love had me on the horny side of lonely, and that was always dangerous.

A shoulder bumped into me, and I went flying towards Ryker again, but his hands came out to catch me before I fell. "Are you drunk?"

I glowered, staring up at him. "Just because you're gorgeous does not mean you get to be an asshole."

He chuckled, and dammit, this man did not need a dimple.

I lurched forward again, and I turned, ready to tell off whoever kept bodyslamming me, only to come face to face with Julian and Lily. I recoiled, stepping towards Ryker as I put distance between myself and the couple who were so deep into a makeout session they hadn't noticed me.

"She can't be enjoying that." I pointed at the way Julian's tongue darted into her mouth, surely cutting off Lily's air supply. "No finesse. All force. She's gasping, and not in a good way. I'd give it a 2.5 out of 10."

"Takes some males a couple hundred years to put their needs second," Ryker agreed, throwing Julian a look of disdain before his eyes slid back to me. "To realize the more they give, the more they get. Isn't that right, Khaleesi?"

For a split second, his eyes almost seemed to glow, but maybe that was a trick of the moonlight. Whatever it was, the air between us grew tense, and my mouth went dry at the implication behind his words. A bead of sweat dripped down my chest, trailed by the molten heat his attention spread in me.

"Hm," I offered intelligently, taking a long gulp of my empty cup as I tried to gather my wits. Smooth, Selene. "Hard to say. It's been a while."

Ryker tilted his head, his gaze sliding past me to where vehicles had parked at the edge of the beach — among them, his gleaming Harley. "I'll change that."

I choked on the last of my drink, struggling to swallow, and Ryker's thumb lifted to brush across my lips, cleaning up the alcohol that had dribbled out. It shouldn't have been sexy, but the swoop in my stomach begged to differ.

He stepped past me, deliberately brushing against my shoulder with his giant Viking chest, then stopped a few paces away. Brow cocked. An invitation, or a challenge.

I moved to follow him, but not before "accidentally" tripping, my cup of ice miraculously falling directly down the back of Julian's shirt. He yelped, pulling off Lily's face, but by the time he looked around to find the culprit, I was gone, hidden by Ryker's massive form.

"Sneaky witch," he murmured, his breath ghosting the shell of my ear.

I opened my mouth to reply, but warm hands grabbed

my waist, lifting me into the air and depositing me on the back of Ryker's bike.

A helmet was shoved into my arms, and Ryker climbed on in front of me, the engine roaring to life.

"Ready for the ride of your life, Flores?"

Chapter One

SELENE

Lifting the hem of my emerald midi-dress, I leaped over the mountain of snow on the sidewalk. For the millionth time, I wondered what had possessed my mother to move us from warm, sunny, tropical French Polynesia to the Arctic tundra of New England. It was a question I'd asked her many times throughout my childhood — our living room walls adorned with photos of sandy beaches and palm trees as her reminder of home. She'd always said she wanted a fresh start and to be with her kind — witches.

Later, I learned she'd needed that start, not having the best living situation back home. First, her family was not accepting of having a practicing witch in the family. Then my biological father — or, as I typically thought of him, *sperm donor* — was far from honorable.

But these pointless questions aimed at my mother's spirit were nothing more than a distraction from the question I needed to ask myself: Why was I even bothering?

My breath fogged as I stopped, staring up at the night sky as I headed out to yet another internet date. Nimue's wedding in November had been a rude awakening that it was time to put myself back out there. Suffice it to say, I was in the middle of a string of bad luck.

My last date? An amateur taxidermist. "I find the carcasses myself," he'd informed me proudly. *Gag.*

The one before that didn't know how to shut up about himself. After five minutes of him talking nonstop about his start-up, I'd discreetly started the timer on my watch. It took him twenty-five minutes before he directed a single question my way, and that question had been, "Do you want to see our design portfolio?"

No, Todd. No, I did not.

Yet here I was, like Charlie Brown with the freaking football, heading out for another date right after a nor'easter had blown through and left a foot-and-a-half of snow on the ground. It was pretty at first, the fresh blanket of sparkly white, but overnight it turned into piles of grey and brown with stretches of solid ice for good measure.

You had to love Boston to live here. Especially in January.

I was almost afraid to get my hopes up, but I wanted to think this guy seemed promising. Mark was an orthodontist, so hopefully he wouldn't be intimidated by the fact I was a doctor. We talked online for the past week, and, so far, had a good enough rapport to risk an actual date.

He'd picked a boutique wine bar in Cambridge to meet at, so one point for Mark. Steeling myself, I approached and saw him waiting by the cast-iron railing for me, even though it had to be no more than 20 degrees — another point.

"Selene?" he asked in confirmation, and I smiled.

"Mark?" I shot back, and he nodded, the corners of his

eyes crinkling. Not quite a smile, but not everyone was a smiler.

Mark was only a few inches taller than me, which was saying something because I stood just above five feet. His black hair was styled nicely, and his glasses framed a decent, albeit forgettable, face. Everything about him seemed polar opposite to my own tan skin and brown curly hair. But what mattered most was that he had not even an inch of resemblance to the image of someone *else* I'd seen in my head thousands of times since last Halloween. Just as I'd intended. "I hope you haven't been waiting long."

"Just a few minutes," he said and held out a hand to lead the way inside.

We got through all the superficial date talk — siblings, career, favorite travel destinations — in the few minutes it took for our appetizers and wine to arrive, and then conversation stalled out.

I grabbed a pita triangle and took a healthy scoop of spinach and artichoke dip. Just because our date was awkward didn't mean I had to lose out on a decent meal.

"Any hobbies?" I tried, taking a sip of my cabernet as our waitress caught my eye. *Keep 'em coming,* I tried to signal to her telepathically, but that wasn't a power witches like me possessed. We should have just requested the bottle.

"Work keeps me pretty busy," he admitted. "But in my spare time, I do consider myself something of an *'artiste.'*"

Huh, air quotes. Was he mocking himself, or other people who used that word?

"What type of art?" I asked, giving him the benefit of the doubt.

"I like to forge *'historically accurate'* weaponry."

I narrowed my eyes — not at the strange hobby, although that certainly raised some red flags, but at the second seemingly out-of-place use of air quotes.

"Oh, really?" I asked, tilting my head politely. "Where can you even do that?"

"There's a community artisans' workshop in Somerville."

Of course there was.

"They have all sorts of *'equipment'* you can use with a monthly fee to specific studios."

There they were again. Was this a nervous tick? I tried to ignore it. "What sorts of weapons? Or era?"

"Well, I have a personal penchant for the traditional 14th-century *'longsword.'*" He raised his eyebrows.

Was that an innuendo? And the air quotes again! I pulled my hands down into my lap, gripping them tightly to keep myself from reaching across the table and batting his hands out of the air.

"Fascinating," I said, hoping my voice didn't sound as flat to him as it did in my head. As he continued rattling off about medieval weaponry with unnecessary air quotes, I glanced at my watch under the table and set my timer.

The clock was still running — thirty-four minutes, fifty-two seconds of non-stop weaponry monologue — when my watch showed an incoming call from Orion, of all males. My eyes widened in shock, and I held up a hand to silence Mark. A stunned expression crossed his face at my audacity for interrupting his seminar about how the longsword later came to be replaced by the Swiss saber in some parts of Europe. Not waiting for him to acknowledge my silent request, I whipped out my phone and slid to answer the call.

There was only one reason the Mayor of Deadlights Cove would call me unexpectedly.

"What's happened?" I asked, mindful of the way the to-the-point mayor preferred to communicate.

"You need to get up here immediately," came his deep, solemn voice with not a note of inflection. "If you're not at home, get to a discreet location, share it with Blaze, and he'll pick you up in a few minutes." He paused before continuing, his tone sharpening in a way that had my heart rate speeding up. The male was distraught. "We have an emergency."

He hung up.

"So," I dropped my phone into my purse, already standing. "This has been… Well, I have to go. Medical emergency." He stood too, brow furrowed.

"Oh, okay," he said, perplexed, probably thinking I'd scheduled an emergency call with a friend in case the date was a disaster. Not a bad idea for the future, if I was being honest. "Was it the *weapons*?"

Well, it wasn't *not* the *'weapons,'* Mark.

"Sorry, I just really have to go." I was already pulling my coat back on, thankful I hadn't checked it. I needed to get somewhere no one would see Blaze and me disappearing into thin air. "Listen, I'll text you, but I have to run."

With that, I turned to go, figuring I could probably find a dark enough alley to hide from passersby, Mark spluttering behind me.

Back out in the street, for once I was glad it got dark so

early here in January, and I ducked around the corner of a brick building to slip behind a dumpster in the alley. I shared my location with Blaze, one of the demons in Deadlights Cove who was something of Orion's right-hand-male as well as being the one dating my best friend and former roommate Petra, and waited.

Whatever was going on, it couldn't be good. Orion had never called in my contract before.

The supernatural government agency, the Paranormal Regulation and Interspecies Council, that oversaw all supernatural towns and laws had technically paid for my education — from my first year at Bishop College through my medical training — and in return? All they asked was that I would be available anywhere, day or night, in case of a medical emergency to the supernatural community. As a witch *and* a doctor, I was one of the few supernaturals in the world who had the breadth of training to handle almost any situation that might come up, whether I needed to use magic or medicine.

Since most supernaturals possessed enhanced healing abilities, it had seemed pretty far-fetched that they would ever need me, so I'd taken the deal. I figured they just liked to have an insurance policy — a few supes around the world who could use both interchangeably, just in case something ever happened.

And now, obviously, something had.

Just then, Blaze appeared out of thin air in front of me — flickering, as demons called it — the usually olive complexion of my half-demon-half-witch friend paler than I'd ever seen it. His brown hair, while typically windswept, was even more unkempt than usual, and the corners of his eyes seemed crinkled in concern rather than amusement.

"Is that —" I pointed to his grey t-shirt, where I could have sworn I saw blood splatters.

"Yes," he said, gripping my forearm. He surveyed where we were standing. "Wait, this is where your date was? No wonder they've all been shitty." He eyed the dumpster with disgust. Clearly, Petra had spilled the tea about my series of dating mishaps.

"Not here," I waved at the building. "Inside."

"Right," he said, still sounding unconvinced. "Anyway," I closed my eyes — flickering was not my favorite mode of travel — but his next words had them shooting right open again. "Ryker's been shot."

Chapter Two

RYKER

Sixteen hours earlier

The night was silent around me as I soared over Siksa Village, invisible to those below. After a thousand years, my glamour's reach had extended beyond just humans to conceal me even from supernaturals. As a dragon the size of a semi-tractor trailer, I greatly appreciated this. Nothing mattered more to me than my freedom.

Here, on the coast of Alaska, the crisp Arctic air reminded me of home. Of a time long forgotten by everyone but me.

My wings beat in the night air, heavy with an incoming storm carrying snow from the coast. Soon, everything below would be dusted in a fresh coat of white.

It had been four months now since Morgaine had called in her favor last September, and I'd returned to Deadlights Cove. Four months hunting witches and demons. Four months of uncovering answers and dead-ends, in turn.

It was infuriating.

By the time the angels were done questioning the witches at the trial in the Cove last November, they'd exposed more of their plan to pull magical power from the ley lines, and I'd taken the opportunity to leave without a second thought. I needed to be free of the small town.

Errakal, Blaze's brother and the demon-witch at the center of all of our magical problems, was still on the run, and each day that he avoided capture felt like waiting for the other shoe to drop. Magic hummed under my skin in a too-long game of Whack-A-Mole with the male, drawing me down to the town below. I dipped my wings and lowered myself to just above the water, floating on air as an orca surfaced, sending a spout of water directly into my mouth.

Not an orca, then, if it could see through my glamour. A sea nymph, and a powerful one at that.

I rose up to avoid the sea plane parked at the dock amongst the fishing boats, and skirted the tops of the buildings, heading for one I'd become familiar with over the years.

Without missing a beat, I landed smoothly on the roof, intentionally built as a landing pad for this purpose. Instantly, my large dragon form shrank, pulling back into my towering human frame. What little moonlight shone through the clouds glistened off my naked skin as I held out my palm, waiting for my magic to summon my clothes back to me. Black jeans, just as I preferred. I pulled them over my tattooed legs and fastened them right as the door from the building onto the roof opened.

"Timed that correctly, I see." Tulok's deep voice carried over the night, his hand blocking my half-dressed form through cracked fingers. I pulled my long blond hair into a knot at the top of my head as I took in the male: his tan skin clear and ageless, his long, black hair parted in the center and worn loose, hanging nearly to his waist. He wore jeans and a puffy vest over just a t-shirt, despite the fact that the temperature was in the teens with a biting wind.

"What's the matter, Tulok?" I asked as I summoned a black tee into my hand. "Intimidated by my wingspan?"

Tulok dropped his hand as he walked towards me, deliberately avoiding my comment, and warmth seeped through me at his lack of acknowledgment. While he wasn't as uptight as Orion, the mayor back in Deadlights Cove, Tulok, an eagle shifter, was far from relaxed. I wasn't as bad as Blaze when it came to needing to ruffle feathers, but I got a sense of satisfaction in reminding everyone just how unique I was. A normal human might have smiled, but I was far from normal. And definitely not human.

"Yura said you were hovering today, and I want to know why."

I nodded, still holding my shirt in my hand, solely to make Tulok uncomfortable. After all, he was the one who'd barged in on me. "I was checking the ley lines for any sense of disruption."

"Disruption?"

"Any of your shifters lose the ability to shift, or notice any other differences in their senses or powers?" I clarified, pulling the shirt on and magicking my boots back as well before he led the way to the door down to the lobby of the town hall. Siksa Village had a much smaller operation going than Deadlights Cove — one office unit in a block that housed town hall, a combination general store/post office, and a restaurant/movie theater.

"Unable to shift? Shit," Tulok's voice echoed in the stairwell as he thought it over. We emerged down in the main lobby, its decor much more rustic than the town hall in the Cove. The furniture was made of carved logs, every painting was of the surrounding Alaskan landscape, and multiple buck heads adorned the walls. Since it was night, the rest of the place was empty but for us.

Crossing the main floor — a couple chairs strewn about in case of meetings — Tulok made his way behind a counter, sliding open a drawer to pull out a bottle of vodka and two glasses. With a flick of the lid, he poured us each a few ounces, then slid one across the counter to me as he sighed.

"I haven't heard any complaints," he said, leaning his elbows on the counter. "But I can ask around in the morning. What have you heard?"

"There's a half-demon-half-witch pulling magic from the ley lines," I told him, taking a healthy sip. Tulok's deep brown eyes flashed a light yellow before they turned back. "Half the shifters in Deadlights Cove were stuck for several days until they sorted it out."

"Shit," he breathed. "What makes you think that demon would come here next?"

I shook my head. "Maybe not here, but Errakal will try again somewhere. We interrupted him in the Cove before he was able to finish his spell, but he escaped, flickering out at the last minute. I'm checking in with every supernatural community that has a significant concentration of ley power.

I stopped in Timber Creek, Colorado on my way over, and Larkin said a few of his lone shifters on the outskirts have noticed that shifts seem to take longer than usual, increasing the pain between forms, but nothing like what happened in Deadlights Cove."

Tulok finished his drink, holding up the bottle to ask if I wanted another, but I waved it away. "Sticking around till morning to ask the villagers yourself, or should I just text you tomorrow?"

Rolling my neck, I took a deep inhale of the crisp pine air that pervaded every inch of this village. Well, that along with the sea salt and fish. "I'll stay the night; I've been flying for a few days straight."

He shot me an unreadable look before beginning, "I think Aoko is in town —"

But I cut him off with a look. It was hard for most other shifters — predominantly pack creatures — to fathom that Aoko and I, two of the last dragons in the world and certainly the only two on this continent, didn't much care to seek each other out. We were a solitary species to begin with, but even more than that, Aoko and I had never seen eye to eye. In fact, most dragons didn't really get along with each other. We tended to be arrogant, prideful assholes. In Aoko's and my case, she and I were like fire and water. Literally.

"Right." He cleared his throat. "Well, the trailer is free."

A downgrade even from The Last Resort in the Cove, Siksa Village had a single guest trailer for visitors — really rolling out the welcome wagon.

"Perfect." I deadpanned, but he knew me enough to know it was sarcasm. Maybe.

With a final swig of vodka straight from the bottle, Tulok screwed the top back on and slid it back in the drawer. I followed him out of the building, using my magic to pull a leather jacket to me for the brisk walk to the far edge of town.

The next morning — if it could be called that, since the sun wasn't coming up for a while — Tulok gathered some of the heads of the local shifter communities back at Town Hall. Relaying the news I'd brought, he asked if any of them had noticed anything unusual. Unfortunately, none of them had.

I exhaled sharply through my nose — in dragon form, it showed my frustration more expressively, since sparks came out with the air. How many more towns would be dead ends?

Two months now I'd been on this pointless mission, flying around, following ley lines, pinpointing nexus points to feel for changes in the power, and worst of all — *talking* to people. Lots of them. I tried to suppress my scowl that there would be more of that to come.

Two months of tracking Errakal, and missing him by days, sometimes hours, each time. Even trying to be proactive, like my visit here to the Village, hadn't gotten me any closer to him. Errakal didn't seem to have a pattern to his movements, and the few attacks he had made were briefer than they had been in Deadlights Cove. No bodies had been left in his wake, unlike in the Cove. But rather than being reassured by this, I couldn't help but feel like he was building up to something bigger, something *more*. With each near miss, my anger for the demon-witch grew.

"I'll keep you posted if we hear of anything strange happening," Tulok said as I hopped up the steps to the roof. "Take care of yourself, old friend."

I grunted in agreement, and shifted to my dragon form. Pale, tattooed skin transformed into black and gold glittering scales, the hum of power surging in my veins as it did every time I shifted. Wings unfurled, snapping in the wind as I glanced out at the snowy landscape one more time, then leaped into the air.

Fed up with yet another inconsequential stop, I decided to head straight back to the Cove. I needed the long flight ahead of me to clear my head, and think of a new plan of action.

Somewhere over the Great Lakes, I felt a strange buzzing along my power, like a tingle of electricity deep in my veins. Nothing like that had ever happened before, so I scanned the world below me, searching for anything out of place.

My vision in dragon-form was far superior to that of a human's, but still, I couldn't see anything.

As the buzzing continued, I dipped lower, hovering just above a small town on the water's edge of Lake Erie, concealment glamour still in place. Nothing of any interest showed here in Ohio, but I searched for *anything* as my intuition began rapid-firing that something was wrong.

Just as I spotted movement to my right, I turned.

My leg exploded in pain.

The bullet that was aimed for my heart hit my thigh, and pain like I'd never experienced shot through my body. I bellowed, fire erupting from my mouth as I careened through the sky, and I felt my glamour shift, releasing its hold.

Shit.

Humans cried out below me, and I beat my wings hard, inching back into the clouds to hide myself.

I just had to make it to the Cove.

Keep going.

Keep… going…

Chapter Three

SELENE

A wave of heat exploded over my skin as Blaze flickered us onto a rooftop overlooking the Cove. I rested my hands on my knees as I tried to get my bearings and stop the head-spinning that always accompanied flickering. Moonlight sparkled off the water in the distance, but we were pretty far out from the rest of town. This was Ryker's roof.

"Ah, shit," Blaze mumbled, pulling me further away from the scene before me.

A massive black dragon lay sprawled on the roof, a dark pool of blood beneath him, the gold tips of his wings shimmering in the moonlight.

"Ryker," Orion said where he stood closest to the dragon, albeit still at a distance. Despite Orion keeping his white wings tucked tightly behind his back, his feathers still ruffled in the air from Ryker's breath and the twitching of his giant wings. The fact that the angel was in grey sweatpants and matching crewneck sweatshirt told me he must have rushed out of bed straight here — I'd only rarely seen him out of his usual business casual. "You have to let us close enough to help you." Orion held his hands out in front of him, showing the immense predator that he was unarmed, but an angel didn't require weapons to be dangerous. And the dragon knew it.

The black and gold dragon roared again, and I flinched. Even knowing Ryker was a dragon shifter, nothing had prepared me for how massive his dragon form was. I would be about a half of a bite in his jaws, not even a snack to a giant like this.

Ryker was terrifying.

His neon green eyes flashed in the night, taking us all in. A rush of adrenaline surged through my body as I tried to discern how I could be of any help.

"Blaze," I whispered, "I don't know what Orion wants me to do, but I can't work on animals. If Ryker needs medical attention, we have to get him to shift back to human."

"Right." Blaze nodded absently. "Any ideas on how to do that?"

"How would I know?" I nearly cried. "I hardly know the male."

Blaze glanced my way, a shrewd look in his black eyes. "And bears don't shit in the woods."

I slapped his arm, but didn't break my attention from the dragon.

Orion was having zero luck approaching Ryker. From where I stood, I could see that his wound was still seeping blood. I chewed on my lip, stepping away from Blaze's side and towards the dragon.

"Selene, what are you doing?" Blaze whisper-shouted, but I ignored him. I'd spent years practicing how to stay calm in crisis situations, and it was time to put all of my learning to use. I had to stop the bleeding before this got much, much worse.

"Ryker," I called, loud enough to draw his attention to me. The last thing I needed was to surprise an injured dragon. "It's me. Selene."

His bright green eyes focused in on me, glancing between where I inched towards him, hands out, and where Orion still stood. Orion took the opportunity to back away, and rejoined Blaze at the far side of the rooftop.

"It's me, Selene," I repeated, smiling up at him. "You're bleeding a lot, Ryker."

Smoke billowed out of the black dragon's nostrils, and I paused, feeling the heat wash over me. It smelled like sparks and steel and something unmistakably *him*, but I couldn't let the memory of being wrapped up in that scent distract me.

"Please don't hurt me, Ryker," I said as I took another tentative step forward. "I just want to help you. But I can't do that when you're shifted."

A weird chuffing sound came from deep in his throat, his eyes still intently focused on me, but the dragon made no aggressive moves.

"How can I help you shift, Ryker? I need to stop the bleeding, and you're not healing on your own. Something is wrong."

The same sound came again, almost as if he was trying to speak to me, and was frustrated I couldn't understand him.

I was within arms' length of him now, barely standing taller than his large head, and petrified all the way down to my bones. But my hand was steady as I reached forward, delicately placing my palm on his jaw. The scales along his face had a smooth, glossy feel, and I gasped as my fingers grazed across him.

"I need you to shift, Ryker," I whispered again. "Please let me help you."

With a burst of magic, Ryker's form shifted, and left behind a very large, very bloody, very *naked* male who crumpled to the floor.

"My leg," Ryker bit out between clenched teeth. His skin was pale and clammy, sweat beading on his brow, his long blond hair sticking to his face. "I was shot, and it's in my leg. I can't heal it."

I nodded in understanding, glancing down at his right thigh where blood pulsed rapidly from a large gash. From what I could see in the dim light, it also looked like his tibia was probably fractured in his calf. Stripping out of my jacket, I bunched the fabric, pushing it into his leg. He roared in pain at the touch, and I winced.

"We need to get you downstairs so I can see better." A doorway behind me led down from the roof, but there was no way Ryker would be able to put any weight on his leg to get downstairs. "Will you let Blaze close enough to flicker you downstairs?"

Ryker growled, but didn't say no.

"You owe me for this," Blaze said as he knelt, gripping Ryker's hand, and flickered out of the space.

I sprinted to the steps and down the stairs with Orion at my heels, headed to the bedroom I'd revisited so many times in my dreams. Ryker already lay sprawled on the bed, groaning in pain.

Orion started gathering any towels he could find, and I

grabbed an armful from him gratefully, rushing towards Ryker on the bed to soak up the blood.

"I'll need water," I called out, and Blaze ran off to find some. So much of the blood had already dried, I'd need to wash it off. "Remind me why you couldn't heal this?" I asked Orion next, and grabbed the bowl of water from Blaze to begin clearing off the wound.

"I tried," Orion said as Ryker snatched a towel for himself with a growl and draped it over his hips. "It wouldn't heal — whatever he was shot with was magical. Iron probably. And he flew for so long with it in, it spread quickly through his system. It's repelling any magical attempts to retrieve it or heal him."

Great. "I need supplies. There's an emergency kit I left in Town Hall. Blaze?" I said, realizing we would have to do this the old-fashioned way. Blaze disappeared immediately to retrieve it. "Find a belt or a rope." I directed at Orion, and a minute later he passed me a belt that I used to tourniquet the leg, trying to stop the bleeding until I could get a better handle on the situation and figure out if there was still a bullet in there.

"*Fuck*," Ryker hissed as I tightened the binding, and I grimaced, but didn't stop. It had to be tight.

"Orion, can you do anything for him for the pain?" This would definitely go better if the male wasn't griping and writhing around the whole time.

"It's fine," Ryker gritted out, but I cut him a look that silenced him.

"I'll try." Orion moved closer, placing a hand on Ryker's head, and the shimmer of electricity in the air told me he sent a burst of magic into the male. "Better?"

Ryker only grunted, but we took that as an affirmative. I moved off to wash my hands at the bathroom sink, and a breath of relief left me as I heard Blaze return.

"Hope you'll ignore the breaking and entering this once, O," came his voice from the bedroom holding my kit. "I tried not to shuffle your papers on your desk, but can't make any promises. Is this what you needed, Selene?"

Drying my hands, I came back in the room and gave him a nod. "Thank you. Gloves?"

Moments later, Ryker was sweating and swearing again as I poked and prodded the wound, searching for the bullet.

"This is strange," Orion's voice came from behind me, low and confused.

"Right?" Blaze agreed. "Ryker, you've seen *10 Things I Hate About You?*" Blaze stood at Ryker's bookshelf, where he had a few scattered books and DVDs. I pressed my lips together to hide my laugh as Ryker growled at him.

"Christmas gift," Ryker grunted out. "Didn't have time to get rid of it yet."

Blaze laughed, eyes glittering. "From who?"

Ryker's jaw clenched tighter, but I was glad Blaze was distracting him. Having a person rooting around in his quad couldn't have been fun.

"Devanna."

Blaze cackled all the harder, and I could practically feel Orion scowling at him.

"I meant Ryker," Orion cut into Blaze's laughter. "Even though I couldn't heal him, I should be able to dull the pain, at least. He shouldn't be in this much pain after my magic."

All of us sobered immediately.

"What do you mean?" Sweat was beading on Ryker's

brow, his voice pinched and tight; it was clear he was still hurting.

"With the amount of magic I just dumped into your system, you shouldn't be able to feel *any* of this," Orion admitted, coming forward again to stand by my side where I worked. "I don't know why my magic isn't working."

"That sounds bad," Blaze muttered at the same moment as I shrieked, "Aha!"

The three males startled at my exclamation, but I hardly noticed. I'd found the bullet. Grabbing a pair of forceps and a clamp, I pushed the skin and the muscle aside to have a clearer view, mindful to avoid the vein that would be running through the same area. I had a feeling there was an artery nicked here somewhere, based on the extent of the blood, and we didn't need it to get any worse.

Spying the offending metal, I gripped it with the forceps and gently pried it out, the bullet nearly the size of a golf ball — much larger than anything I'd ever seen in a human hospital ER. Orion held out a hand with a washcloth and I passed it over, exhaling as the first step was over.

"Iron," Orion muttered, cleaning off the bullet. "With it in his leg for so long, he's going to be dealing with some iron poisoning for a while."

I nodded in agreement. Iron poisoning for a supernatural was no joke — it rendered the injured practically human until the last of the iron was out of their system. With an injury like this, a full-strength shifter could have healed themselves, but with iron pumping in their bloodstream? It could have been fatal.

From there, I worked steadily to close up the rest. The tear in the artery looked small, despite the amount of blood coming from the wound, so I applied pressure until it stopped leaking. As long as he kept the limb immobile, it should close up on its own. When I couldn't find any other sources for potential bleeding, I met Ryker's glowing neon eyes. He must have been watching me intently this whole time, but I'd been too busy to notice. Now, my breathing hitched, his eyes flickering from round to slitted pupils every few seconds.

"I need to remove the tourniquet now," I told him, trying to keep my voice steady, but it was like making eye contact with a radioactive magnet. I felt drawn in to him and like I should run the other way all at once. "This is going to hurt."

He only blinked and grunted.

"I might need your help," I called over to Orion and Blaze. Once we removed the tourniquet, blood should hope-fully flow normally, but there was a chance there was some-thing I missed and he could start bleeding again. Then of course we still had to set his broken tibia.

Blaze moved around to the other side of the bed to await instruction, Orion still by my side, and I held my breath as I loosened the belt, letting it drop off the bed as we all waited to see if I'd messed this up. Ryker hissed through his teeth as blood flooded back into his leg.

I tracked every blood cell for a moment, my eyes racing over every part of exposed muscle, bone, artery, or vein I could see. A moment later, I let out a breath. There was still some blood loss — his leg was still cut open, after all — but the gushing from earlier was gone.

"Well, that was the fun part," I said lightly, smiling at Ryker who glowered back. "Blaze, can you hold his shoulders down?" Blaze moved into position with a grimace. "Orion, hips?"

Grumbling something under his breath, Orion moved to hold Ryker's hips down, the dragon growling at him again, covered only in his towel. He could get over it.

I moved to his feet, hoisting his leg into position and silently cursing myself for my arm-day workout this morning, as this single limb of his probably weighed fifty pounds.

"If the bullet got your thigh, how did you break your tibia?"

He was hissing as I moved his leg, but managed to bite out, "Crash landing on the roof."

"You know, I've been meaning to tell you this for months," I said casually, reviewing the next few moves I would need to make in my mind's eye and taking a few steadying breaths. "But as far as bikes go, a Harley-Davidson Super Glide has got to be *the* most cliche choice. What, did you buy the first one you saw in the shop window? Do you have a matching SAMCRO jacket?"

His eyes turned to slits, glaring at me. "*What?*"

With a crack, I yanked his bone into place. "Psych!"

"*FUCK!*"

Chapter Four

RYKER

My eyes were heavy, caked shut and groggy as I fought to return to consciousness. Something cool and damp slid across my forehead, jerking me upward, and to attention.

"Easy," a soft, sweet voice said above me, and I turned my head to find the speaker.

"Flores."

"Hey there, big guy. Welcome back to the land of the living." Selene smiled down at me, and I frowned. She stood, walking to the kitchen across my loft that was covered in items I didn't recognize.

"How long have I been out?"

"All night." Selene reemerged from the kitchen with a glass of water, the faint morning sun illuminating the side of her face from the large wall of windows that overlooked the ocean. The golden glow made her light brown skin radiant, and her dark hair looked as soft as I remembered. She was in a grey Red Sox shirt and a pair of light aqua scrubs pants that hugged the curves of her ass beautifully.

All night? Her words finally sank in as I drew my gaze away from her and registered the sunlight. Someone had slipped a pair of loose black shorts on me, and I wasn't sure if I hoped it was Selene or not. I slid my palms down to my bed beneath me, pushing up against the soft mattress to a sitting position. Pain radiated from my leg, and I exhaled sharply.

"Shit. Slow down," Selene rushed back to my side, helping me to sit. "You're going to be one of *those* patients, aren't you?"

This time, my frown was a full-on scowl. "I have never been a *patient* before in my very long life, and I won't start now." I pushed to slide further to the edge of the bed, and my vision blacked out as pain shot through my body.

"Yeah, well," Selene answered in a know-it-all tone, "first time for everything. Lay your ass back down."

"Some bedside manner you have," I growled, but did as I was told. She handed me the glass of water and a couple pills, and I scowled again. I'd never had to take so much as an aspirin before. I swiped them from her palm and swallowed them down.

"You weren't complaining about my bedside manner last Halloween, if I recall correctly."

And there it was. I knew this would come up eventually. Selene had come home with me after Blaze's party, and we'd spent the evening having the most mind-blowing sex of my life. I'd been tempted more than once to call her again, but dragons were solitary creatures. And I already knew what type of woman Selene was.

Good.

Too good for me.

"Listen," I started. Was I about to apologize? I *never* apologized. "I—"

"Forget it." Selene huffed a laugh. "It meant nothing. It's fine."

Well, shit. I didn't know if I liked the sound of *that*.

"Besides," Selene went on, and I glanced sideways at her. "It was *fine*, but, I mean, it wasn't that special. Not like I need an encore performance."

"Bullshit," I spat before I could even think through my own train of thought. "I gave you the best orgasms of your life. *Plural*."

Selene laughed lightly, her hands resting on my thigh as she checked my stitches, which she must have done after I'd passed out, her warm brown eyes trailing over my leg in assessment. The fact that she didn't even argue, or take the bait, had my blood boiling.

"I'll prove it to you." I arched a brow in challenge.

"In case you haven't noticed —" Her hands wrapped around my thigh as she wove the bandage around it tightly, and I practically hissed as I pressed my eyes shut. Not at the pain, in fact, that barely registered. Her gentle fingers were just so close to something *else*, I thought my brain might short-circuit. " — you're a bit too injured to use anything south of the border right now."

As if that was the only way I could blow her mind. My eyes snapped open again as I looked at her dead-on. "Then take off your pants and sit on my face."

Selene jerked back, her hands falling to her side as she stared down at me. My lips tipped up on one side as I held eye contact, letting her know I was serious.

Nervous laughter erupted from her as she stood, turning her back on me and walking over to the table.

While she may not have taken me up on my very serious offer, the image I'd planted was sure to remind her just how *special* I was.

Not that special, my ass.

Chapter Five

SELENE

It was a stressful, mostly sleepless night for me, even after I stabilized Ryker and he knocked out. To distract myself, I set up my laptop, spending the time in between checking on Ryker trying to brush up on actual witch healing spells. Orion might have said the injury hadn't responded to magic at first, but I had to hope that now that the iron bullet was out, it would be more responsive.

It didn't help that I hadn't done this kind of magic in years. If I was being honest, I rarely tapped into my *witchiness* at all. Maybe once in a while I'd use it to help ease a patient's stress or read the severity of an injury, lower-level stuff like that, but for full-on healing? To say I was rusty was an understatement.

My choice to practice human medicine instead of healing magic was something many of the witches in my Coven hadn't understood, and had been one of the reasons I'd left the Cove to begin with. For most of them, like Devanna and Morgaine, magic was as much who they were as any other part of their personality. Intrinsic. Dev had stared at me like I'd sprouted two heads when I'd finally told her I was accepting Orion's terms to train in human medicine in exchange for my turn-on-a-dime medical services whenever needed.

But the truth, which I suspected Dev understood more than she let on, was that using magic always reminded me of my mother. And the pain of losing her was still too fresh.

To get out of the Cove and back to Boston, though, I'd face it.

Assuming I could figure out how.

I'd been staring at my laptop, squinting at various symbols and ingredients I'd managed to research and making notes for myself, when Ryker had woken. And now, in addition to trying to get the image of straddling his face out of my head, I had to deal with his incessant grumbling while I tried to work out a spell.

I didn't have all the supplies I'd noted down, but I had enough to give it a shot and see if *something* happened. If it did, then I could text Orion or Blaze to bring over the rest later.

In the kitchen, I gathered the salt shaker (generic, but better than none), a candle (I was dying to know why Ryker had a Christmas Morning-scented candle, but I'd never ask), and a lemon-verbena tea bag (Blaze had brought the tea for me, to help me relax, but I could sacrifice one). Carrying the items over to the bed, I set them on the night table as Ryker eyed me warily.

"What are you up to, Flores?"

I explained my reasoning about trying magic again now the bullet was out, and Ryker nodded. Realizing the one item I'd forgotten, I cleared my throat. "Can you light this?" I waved to the candle.

Green eyes slid from me to the candle and back. "Not unless you want the whole room burned down."

Right. "Lighter, then? Or matches?"

"Drawer to the left of the fridge."

I popped up, scrounged around in said drawer, and returned a moment later with the lighter, flicking it on to light the candle. The smell of balsam fir wafted into the air, and I could have sworn I saw a fleeting look of longing pass over Ryker's face, but maybe it was just a shadow.

With the candle lit, and the other items arranged hopefully the way they were supposed to be, I closed my eyes and tried to reach for my magic.

Deep breath.

Hmm.

Okay, maybe I needed to burn the verbena? That seemed like a witchy thing to do. Pursing my lips, and doing my damnedest not to let on to Ryker how unsure I was about all of this — I'd learned long ago never to show uncertainty in front of patients — I blinked my eyes open and picked up the tea bag. Tearing it open gently, I fished out the largest piece of verbena I could find and held it up to the flame.

Ryker narrowed his eyes. "You sure you know what you're doing?"

I laughed lightly, smiling. "Of course."

Several more minutes ticked by. The leaf burnt completely to ash.

Still nothing.

"You *are* a witch, aren't you?" Despite the fact his tone

held more concern than disdain — for once — the question irked me.

Maybe because it was the very one I was asking myself.

"Yes." I said it through gritted teeth, but I was still smiling. Hopefully. "Just give me a minute."

He gave me five minutes. I'd burned through all the leaves that were big enough to hold without burning the tips of my fingers in the process, sweat collecting on my brow, but had nothing to show for it.

My magic wasn't working. Whether that had to do with the same block that seemed to be affecting Ryker's and Orion's magic, too, or my own issues with my practice, I couldn't be sure.

For the first time, my *in*ability to access my magic actually hurt more than using it. My eyes suddenly felt very dry, and I blinked rapidly as I scooped up the items.

A very large, very tattooed pale hand covered my entire light brown forearm, stilling my movements and forcing me to meet the acid-green gaze of its owner.

"Flores."

I blinked again, and forced a casual shrug as I brushed off his hand and stood, carrying the items back to the kitchen table.

"It must be whatever is affecting the town magic," I called over my shoulder, willing more strength into my voice than I felt. "Guess we're stuck with the human medicine for now."

Ryker grunted, but didn't push it. If he could tell there was something more bothering me, he didn't let on. Maybe he had a little decency after all — deep, *deep* down.

Chapter Six

RYKER

"You've got to be fucking kidding me."

Orion crossed his arms, now outfitted again in his usual grey slacks and blue button-down fitted magically around his wings. Staring down his straight nose at me, he stood over where I sat on the couch, my leg propped up on the coffee table. "What does it matter? You're too injured to go anywhere anyway."

"Over my dead body will I agree to be *grounded*." I let my eyes shift to dragon, but the male wasn't backing down.

It was late afternoon — turned out Selene had slipped me a sleeping pill this morning to get me to rest, last time I took something from that "doctor" before inspecting it more closely — and Orion had just come over. Selene was working at the kitchen table, bent over her notebook as she scribbled something, completely ignoring both Orion and me. This whole revolving door of visitors was insufferable and needed to end. Orion had brought the unwelcome news that I had epically fucked up.

Apparently, when I was shot, some of those pesky

screaming humans had managed to snap a photo of me, and suddenly I was all over the internet.

"I did everything I could, Ryker," Orion said, his face grim. "Headquarters is working on cleaning it up, gathering evidence against you for the infraction. Until they call you to a meeting, you are to stay put in the Cove." I pursed my lips, all too familiar with the *Code* the angels liked to enforce, that none of the rest of the supernaturals had ever agreed to. "Revealing the supernatural world to humans is a serious offense. You know this as well as I do."

I grunted, no real argument against it, but knew this would mean nothing but trouble for me. Dragons and angels had never exactly gotten along — we didn't fit into their pretty power structure guidelines, far more magical than other shifters, especially as we aged, but that was beside the point. Whether I'd meant to or not, I'd broken the Code.

"The Council is already at work convincing the world the photos were doctored and tracking down the eyewitnesses to alter their memories, but it spread like wildfire, Ryker. This will take some time."

I rolled my eyes, annoyed that I couldn't get up and walk away to end this conversation.

As if sensing my train of thought, Orion reached over and picked up my crutches, moving them slightly to the side and out of reach. "You either agree to their terms, or they'll have someone out here tonight to put a tracker on you." Orion's steel grey eyes cut into mine.

Angels were such tightasses. Could I go anywhere even if I wanted to? No, but that wasn't the point. It was the principle of the thing. I remembered the days *before* they got it into their overbearing little brains to try to regulate supernaturals, when we didn't have to answer for shit like this. Not like I'd ever agreed to their forming their little Council, nor had I ever submitted to their Code. No one told me what to do.

"Hold this." Selene pressed an ice pack against my leg, waiting for me to take over before removing her hand and heading back to the kitchen table, writing something down in the notebook she was keeping.

"So, I can tell the Council yes? You understand the severity of this infraction, and you'll stay put?" Orion eyed me, though his gaze shifted to something unreadable as it flitted between me and Selene.

My teeth ground together, though that might have been because I was pressing the ice into my leg rather aggressively. "I'll stay put because *I'm* choosing to."

Orion rolled his eyes. "Right. Works for me." He turned to Selene, calling over to her. "Do you need anything else here, for him or yourself?"

My forehead wrinkled. "Why would she need anything? She's not staying here."

Selene popped a hand on her hip, and flashed me a syrupy smile. "You're *so* hospitable."

"If you haven't noticed, you can't even walk," Orion informed me flatly.

"So what? Leave me a bottle of vodka. I'll be fine in a few days."

Selene scoffed lightly, turning back to her notebook. "No magic, Puff. Remember? It's going to take you several *weeks* to get back on your feet."

I blinked. "The fuck did you just call me?" She ignored

me, so I continued, turning back to Orion. "Even if that's true —"

"It is." Oh, now she was chiming in?

" — I don't need a doctor, just someone to help me move from A to B." My eyes bored into Orion. *Anyone but her,* I tried to tell him, but of course, I hadn't been able to communicate with anybody that way in centuries.

Orion scraped a hand along his sharp jaw. "Shockingly, there weren't a lot of volunteers for this position." I shot my eyes to Selene, who still had her back to us. *She volunteered?* Before I could think too much on why my chest warmed at that thought, Orion set me straight. "It was part of Selene's contract to help out in case of emergency, so she'll be here until you can function on your own."

The angel was stubborn, but so was I. "Doesn't she have a job?"

"She can hear you," Selene sing-songed back at us, but still didn't turn around.

Shrugging, Orion turned to go, apparently done with our conversation and dealing with me for the day. "It'll be there when she gets back."

"There isn't even anywhere for her to sleep here," I shot at his retreating back. I had very limited furniture. There was my bed — a bad idea for numerous reasons — or the couch, which I doubted she'd be thrilled to sleep on for *several weeks*.

"You'll figure it out," Orion tossed back, and left the room.

Chapter Seven

SELENE

"What are you doing?"

I ignored Ryker, setting my chilled sauvignon blanc on the coffee table and reaching for the remote. I'd had a long day dealing with him, and he could shut it.

It did *not* help that Ryker's place was essentially one large studio loft. The upstairs where we were was a very modern, sparsely decorated bedroom, living room, and kitchen that was all open and overlooked his garage, which housed an extensive collection of vehicles. I had peeked over the railing at the line-up of black cars and bikes, but had been itching to get down there and take a closer look. The last time I'd been in his home, I was more than a little distracted by everything *else* to pay close attention to the vehicles. When his next sleeping pill kicked in, I was going to explore. That is, if I could trick him into taking it again.

The surly dragon had been complaining since the moment he woke up around three in the afternoon — note to self, dragons need the extra *extra* strength sleeping pill — and I was over it. If I had a time clock, I'd be punching out, but as it was, I had to do it mentally. I could take two hours to myself to enjoy a movie.

You'd think someone had chopped off his leg the way he was carrying on.

So I had tuned him out, cooked myself dinner — chicken parmesan — chucked his plate at him, and headed for what sufficed as his living room, which was just a couch, coffee table, and a TV.

Stopping to glance over his movie selection, I smiled as I pulled one from the shelf.

"Don't put that on, Flores," he warned between bites. Had he thanked me for dinner? No. And I didn't *have* to cook for him — that was nowhere in my contract.

"Oh, this?" I said, punching in the DVD deliberately. "Oops."

He grumbled something in retort, but I slid the volume way up and kicked my feet on the coffee table as I settled into my dinner.

The Barenaked Ladies morphed into Joan Jett's *Bad Reputation* as the opening scene of *10 Things I Hate About You* started up. I smiled to myself as Ryker only grumbled louder.

"You know, I'm not making you watch it," I called over to him.

"What else am I supposed to do with the volume maxed out like that?" he snapped, and I chuckled into my wine glass.

"How about another sleeping pill?"

I could feel his eyes boring a hole into the back of my head. He was so easy to rile.

"Why did Dev get you this anyway?" I asked later, feeling a little looser after my second glass of wine. Or maybe it was my third. I shifted on the couch, trying to get comfortable, but it was the most miserable piece of furniture I had ever sat on. What little sleep I'd stolen last night on this couch had left me with an excruciating backache all day, and I was dreading another night on it.

After his fourth complaint that he couldn't see the screen, I'd helped him hobble over to the couch, just to shut him up. Easier said than done considering he was over a foot taller than me and twice my weight, but we made it.

Leg propped up on the coffee table and his blond hair messily knotted on his head, he gave a disgruntled wave of *Fuck if I know*. He tilted his head back into the leather sofa, exposing the tattoos over his neck, and I had to forcibly shift my eyes back to the screen and away from temptation.

"I'm a little surprised you still have DVDs and don't just stream everything," I said into the heavy silence later.

"Not here much." Ryker shrugged, dropping back into silence, which left my mind to wander on its own.

I'd be lying if I said I hadn't thought about his *offer* a time or two since he'd made it earlier, but I knew we couldn't cross that line again. I was here as a medical professional, and he really did need to rest. Still, eyeing the large male to my left, I had to wonder how that trim, full beard would feel tickling my thighs.

Not that I really had to *imagine* what it was like. I mentally glared at myself for bringing that night up again.

As if I could ever forget it. No matter how I taunted him, it had been one of the best nights of my life. But Ryker was bad news, and I knew it.

He must have felt my eyes on him, for his green gaze slid to mine with a smug look, like he knew *exactly* what I was thinking about.

"I know *exactly* what you're thinking about," he murmured with a flick of his eyebrows and that hint of a dimple that nearly undid me.

I laughed, pouring myself another half glass. *Huh, was the bottle empty?* "That you probably looked just like baby Heath in your youth?"

He chuckled, the sound a low rumble that went straight between my legs. "Sure, Flores."

Taking a healthy sip of my wine, I tried to hide the flush that rose to my cheeks as I remembered, as a shifter, this male would be able to scent things the average human — or witch — could not.

It was going to be a *very* long few weeks.

Chapter Eight

RYKER

No matter how hard I tried to act like I was fine, my leg was excruciating. Never, in my thousand years, had I felt such incessant, never-ending agony. How did humans survive living like this, *all the time?* Pain radiated both from where she'd extracted the iron bullet and stitched me up, as well as my broken calf.

The movie ended, and Selene's eyes drooped where she sat, still holding her wine glass. I reached over, gently taking it from her hand, and even that small motion was enough to send a shooting pain down my entire body.

I groaned, and the sound roused Selene to attention. "What's wrong?" she asked as her eyes expanded, snapping to me still leaning over her, unable to right myself.

It brought my face right in front of hers, and I couldn't help but inhale her sweet scent of vanilla and bergamot. She smelled amazing.

"You okay?" she whispered, her eyes taking in my features in a much more clinical way than my own. Me? I was staring right down at her chest, whether I wanted to or not.

When I didn't answer, because fuck if I ever was going to admit I needed help, her hands came up to my arms where I was propping myself up, and gently pushed me back up into a sitting position.

I hissed through my teeth in pain, closing my eyes as I fought the wave of nausea that accompanied it.

"You need to lay back down," she said, doctor voice back in full force. "Let's get your leg elevated, and some more pain meds in your system."

"I told you I'm not taking that shit," I growled.

"And I'm telling you, I'm not taking *your* shit," she shot back, standing to her full height. Which was barely above mine, while I was still sitting. Her brown eyes squinted down at me, not budging on this, and yet again, I grumbled.

Gods, I was annoying even myself.

When I didn't argue further, she jogged across the loft, giving me the perfect view of her rear as she grabbed the crutches leaning in the corner.

"I'll help you stand, and then you can either use these, or we can suffer through you using me as your crutch again while we get you back to the bed," she said, and I just stared at her.

She held out the crutches, and I snatched them from her. "I don't need you."

"Keep telling yourself that, Mushu."

It took me far too much effort to get up and onto the damned crutches, nearly blacking out again as I stood. After the millionth time Selene told me to not put pressure on my leg, I snarled at her to leave me alone.

She threw her hands in the air, marching back to the kitchen, but I could still feel her eyes lingering on me, even if she tried to hide it.

I finally figured out the rhythm needed for the crutches, then made my way to the bathroom first — a task I did *not* want her help on, ever — and then to the bed. I sat down with a wince, then slid back on the pillows.

Selene's gentle hands helped lift my deadweight leg up and over, and my eyes flashed to dragon, feeling defensive to have someone near me while I was injured. Fire boiled in my veins, making it hard for me to breathe evenly until she settled my leg on several stacked pillows, then let go.

"You need to keep it elevated above your heart to minimize the swelling and inflammation," she instructed.

"This is ridiculous," I mumbled under my breath, but her eyes shot to me in an annoyance.

"Ready for those pills?" She held them out to me in her dainty palm, a satisfied smirk on her face as I fought to hide the pain.

With a heavy sigh, I grabbed the pills and swallowed them dry. Before I knew it, I was out.

A soft weight on my chest had me jerking awake some hours later, and I lifted my head off the pillows to glance around the dark room.

My vision switched to dragon momentarily to search out any danger lingering in the dark, but nothing was there. As I settled back into my pillow, a soft sigh had me turning my head once again.

Selene had joined me on the bed sometime in the night. The weight on my chest? Her hand. Resting over my heart. Whether that was intentional for some medical purpose, I didn't know. Maybe it had just been unconsciously in her sleep, seeking out warmth. Or maybe she was a liar, and she thought about Halloween as much as I did.

I stared at her sleeping form a moment more, taking in the way her long eyelashes rested on her high cheekbones, and the way her curly brown hair haloed her head on the pillow.

Selene was stunning. And the way she was always so relaxed and at ease in her own skin, even wearing just a simple tee and scrubs like she was now, only accentuated that fact even more.

More often than I cared to admit, Selene had been featured in my dreams, both G-rated, and *not*.

Part of me recognized that having her here in bed with me was a terrible plan — she would get attached, and it would make it that much worse when I left again — but the other part of me… well. He kind of liked it.

I closed my eyes, willing myself back to sleep, and gently placed my hand over hers on my chest.

Chapter Nine

SELENE

Stirring awake as sunlight flooded in through the wall of windows, I jolted, then cringed, then sank into a mountain of… pillows?

Oh no.

Why had drunk-Selene crawled into Ryker's bed? I could hex her for being so stupid.

Damn, it smelled so good in here.

No. None of that.

Maybe if I moved really, *really* slowly —

"Morning."

Damn it!

Scrambling out of his bed, I darted for the bathroom, throwing a far too high-pitched "Yup, morning!" over my shoulder before I all but slammed the door behind me.

Pressing my back against the door, I closed my eyes for a minute and took a breath, then grimaced as the full force of my hangover caught up to me, the room spinning.

But damn if he didn't sound sexy in the morning, his voice all low and raspy and —

Get it together, Selene.

After I'd washed the hangover and embarrassment off my face and made Ryker take a few more pain pills — though I hadn't mustered the courage to meet his gaze yet — I told him I had to run an errand and fled from the loft.

Once outside in the driveway and making my way down to town, if only for a walk in the freezing January air to take a breather from him, I pulled out my phone and dialed my last resort.

Not *The* Last Resort, of course — the only motel in town was no doubt still the shambles it had always been, probably even more than usual after the showdown with Errakal and the witches a few months ago.

"Good morning," the cheery, sing-songy voice on the other end of the line raised my hackles as Morgaine, a local witch I'd known my whole life as *the* worst meddler in history, jumped to Number One on my suspect list for the turn my life had taken. "How was your night, dear? Tell Auntie Mo everything."

I could *hear* her wicked grin, it was that powerful.

"You set this all up, didn't you?" I accused, my eyes narrowing as I carefully wound my way down Ryker's slippery, endless driveway.

"Oh yes, *I* was the one that shot him down," Mo laughed breezily. "Ryker needed help, so I simply reminded our dear mayor about your occupation and contract. Thank goodness for my fool-proof memory, or who knows what could have happened to the poor dragon?"

"Uh-huh." I rolled my eyes. The woman was shameless.

"Can you stop by?" Mo cut in before I could get around to my reason for calling. "Book Club is about to begin, but I'd love to catch up. See you soon!" She hung up without even waiting for a reply.

I stared down at the blank screen of my phone, rolled my eyes, and tossed it into my bag. The further I walked from Ryker's home, the easier I breathed, so maybe some time and space would be good for me. Decision made, I turned left onto Ocean Avenue, and stomped into town.

In the half-hour it took me to walk into town, I lost all feeling in my toes. Snow was piled high on the roof of the magenta and turquoise residence, making it look like white frosting on a overly-decorated gingerbread house. I made my way up the icy steps, letting myself right in as was the custom with Mo's home. The walk had worked to clear my head as intended — I couldn't think past the loud chattering of my teeth.

"Where are you, you unapologetic —" I turned the corner at the end of the hall and nearly tripped over a girl in her late teens, cutting off my shout in surprise. "Oh. You're not Mo."

Her skin was lighter than mine, but I'd assume she had some Latina blood in her to be this tan in the middle of winter. Her deep black hair was dyed fire-engine red at the ends, perfectly coordinating with her feminine-grunge style. At least, that's what I'd call the red floral dress topped with a black sweater, paired with black tights and motorcycle boots.

"I'm Ruby!" She offered a kind smile, pointing down the hall. "Everyone's in the living room. Here for Book Club?"

"Selene. Nice to meet you. And no, just needed to chat with Mo for a moment."

"Well, come join us. I don't know anyone else in town yet, and you're the first witch I've met so far that was born in the same century as me."

A laugh bubbled out of me. "How long have you been in the Cove?"

Before Ruby could answer my question, a voice drifted out to us from the living room. "All I'm saying is the *logistics* don't make sense here —"

"It's *not* too many people if they — Oh, we'll just show you, heaven's sake, Eva —"

We rounded the corner into the living room, and I instantly slapped a hand over my mouth to suppress a surprised laugh.

In the middle of Mo's floral-upholstered living room, coffee table pushed aside, Peg Fernsby, one of the ancient Historical Society witches, was in a Twister-style tangle of limbs with Caedmon and Val, the coffee van guys; Zaphiel, a young angel I didn't know well; and Endymion, the demon who ran the General Store, when he felt like it.

"A little to the left," Peg instructed Endymion, who shifted a few inches over. "And Eva, remember these humans aren't contending with the wings —"

"Wait," Mo consulted the paperback in her lap. "Zaph, your character is actually facing the other — Oh, Selene! You made it!"

All heads turned to me, and I raised my eyebrows. Endymion lay on the floor with Peg on top of him, chest to chest. Val knelt between Peg's legs, Caedmon lying down next to her, and Zaph was pivoting into a new position over her head, white wings ruffling. "What kind of Book Club is this?"

"We're getting a head start for February's Romp and Romance month," Peg said from the floor, eyes glittering, her wrinkled face entirely too close to Zaph's denim-clad crotch. "*Her Five Mates.*"

"Apparently," Eva leaned forward into Zaph's wings conspiratorially, "this is called a *reverse harem*. Ever heard of one, Selene?"

I coughed to cover up my choking on nothing, pointedly *not* responding to that question.

"Come, sit!" Mo patted the floral couch she perched on, not sparing me a glance. Her adopted daughter Nimue — another demon in town and one of my all-time best friends — sat on the other end, black eyes wide in shock as she mouthed, "*Run.*" But I was on a mission, and I couldn't leave yet. "Check and see if you think we got this positioning right."

Mo held out the paperback for me as I hesitantly made my way around the room, trying to look anywhere but the pile of bodies in the middle of the floor.

"Reminds me of that one time we all went to Rio de Janeiro, right Endymion?" Mo sighed wistfully, and I tripped, crashing into the corner of the couch.

"Careful, dear!" Mo jumped up to help. "Although bent over the couch like this is what happens in Chapter 12. Zaph, come here for a moment, and —"

"Nope!" I called out, quickly placing myself on the couch to avoid becoming part of the next demonstration.

Nimue slapped a hand over her eyes, groaning in embarrassment as her long brown hair fell down over her face. Mo tried to pass me the paperback again, but I stilled her with a hand as the others' conversation went back to explaining the logistics to Eva. I was not about to be a part of whatever was going on here, and I had more important things to discuss anyway.

"Listen," I dropped my voice, letting the exuberant orgy discussion cover up my desperate request to Mo, "Can I stay in the carriage house while I'm needed in town? I can't stay up there, with him. He's impossible."

"Oh, I'm *so* sorry." Yeah, she sounded sorry. "But Petra's still renting it."

"Petra can stay with Blaze," I pointed out. "In fact, I happen to know that Petra *already* stays with Blaze at least eighty percent of the time."

"Well, that's none of *my* business," she said, as if Mo didn't boldly insert herself into every budding romantic relationship in town. "But no, I couldn't kick her out, we agreed. She made me sign a lease and everything. So organized, our little Petra."

"What about your spare room? No one ever stays there."

"Oh, dear, I *wish* that were free." Her sympathy fooled *no one.* "But Ruby's staying here; she just arrived from Timber Creek." Mo nodded past me at Ruby, who was perched on an armchair, brows furrowed slightly as her sharp amber eyes tracked from the book open in her hand to the reenactment in front of her. "She's living with me for the next six months while we work on her magic."

"What about your smaller living room? I could just crash there?"

"Oh, I'm afraid not. I'm — well, Blaze is, actually — repainting it, so it's a total mess. I wouldn't want to put you through that — fumes and all, you know? Very bad for your health. Well, of course, I don't have to tell *you* that, *Doctor Flores* —"

I sighed. "Morgaine."

"Selene." We faced off, her eyes alight with mischief, and she patted my knee. "It will be good for you, dear. Trust me."

Well, she was going to be absolutely no help at all.

Good thing I knew everyone in this little town. Nimue followed me into the kitchen, leaning on the butcher-block counter. The bright yellow cabinets next to the turquoise appliances and multi-colored kitchen chairs were just as flamboyant as their owner, and held a homey feeling I couldn't help but enjoy, even with the chaos in the room beyond.

"That bad, huh?"

"Nimue." I deadpanned. "Have you ever heard of the man flu?"

She chuckled, nodding.

"Ryker isn't a man. He's a *dragon*. It's 100 times worse."

Nimue cringed. "Wish I could have Kit give you the keys to the apartment," Nimue said. After their wedding in November, Kit, local fox skulk Alpha, had moved into Nimue's carriage house behind Blaze's cottage while the newlyweds were building their house out on skulk lands. That *should have* left his old apartment over the tea shop free. "But, since he has more Alpha duties now, Nadir has taken over running the shop, and he and Emerson decided to move in."

My heart sank a little, but not to worry. I had more options.

Extricating myself from Mo's house before they could start demonstrating the next chapter's scene, I scrolled through my contacts while I trudged up the street. Next up, Blaze. Of course, no way he was awake yet, despite it being mid-morning, so I dialed Petra.

"Selene, how's Ryker?" she asked, answering on the third ring.

"Oh, he's a delight. Listen, wake Blaze up and get him on the phone, would you?"

"Um, sure —"

There was some rustling on the line, then a yelp, then a deep sigh, and then Blaze's voice came over the line. "Kept him alive, then?"

"Don't distract me right now, demon. Can I stay in your spare wing?" I was snapping at him, but I was annoyed.

"Sorry, it's not done yet." Okay, he *actually* sounded sorry, so I softened towards him. A little. "He's driving you crazy?"

"He's *impossible*. I'll never survive." I might have let out a pathetic whimper to earn sympathy, but it failed.

"Wish I could help you out, but it really is a disaster in there. We need to redo the wiring. Hadn't been updated since the '50s."

Fuck my life.

I debated calling Devanna, another local witch and a longtime friend, but in all honesty, the woman was just as grumpy as Ryker, if not more so. I wasn't sure that was a better option. She'd probably just be on my ass to grow a pair of ovaries and ride the male.

Her words, not mine. Repeatedly. Every phone call, in fact, since Halloween.

So that was it. I stared down at my phone, trying to come up with anyone else I would be willing to beg a room from. I even debated stopping by The Last Resort — the irony was not lost on me — but the whole roof caved in, flooded motel, no electricity thing kind of ruined it.

The rest of the morning, I meandered through town, needing to clear my head and convince myself I could handle going back to Ryker's. About an hour later, feet thoroughly re-numbed, I decided to hunt down the coffee van, assuming Mo's horrifying Book Club was over by now and the guys would have set it up somewhere afterwards.

Ryker was a patient, and he needed my help. That was all.

I was a professional. I could *be* professional.

I nearly shrieked when I rounded a corner and saw Winston, the town moose, in the middle of the road, my hand flying to my heart. He was a local and mostly harmless — some witch had spelled him to be more docile so the rest of us wouldn't have to live in fear of his impressive antlers, now shed for the winter — so I edged around him carefully.

At least this meant the coffee van was close by. Winston had a penchant for stealing donuts when Val and Caedmon passed out asleep on their beach chairs, and I could have sworn I spotted a little pink frosting tingeing the moose's lips.

As predicted, and for once actually in the center of town, the van came into sight as I turned into the square. It was an old aqua and white VW van that Val and Caedmon had gutted and turned into a food truck. Today, they had it parked right at the edge of the square, practically on the beach overlooking the water.

"Hello again," I called over to where they had set up their beach chairs on the pebbled shore after Book Club, and they waved back. They dressed almost identically — board shorts and flamboyant Hawaiian shirts, even though there was snow on the ground; fedoras to keep off the sun with their white hair peeking out — but where Caedmon was pale as a piece of paper, practically translucent despite all the time he spent sitting in front of his van in the sun, Val's skin was a warm, deep brown.

Caedmon stood from his chair, giving a long stretch before walking up to me and heading into the van.

"Going to join our Book Club while you're in town?" he asked, then stopped and choked out a surprised sound. Following his eyes, I saw a suspiciously empty tray sitting in the pastry display case, spots of pink frosting all that remained.

"Valerian! Winnie got our donuts again!"

"What? No, I closed the case before we left for Mo's!" Val half-turned in his chair.

"I *knew* he figured out how to open it!" Caedmon shook his head, putting together a bag of pastries for me, even though I hadn't actually ordered any yet. "That moose is incorrigible."

"At this rate, we'll need to find Winston a moose dentist! Is there such a thing?" Val asked, his expression too serious for this conversation.

"I hate to interrupt you," I finally cleared my throat, "but I am in desperate need of a vanilla latte."

"Right, right," Caedmon answered with an absent-minded nod. "What size?"

"Biggest one you've got."

While he steamed the milk for my latte, I decided to shoot one last shot. "You two happen to have a spare bedroom?" I asked, a forced grin spread wide on my face. In all honesty, I wasn't even sure where they lived, which was strange considering I'd lived in Deadlights Cove for eighteen years, and they'd always been a staple of the community.

"Sure!" Val answered excitedly. "But you should know, once the door shuts, the clothes come off. Orion can't ticket us for nudity in our own home."

That was a visual I did *not* need. Next stop, Orion. I needed to have my memory scrubbed, ASAP.

One muffin and half a latte later, I had accepted my fate. Sitting in the gazebo where I'd been racking my brain for any other options, I was biding my time until a certain angel showed his face. Town Hall was closed every day for lunch from twelve to one, so I tried not to fidget. Right as predicted, at twelve forty-five — Orion was a *fifteen minutes early is on time and on time is late* sort of male — he appeared in the square, heading right past the dangling sign and up the steps to Town Hall.

"Orion."

He turned, his silver hair perfectly styled, not a wrinkle in sight on his dress shirt and slacks, every feather precisely groomed in his white wings.

At least he had the decency to look a *bit* chagrined.

"How was the rest of the night?"

I didn't wish to recount it again. "I made a list of things I'll need," I said instead, handing over the list I'd made on the outside of the pastry bag. Most of it was for Ryker — I needed to get an actual cast on his leg, for instance, to make sure it healed properly.

His steel grey eyes assessed me for a moment before he took the list and read it with a nod. "You'll have them." His gaze snagged on the last item. "Air mattress?"

"Yeah, get a good one, too," I told him. "If I'm going to be here a while, I don't want some little dinky one."

Expression unreadable, Orion folded the paper and put it in his pocket. "You'll have everything by this afternoon."

Good. I might have to stay at Ryker's, but there would be no more bed sharing for *this* witch.

Chapter Ten

RYKER

This was ridiculous. I didn't need Selene's help.

I struggled to get out of bed, never feeling so uncoordinated as I tried to maneuver the crutches without sending jolts of agony through my entire body. But I could figure it out, I *would* figure it out, and then I could send Selene on her merry way.

Waking up with her in my bed had been… We couldn't do that again. I knew she'd probably been too drunk to realize it was a bad idea, but that was playing with fire.

I had to get her out of my space as quickly as possible.

I'd just made it to the bathroom when I heard a faint knock from downstairs, followed by an overly cheery, "Yoohoo, Ryker, dear."

"Great," I muttered to myself. Someone had disabled my high-tech security system, and now anyone could just barge right in. I knew any response on my part would be unnecessary, as the meddling old witch would just let herself in no matter what.

Sure enough, by the time I emerged from the bathroom, Morgaine had seated herself at my kitchen table, an array of items spread across its worn surface. She wore her typical, overly bright and contrastingly patterned attire, today in an oversized pink and yellow floral sweater, black and pink pin-striped pants, and thick bright orange glasses.

"Good morning, dear, glad to see you up and about." She pushed a strand of her short white hair behind her ear and rolled up her giant sleeves. "Have a seat."

I narrowed my eyes where I stood. "What are you up to?"

"Moi?" She gave a hurt gasp, like she was shocked I could possibly think her up to no good.

"There's obviously something going on with your magic." She indicated my crutches and bandaged leg. "I'm going to try to get a reading."

Okay, maybe she had a point about that. But I still grumbled at her as I made my way over to the table.

"How was your night with Selene?"

"Can it, witch."

She grinned anyway, her eyes gleaming.

An hour later, I'd been pricked for blood, plucked for hair, and had my palm examined repeatedly, but Mo was no closer to figuring out what was wrong with my magic. Each new spell or incantation merely resulted in another infuriating *Hmm* from the witch, and I was losing my patience.

"If you can't figure it out, let's just call it quits," I muttered after her latest conundrum, pulling myself to my feet. I needed coffee. Or vodka. Or both.

"Oh, look." Mo leaned back, gazing up at me excitedly. "Your aura is brown!"

My brows dipped in confusion as I leaned on my crutches. "What does that mean?"

"Must be from your shit attitude." She hummed to herself, content to keep working.

I rolled my eyes.

"What you *need*," Mo answered as if reading my thoughts, "is to open your eyes. And maybe to get over yourself."

"Last time I checked, they were fucking open." I swung my angry gaze back to her, letting my dragon flash momentarily. "And thanks for the helpful wisdom."

"You're welcome!" She smiled, picking up her supplies and wildly ignoring my sarcasm as she prepared to leave. "Glad to see you found your manners after a thousand years."

"Do you have anything useful to say after all this?" I took a page out of her book, and also ignored her jab.

She bent over the table, scribbled a note on a piece of paper, and slid it towards me. "Tell Selene to try this spell every once in a while to check the iron levels in your blood, and to keep me updated."

I squinted, trying to read the writing from where I stood across the room, but my vision seemed to be pretty damn human right now, other than the whole dragon-eyes every once in a while.

"That's it?"

"I already told you." She shook her head. "I can't see anything with the defenses you've built around yourself. Let us in, Ryker, and get over yourself. Then maybe I can work around the iron to help you fix your magic."

Mo patted me on the arm, then proceeded to hop down

the steps to the door. I stayed standing there for several more minutes, trying to figure out what that meant.

I'd just settled myself on the couch to watch TV when the exterior door slammed, and a moment later Selene appeared at the top of the stairs.

"Wondered if you'd have the nerve to come back."

She didn't look at me or make any sort of facial expression in retort. No, she had that calm, detached, *doctor* look on her face.

Impersonal.

Placating.

I hated it.

"I went into town to request a few items from our esteemed mayor."

I cocked my head to the side, filling in the blanks as to why that had taken almost all day. Why was she being so formal? She'd been awkward this morning, too, but I figured by now, sobered, she'd be laughing our morning off. Why wasn't she laughing it off?

"Everything should be here shortly."

Fuck this.

"Flores."

She slipped her coat over the back of one of the kitchen chairs, placing her purse on the table, and still all but ignored me.

"How's the pain on a scale of one to ten?"

I didn't answer, staring at her until she finally lifted her eyes to mine.

There. Better. Even if they were guarded.

"Seven."

She nodded clinically, flipping open her notebook to scribble something down before pouring out a few more pills and bringing them over.

"Morgaine was here," I said when she was standing just to the side of my leg resting on the couch, handing over the meds. "She tried to read my magic." I told her what Mo had found — or rather, mostly *not* found. "She left directions on the table for a spell she wants you to try once in a while, to test for any changes as the iron leaves my system."

"I'll take a peek," she nodded again, but was still avoiding my gaze.

"Did you bring back any food?"

With that, Selene's eyes locked on mine, and I could swear anger simmered there. "I'm not your maid, you know."

I wish I could say that she was less attractive when she was scowling at me, but I tried not to lie to myself.

Selene was stunning.

Chapter Eleven

SELENE

"You're lying to yourself if you think you're ready to skimp on the pain pills already," I huffed later that afternoon. I'd just finished Ryker's permanent cast — black, not that he'd thanked me for not choosing hot pink — and he was lying on the bed, face paler than usual. A light sheen of sweat glimmered on his forehead, but I was so annoyed with the stubborn male, I almost didn't care.

Almost.

With a heavy sigh, I grabbed the wet cloth next to the bed, wiped down his forehead, and took his temperature. All was fine, except for the intense denial this stupid dragon lived in daily.

Even though I was annoyed with Ryker's entitled comment earlier asking if I had any food — I wasn't his housewife, for fuck's sake — I had asked Nimue to flicker down to my favorite market in Boston for several things.

Luckily for my rude patient, cooking helped to calm me. I dropped the pills in my hand onto his nightstand, then stood, done with his obstinate ass.

The male was smart enough not to ask questions as I began to pull pots and pans from the cabinets, and prepped ingredients for scallops and mashed potatoes. Because *I* wanted to eat them, not because I was trying to feed Ryker.

Ryker grunted and growled as he rose from the bed, and I watched from the corner of my eye, but didn't move to help. Slowly, he made his way over to the kitchen table, and pulled back a chair.

"Put your foot up," I instinctively said over the sizzling of the scallops in the pan. As soon as he followed my instructions, I returned to the potatoes.

"It smells amazing." Ryker turned towards me. "What are you making?"

I chewed on my lip for a moment as I fought the urge to snap at him — he had been rude all day, and I was sick of it — but his expression almost seemed like he was *trying*.

"When Orion sent Nimue to my house in Boston to retrieve the supplies I needed, I asked her to stop in at Olmsted Market. Barrett works the counter, and he posted his Cut of the Day this morning was going to be scallops. I plan my meals around what he's got in fresh."

"You're on a first-name basis with the butcher at a market?"

"Yep." I nodded, not even bothering to glance his way at the surprise in his voice. More than likely, Ryker could count on his hands the number of people he was on a first-name basis with. Despite the fact that he was so hot I could cook these scallops on the washboard abs I knew hid beneath that black shirt, his personality was as warm as the Arctic tundra.

"You like to cook?" Ryker asked, and this time I did look

over. Now, he was *definitely* trying to be nicer. This was a lot of conversation without grunts mixed in for him.

"I do," I answered as I chopped the scallions to mix into my mashed potatoes. "My mom was a fantastic cook, and it was just the two of us growing up. I helped a lot in the kitchen."

Ryker grunted — I knew one would be coming soon — and turned slightly as he watched me finish cooking. I decidedly focused on the food in front of me, artfully arranging it all onto my plate, and carried it over to the table.

"If I make you a plate, too, can I convince you to take some more meds?" I asked softly, holding the plate above the table. "If we can't get your magic back soon, you have a long road to recovery in front of you. It does neither of us any good if you wear yourself out so much these first few days that you then crash and burn."

With a heavy sigh, Ryker reached up and took the plate from me. I took that as an agreement, and smiled.

The rest of the scallops and mashed potatoes I placed on a second plate — even if he hadn't agreed to take the pills, I'd still made enough for both of us — and grabbed my glass of pinot grigio. Just one, tonight.

Apparently, drunk Selene had it bad for Ryker.

After dinner, Ryker took his meds, and I did a little mental jig at my success. I rinsed off the plates, and cleared the table before helping him to the couch.

Once he was settled, I circled the couch, heading for the pile of bags Nimue had given me earlier. In it was an air mattress Mo said I could borrow. Why she hadn't mentioned that when I was at her house this morning was beyond me, but I was glad to have it.

"Not going to watch with me?" Ryker asked over his shoulder.

"I will in a minute." First order of business was this air mattress. Knowing myself, I needed to have this baby up and ready before I got too tired and wound up back in Ryker's bed.

The loud whir of the air mattress pump had Ryker spinning in his seat, flashing me a confused side-eye. Right then, the theme song to *Gone in 60 Seconds* blared through his surround sound speakers, and I stopped the motor on the mattress, rising up on my feet to peer over the couch.

I sat like that for several minutes, watching the opening credits raptly. From the few peeks I'd seen over the railing, several of the cars featured in the film were parked down below us in Ryker's garage, so I wasn't too surprised by his choice of movies. The male was relatively predictable.

Air mattress forgotten, I circled the couch, drawn in by the opening scene, and sat on the far end — as far as I could get from him.

We were quiet for a long time, right up until the crew stole the first Aston Martin. "I never understood why they chose that model. I've always preferred the DB5 to the DB1 for classic Astons. James Bond had it right."

Ryker's eyes swung to me, but I stared ahead, watching the movie intently.

Eventually, I got up and made my way to the kitchen, grabbing a block of salted dark chocolate from my bag of groceries from the market.

"The body of that Chevy Corvette Stingray might be the sexiest of the muscle car era. Don't ever tell Blaze I said that," I mumbled around my bite of chocolate. I dropped back down on the couch, tucking my feet underneath me as I broke off another piece, and held it out in my hand for Ryker. I kept my gaze on the screen — either he'd take it or he wouldn't, didn't matter to me. His fingers brushed mine as he took the piece, and I'd be lying if I said just that simple touch didn't send a ripple of electricity across my skin.

"I don't get the infatuation with Lambroughini's." At this point, I was talking to myself, which was fine with me. But this statement was enough to draw his attention.

"What do you have against Lambos?"

I shrugged. "They're so Hollywood now. Every little YouTube star drives one as a status symbol that they've made it because *look at me, with my matching purse and car*. Not a single one of them probably even understands the insanity of the engineering that goes into those cars, and that kind of ruins the brand for me."

Ryker grunted, but the sound seemed more surprised than anything. "And how is it that you know so much about cars? Was that a thing with your mom, too? Or an ex-boyfriend?"

I laughed and shook my head. "Would you like some bait since you're fishing?"

His expression was more perplexed than remorseful, so I decided to answer honestly.

"Medical school was overwhelming." I sighed, breaking off another piece of chocolate. "I was driving an old Honda then, and it kept breaking, so I started watching YouTube videos to see if I could fix it myself. Figured bodies and cars couldn't be that different, right?"

Ryker's eyes were heavily focused on me now, but I stared back at the TV, waiting for Blaze's Mustang GT500 — Eleanor — to appear at the finale. "I couldn't fix it on my own, and ended up making it worse rather than better. But at this point, I was frustrated. Rather than take it someplace to be fixed, I enrolled myself in trade school to learn how to fix it myself." I chuckled at the memory, shaking my head at my own stupid decision. "Like I didn't have enough on my plate."

"So you fixed your car?"

"Nope." I laughed. "Turns out cars and bodies are, in fact, *very* different. But I learned how to appreciate them all the more. And then, like everything else in my life, I became a little obsessed."

"A little?" Ryker asked, humor lacing his tone as he pulled a pillow into his lap, draping his arm across it. I kicked myself for noticing his dimple showing. A man should not be allowed to be that attractive.

"Well, like the body, I want to understand it. As a single woman who's been on my own for most of my adult life, I like to know what they're talking about when I take my car in to the mechanic. Even if I can't fix cars myself, they are to be appreciated and well taken care of. I admire the craftsmanship that goes into each one, and can appreciate the nuance that sets each apart. Especially with classic cars. They're my favorite."

"Hmm," Ryker mumbled, turning back to the TV.

His long arm extended over the back of the couch as he

stretched, and I fought not to pull away from his touch. Or maybe lean in. Undecided.

The movie ended shortly after, and I helped Ryker up onto his crutches. He made his way to the bathroom, and I spread the blankets over my air mattress, settling in for the night.

"Goodnight, Flores," Ryker said as he made his way back to his bed, flipping off the lamp on his nightstand.

"Night."

Chapter Twelve

RYKER

I settled into bed after I'd flicked off the light, but even the pills Selene had given me at dinner couldn't put me to sleep yet. My mind was reeling, and it had everything to do with the female lying a dozen or so feet away from me.

First, the cooking. Those scallops had been one of the best meals I'd ever had, and she was so casual and flippant about it. Selene could be on Top Chef and win the whole damn thing if she wanted to. And that wasn't even her *job*.

Then, the cars.

If it weren't for this stupid cast, I'd have pushed her down on the couch and taken her right there. Never had I been so turned on listening to a female talk.

Thinking about it now made me hard again, but there was little I could do about it. This whole *sharing a room* was not exactly the most conducive to meeting my own *needs*.

Staring up at my ceiling, I tried to think of anything but Selene. Tried to forget how soft her skin was. Or how her lips felt on my —

Hissssssssssssss

"Shit," she muttered, and I lifted my head off the pillow, staring into the darkness of the loft. Selene rose awkwardly to her feet off the air mattress and stared down at it.

"Everything okay over there?"

"Yeah," she muttered. "Sorry, didn't mean to wake you. But since you're up, I need to turn the motor back on this thing."

The loud whirring of the pump sounded moments later, and the airbed rose again. Selene flicked off the light on her phone, and lay back down.

Several more minutes went by as I listened intently for her breathing to even out, waiting for her to fall asleep first. I didn't know why that mattered, or why I was concerned about how well she slept, but it did.

Hisssssssssssssssss

"You've got to be kidding me," she mumbled. Once again, she rose to her feet, flicked on the air mattress pump, watched it rise, then laid back down.

By the third time this happened, I couldn't help but smile. Good thing she didn't have night vision like I did. "Problems?"

"I think there's a hole in this stupid thing," Selene huffed, staring back over at my couch.

I'd regretted the purchase of that couch for years, but I wasn't here often enough for it to ever really matter. When I'd chosen it, I had picked based on the modern, sleek design of it more than comfort, and the thing was hardly better than sitting on the wooden kitchen chairs. It wasn't like I had frequent overnight visitors — especially ones that weren't sharing my bed — so I'd just dealt with it on the rare occasion I was hanging out here. A night on it would be little better than the floor.

"Where'd you get the airbed from?" I asked, curiosity getting the better of me.

"Mo dropped it off. Said she felt bad after our conversation earlier, and that I could borrow it rather than buy a new one." Then Selene cursed under her breath. "That woman. Goddess love her, but I could kill her."

I shook lightly with laughter as I followed her train of thought. "She set us up, didn't she?"

"Seems like it." Selene huffed in frustration as she sat on the floor, staring into the darkness around us. "Are we *sure* it wasn't her that shot you so I'd be forced to come back? Seems a bit extreme, but at this point, I'm not positive I'd put it past her. Her meddling is getting out of hand."

"It's late." I sighed. "Just get in the bed, and we'll figure it out tomorrow."

As soon as the words were out of my mouth, I regretted them. Not because I didn't want her in the bed with me, but because I very much *did*. The idea of Selene in bed with me when I couldn't do all of the dirty things now flooding my brain seemed like an extreme sort of torture.

"You sure?" she asked hesitantly.

Rather than answer — I didn't trust my own voice at this point — I scooted as far over on the bed as my leg would allow, and flipped back the covers.

"Just for tonight," she said as she sat on the edge of the mattress.

I grunted, but that was normal for me, so hopefully, she wouldn't think anything of it.

The mattress dipped as she sat down with a heavy sigh.

Never had eight hours passed so slowly. Even with the help of the medication Selene kept forcing on me, I lay awake most of the night. My senses were highly attuned to the female next to me: listening to her soft breathing, inhaling the scent of her shampoo from her hair draped across the pillow, feeling the mattress move as she tossed and turned.

It was sweet torture laying next to her, even on my California king-size bed. She touched me nowhere, and yet my body was alight. The last time I'd felt like this was... well, never.

The beginning of my life was full of warfare and purpose, driven to protect my loved ones with a fiery need. Not all dragons were this way, but my fate had been promised long before my birth. However, my life had been tied to the humans of a world long gone, and a dragon's life span was as close to immortal as a shifter came.

It had been a millennium now that I had been alone, drifting from one spot to another. How I'd landed in Deadlights Cove shortly after it was founded was still a mystery to me, but these people had weaseled their way into my life, whether I'd wanted them to or not. Yet, I couldn't remember the last time I'd been so drawn to another person, even as a friend.

I closed my eyes, pushing away the pain — a different kind than my leg — at the memories that threatened to surface. Of all of the years I'd spent alone.

Centuries had come and gone while I searched for a higher purpose, a ship lost at sea as I floated through life with nothing to anchor me in one place. When I'd come across Henry and Torrance, two of the original settlers in Deadlights Cove, they'd pleaded with me to stay and protect their people from the locals. Together, we oversaw the arrival of more supernaturals than I had ever seen congregated in one place. They called to me, helped me to feel more useful than I had in hundreds of years. So I'd stayed.

Protecting came naturally to me, so once Deadlights Cove was secure, and the threat of witch trials had passed, I'd begun to travel, searching for those who needed me next. Along the way, my glamour had evolved, allowing me to hide from the changing world even in dragon form.

It was both a gift and a curse, these powers I had. On one hand, I was different than the others, even from the other few remaining dragons, my extended glamour giving me a special ability to protect those in need. On the other, I had spent a thousand years alone.

I knew no other way to be.

Listening to Selene share her story — or pieces of it, at least — made me realize for the first time how much of life I was missing out on.

SELENE

I awoke the next morning to darkness. The other side of the bed was empty, and, as my senses came into focus, I realized the shower was running.

Part of me was glad Ryker had enough energy to take a shower — that meant he was on the mend. The caretaker in me wanted to go check on him, to make sure he was keeping his cast dry, but at this point, I knew Ryker well enough to know his pride would be severely damaged if I did that. Plus, the thought of a very naked, very wet Ryker standing in the shower was more than distracting.

Nope.

Better keep those thoughts locked down tight.

I stood, pacing over to the window on the far wall, and peeked out the blinds. Snow fell in heavy sheets, almost a whiteout, and painted the tall pines around his home with a beautiful white glaze.

The water shut off, and subconsciously, I drifted to the bathroom door, waiting on the other side to help if needed.

Several mumbled curses sounded from the bathroom, but no loud thunks or cries of pain.

When the door opened, I jumped back, realizing too late how close to the door I'd been standing.

"Sorry," I mumbled, casting my eyes anywhere but the bare chest of the male in front of me. Easier said than done.

Ryker had muscles on muscles, toned beyond belief, and all of it was covered in gorgeous, intricate tattoos. Some of them seemed ancient, black with an almost blue tinge to them, and painted on his skin in swirls and runes. Others were more modern — spokes of a tire, skulls, several dragons, even a few flowers.

Then I glanced down, afraid to meet his eyes after I'd clearly been ogling his chest, and that was an even *bigger* mistake.

Ryker wore only a towel, draped low across his waist, while he leaned on his crutches.

"Couldn't navigate getting my cast through my pants." He cleared his throat, seeming almost embarrassed. Why was that so freaking *cute?*

"Right." I nodded vigorously, trying to pull my focus back. "Yes. Let me... I mean, can I help? Or, do you have shorts? That'd be easier."

Ryker grunted, which I took as an agreement, and said, "Second drawer."

I jumped to attention, and almost jogged across the room to his dresser, just inside his closet. When I flicked on the overhead light, I shouldn't have been surprised, but the black hole of dark fabrics caught me off-guard. "Do you *always* wear black?" I called out over my shoulder as I pulled open the top drawer. Belts, socks, and boxers stared back at me, all black. "Oops," I muttered as I pushed the drawer back closed and opened the second one, as he'd instructed.

I wasn't snooping.

Would never do such a thing.

I did note there were *far* fewer boxers than I'd have thought necessary, but chose not to dwell on that.

"Shorts." I chanted to myself, trying to focus, and pulled out a black pair of loose sweat shorts for him. They had frayed edges, as if they'd once been long pants and he'd sheared them off at the knee, but were soft and stretchy.

"Need anything else in here while I'm at it?" I called back.

"If you're asking if I need underwear," Ryker's deep voice rasped from right over my shoulder, and I leapt into the air as I gripped my chest, "No. I'm good."

He snagged the shorts from me, and the click of his crutches sounded as he went back to the bathroom, and closed the door.

I stood there, leaning against the closet wall as my heart raced wildly in my chest. Luckily, the sound of my phone vibrating on the nightstand pulled me back from my momentary trance.

"Hello?" I answered.

"Bit breathy," Morgaine chuckled on the other end of the line. "I hope I interrupted something salacious. Have a good night, dear? Sleep well?"

I held the phone away from my ear, deadpanning it as if she could see me through the screen. "Is that why you're calling? To see if your meddling worked?"

"Ah," Mo sighed dreamily. "No. You've been called into a meeting with the leaders to give a report on Ryker."

The sound of the bathroom door opening made me glance over my shoulder towards the male, still bare-chested, and I swallowed. "Okay." I nodded, trying to stay focused. "What time?"

"Thirty minutes from now."

"Goddess, Mo!" I cursed. "You didn't think to give me any more warning?"

"Peel yourself away from that dreamy male, get in the shower so we don't all have to smell his musk on you, and borrow a car of his. Oh, and leave lover-boy at home. He'll only make a fuss. See you soon!"

Mo hung up, and I stared at the phone for several more minutes, trying to fathom how this woman had become this way.

I cut my eyes at Ryker. "How old is Mo?"

He snorted and shook his head. "I'm not at liberty to divulge that information. What was that call about?" He changed topics *real* quickly as he sat down on the couch, leaning his crutches on the armrest.

"I have to go into town for a meeting." I glanced his way, trying not to focus too blatantly on the water dripping off his shoulder-length blond hair, rivulets sliding down his chiseled chest. Even his calves were tattooed, and I fought the urge to inspect them closer. I'd seen all of him before, both way back on the *Night Which Should Not Be Named* and then again during his emergency surgery, but had never taken the time to appreciate the artwork covering his body.

"Right." Ryker shifted forward as he went to push up off the couch. "What time?"

"Well." I cleared my throat, grabbing my clothes from

the bag Nimue had dropped off for me. "They actually said just me."

Ryker's eyes squinted. "What's the meeting about?"

"Uh." I hesitated, suddenly uncomfortable. "I'm supposed to give a report on your status."

"Good." Ryker pushed up, grabbing his crutches. "Then I'm coming."

While I was at a loss for words on how to get him to stay put, Ryker moved to the closet, grabbed a black tee, and pulled it over his head.

"Don't put weight on your foot," I said automatically. He glared in return, but did as I said, foot hovering off the ground with his knee bent.

"I'll just shower quickly." I pointed to the bathroom, rolling my eyes internally at my own commentary, then hurried into the room, slamming the door shut behind me.

"Goddess, you're acting stupid," I muttered to myself. "Pull it together."

"I can still hear you," Ryker answered from somewhere on the other side of the door.

I showered and dried off as quickly as possible, even magically drying my hair, a useless waste of energy usually, and it drained me more than I was used to. I pulled the curls back into a ponytail, and dressed in my black yoga pants, turquoise pullover sweater, and snow boots.

"Where are your keys?" I asked, eyes searching the room. "Downstairs with the cars?"

Silence greeted me, and Ryker's stare blazed an ultra-bright green as he eyed me carefully. "I'm driving."

I laughed, a high giggle escaping me as I looked down to his right leg, then back up. "No. As your doctor, and the person who would be forced to be your passenger-slash-victim, I can't permit it."

"As the *owner* of the vehicles in question," Ryker growled, and my spine straightened, "I never let *anyone* drive my cars."

"Well, unless your wings suddenly work again, and you're offering me a ride," I immediately regretted my choice of words as I felt my cheeks heat, but forced myself to continue on, "I guess we're not going anywhere."

"Flores."

I paused, realizing just now that I hadn't the slightest clue what his last name was. "...Ryker."

Ryker's eyes closed as he inhaled deeply through his nose. I could feel the magic humming off him — it was there, just somehow unusable to him, which seemed strange to me. "I'm going to regret this, aren't I?"

I beamed, sensing what was coming next, and just barely kept myself from bouncing in excitement. "You tell me which one to drive."

With a quick glance out at the blizzard, he inhaled again before a heavy sigh escaped him. "The truck."

It took him several minutes to navigate the stairs on crutches, but we finally made it down to the floor of the garage below the loft. With a swipe of his hand over a panel on the wall, two glass doors slid open. The air was sucked from my lungs as I glanced around the neatly kept, almost museum-like room.

"So many cars." My eyes were blown wide as I ogled them, my fingers itching to touch the glossy black paint. Every single car and bike in his garage was black, to no one's surprise.

"I'm a dragon," Ryker huffed in annoyance. "We don't do minimalism."

I took in the room for another minute — we were running out of time, but I couldn't help myself after I'd been dying to get down here for days. From above in the loft, I could see the four parking spots straddling a wide center aisle leading to the double-wide garage door. But what I hadn't seen yet were the other six spots under the loft. Sports cars and bikes, some modern, some vintage, all dripping in luxury and wealth. The room was set up more like a museum than a garage with lighting placed strategically, casting each car in a glowing aura as one would a priceless painting. A laugh stuttered out of me as my eyes landed on a sparkling black Lamborghini Aventador.

"You have a Lambo," I chuckled, remembering how I'd dissed them last night during the movie.

"It's for sale," Ryker muttered.

"Since when?" My eyes sparkled with mirth.

"We're going to be late." Ryker avoided the question by hobbling over to a very large, lifted black GMC Denali truck in matte black towards the front of the garage. He paused at the driver's door, frowned back at me, and then moved to the passenger side.

A giddy laugh escaped me as I pulled open the door,

waiting for the running board to descend. I needed the step up into the car, but refused to admit it out loud to Ryker.

Once I was seated in the truck, I placed my hands lovingly on the steering wheel, feeling the smooth leather under my fingers. "This is nice."

Ryker grunted in agreement, looking extremely uncomfortable in the passenger's seat.

Dropping my hand to the side of the chair, I pushed on the button to move the seat forward. With every passing second that the seat motor continued to whir, moving from Ryker's normal seat position to where I needed it, Ryker's jaw ticked in annoyance. I paused, feeling mischievous, and waited for him to open his eyes. As soon as he'd relaxed, I pushed the button again, biting my cheeks to hide the smile that fought to escape me.

"Oh, my gods." Ryker slapped his hands down on his lap, head leaning back on the headrest. "You done yet?"

At that, I reached forward, dropping the steering wheel to my level, adjusted the pedals to move forward, and then grabbed the mirror to adjust it. "There. All good now."

"I'm never going to be able to drive this truck again," Ryker shook his head. Just to annoy him further, I reached down and pushed the button labeled "2" on the door, saving my seat position for next time.

Shockingly, he said nothing to that.

Ryker reached over, pressing a button on the bottom of the mirror, and the sleek garage door opened. "If you so much as knick the paint on this truck, I will never speak to you again."

"Got it." I smirked, pushed the ignition, and pulled out of the garage.

Chapter Fourteen

RYKER

If I never saw this damn conference room in Town Hall again, it would be too soon. I had spent centuries avoiding humans and supernaturals to the point it was practically an art form at which I was a master, and now? How many times was I going to let myself get roped into their affairs? Even if this one did concern me, a little.

I almost didn't survive the drive into town, and it had nothing to do with the icy, nearly impassable roads. No government agency was plowing my two-mile driveway, so we had to rely on snow tires and four-wheel drive.

I had to admit Selene was an adequately competent driver, not that I'd ever tell her that. I'd never let another being drive me around, and I hardly knew what to do with myself, just sitting there in the passenger seat like a child. I itched with the desire to take over, especially anytime we started sliding down the hill, but I restrained myself. Instead, I grabbed the *Oh Shit* handle so hard my knuckles were white and clamped my jaw shut.

But my near-fatality had nothing to do with the drive

itself and everything to do with the tiny witch perched in the driver's seat, a smug grin on her face, eyes alight with the joy of the drive. Gods, if she looked that good driving the truck, I wondered how she'd look behind the wheel of some of my other vehicles.

Or astride my bike.

I shifted in my seat at the conference table at the memory, my shorts suddenly feeling a bit too tight.

Orion had frowned when I hobbled into the room on my crutches, but he could fuck right off if he didn't think I was going to be involved in a meeting *concerning me*. Even if I'd had my fill of meetings for the next millennium.

The other heads of town were in attendance as well. Blaze gave a friendly wave from beside Nimue, who was seated between him and her new husband/mate/fox Alpha, Kit. Kit's dark brows furrowed as his eyes scanned my crutches, and I couldn't blame him. A shifter unable to heal for this long *was* alarming. I saw the sentiment reflected on the faces of the other shifters as well — Nadir, Kit's cousin and Second, frowned as he noted my cast; Darius, wolf Alpha and local law enforcement, rubbed a hand through his close-cropped coils; Julian, his Second, leaned forward on his elbows, eyes sharp. Winona, head of the local bears, gave me a sympathetic grimace, but I couldn't handle her motherly shit right now and all but ignored her, even if the female didn't deserve my ire.

Ostara, head of the local witch Coven, raised a greying brow appraisingly, her head tilted in thought. A witch who looked to be in her mid-fifties, but was likely several decades older due to the way witches aged, Ostara always managed to come across somehow both regal and condescending. Her white-streaked natural coils were short and neat, the strands of white contrasting her deep brown skin. Her son and Second, Lysander, had skin several shades lighter than hers and light green eyes that told something about the skin color of his father, though I'd never met the male. However, even aside from those details, I always had a hard time seeing the resemblance between the imposing and haughty mother and her cocky lothario of a son.

I gritted my teeth at their attention. As much as I knew this was why we were here, it didn't mean I was the gods-damned prop for the afternoon.

"Let's get started," Selene called over to Orion from where she sat to my right, and I grunted quietly in thanks. "What is it you'd like to know?"

"Right." Orion sat up a bit as the focus swung over to him. "As you all know, a few months ago we had some issues with the magic in the town —"

"Yeah, we remember," Darius muttered bitterly. The shifters had been unable to change between forms and he, along with a number of other shifters, had been stuck as their animals for several days.

"And while we caught the witches responsible —"

"*Some* of the witches," Blaze interjected.

"*Most* of the witches," Orion continued. "The true instigator was *not* caught, Blaze's brother Errakal. I sent Ryker out to track him down —" he nodded to me, and I answered with a slight nod of the head, "— But so far, Errakal has evaded capture." Orion pressed his lips together before continuing. "We knew it was possible something like this would happen again, and it seems it has. Not only was *Ryker* tracked and shot, but his magic has been unable to heal his wounds as he's dealing with iron poisoning."

My jaw worked at the implication — however subtle or unintended — that I was incompetent at my job and stupid enough to let some half-demon-half-witch get the jump on me.

"He should not have been able to track me like that," I said. "I was fully glamoured at the time."

Murmurs swept around the table until Orion cleared his throat, settling them down.

"Nevertheless," his wings rustled with discomfort, "the Paranormal Regulations and Interspecies Council is investigating the matter of your revealing yourself to the humans."

"Jesus, don't say it like that, O." Blaze shuddered from my left. I had to agree with him.

"It wasn't his fault," Selene spoke up again, ignoring Blaze's comment. "Errakal, or whoever shot him, should be the one under inquiry."

Orion shrugged. "I would be inclined to agree, but seeing as he can't be found, they will be questioning Ryker."

I met Orion's grey stare, but I knew there was nothing he could do about it. The PRICs could come and question me all they wanted. Not like there was anything I could tell them.

"Selene, have you seen any sign of his magic returning?"

Shooting me a quick glance before looking around the table at the others, Selene shook her head. "Not yet. His injury appears to be healing exactly like a human's would."

I knew it wasn't *technically* an insult, but damn if it didn't feel like one.

She rattled off a handful of other medical things that I

tuned out, as did the rest of the table if their glazed expressions were anything to go by. Only Orion listened intently, seeming to take in her every word as he made a few notes for himself.

"My powers have also been off since that night, so I'm wondering if it's more than just the iron poisoning," Orion admitted, laying his pen down. "Ryker shouldn't have been able to feel anything Selene did after I used my magic on him, but he still could. My power has been noticeably reduced since."

Mutterings again, and then he went around the table, asking each group if they'd noticed changes or reductions in power, and making notes.

All the shifters were healing like humans, it seemed, not just me, which gave me some measure of vindication. Even the witches were needing to use stronger ingredients in their spell work to achieve the same results, and some of their spells no longer worked at all. There weren't many demons in town, but Blaze admitted his demon powers had been reduced significantly, and Nimue nodded in agreement.

Orion nodded grimly as he finished taking down their accounts. "I have calls out to the other supernatural towns across the US to see how widespread this is, and if their powers are weakened in the same ways or not. I should hear back from them by the end of the week, at the latest. But at this point, it's probably safe to assume the worst."

"Errakal is trying again." Blaze winced. Though he was nothing like his brother, they were still technically family, and it had to carry the sting of betrayal that Errakal was doing this to all of us.

"Not only trying again, dear." Morgaine glanced from

Blaze to Selene and me. "But he's clearly increased his power and range somehow."

"A half-demon-half-witch wouldn't be able to do that on their own," Ostara's velvety voice mused out loud.

"No," Orion agreed. "He must be working with someone else. Someone *much* more powerful than himself. Which means if we can't find them, this is all about to get worse before it gets better."

Silence hung heavy in the room at his words, but we all knew he was right.

The only question was, how much worse?

Chapter Fifteen

SELENE

"Come for a drink at Scallywags?" Nimue asked after Orion had wrapped up the ominous meeting, having come over to chat when we'd all stood to go. I heard her words, but my attention was on Ryker. He hadn't said anything, but I could tell by the slight tightening in the corners of his eyes that the pain meds were wearing off.

"Selene?" Nimue asked again, and I pulled my eyes to land on her. "Petra's there already."

"I don't know." I bit my lip. "I'd like to, but I think I should drive him back —"

"He can hear you," Ryker muttered from beside me, leaning on his crutches. "And he could do with a drink himself."

"You shouldn't drink on your painkillers."

"I'm a dragon. I can take it. And they've worn off."

I propped a hand on my hip, but instead of making me feel authoritative as it usually did with patients, the way it drew Ryker's bright green eyes to my waist made me feel decidedly self-conscious. "Your magic isn't working, which makes you basically a human."

His eyes narrowed as he drew them slowly up to my face, and I swore I could feel the trail they traced along my body, igniting my nerves with their caress. But the look he leveled me with when his gaze finally met mine was anything but sensual. In fact, it was so downright terrifying I swallowed and nearly took a step back.

"Say that again." His low growl was a challenge. One I was *not* about to accept.

My heart pounded thunderously the longer we stared off, tension I didn't understand — or maybe I did — coiling between us, my throat going dry.

"Fine," I managed to croak out. "*One* drink."

He didn't smile, but there was something of triumph in his eyes that told me he just thought he'd won something.

As he started hobbling for the door, I refused to meet Nimue's eyes, not ready to face the understanding I knew I'd find there.

As soon as we made it to Scallywags, I abandoned Ryker at the bar to drink alone and raced over to the booth where Petra was already seated, laptop, books, and notebooks fanned out around her. Her deep sapphire cable-knit turtleneck set off the blue of her eyes, while her red hair tied up in a messy bun highlighted her slightly-faded winter freckles.

It was still strange to me to see my decidedly-human college roommate here, in the Cove, surrounded by supernaturals I'd known my whole life. Petra had come up here last summer as part of a sabbatical from her job teaching at Bishop College, to do research on the witch history in the area and find new source material to design college courses. Now that she knew the *real* history, I knew she'd been struggling with how to present something useful back to her department without revealing the truth about our hidden supernatural society.

Petra had also told me Morgaine had essentially offered her a job writing an account of the history of supernaturals in general. I knew she'd been considering it for after this sabbatical year, and once in a while I caught her doing a little *extra* research, though she hadn't officially taken the project on yet.

Now, as I slumped into the booth across from her, I was glad she was here to vent to. Nimue was on my heels and slid in beside me.

"What are you working on?" I asked, peeking at the books on the table that all appeared to be about the history of magic.

Petra looked up from her work, one fiery red brow raised in inquiry as she scanned my face to see if I was actually interested. Petra could go on a tangent like no one I'd ever met, so I smiled to make sure she knew the question was genuine.

"Oh, well. I've been helping Mo do some research on linking magics. As far as she knows, it's only a myth, but she's been wondering if there's any truth to it. An old witch legend spoke of a witch and a shifter linking their magic, which then allowed the witch to heal like a shifter could, and the shifter to conduct rituals like a witch. She was wondering if that's what Kal is trying to do in some round-about form to gain power, but I keep coming on dead-ends. She has a whole list of topics for me to research though, so I might table this one for now and move on to the next, assessing the ley lines across the country."

Petra studied me, then glanced to Nimue at my side. "But you're not here to talk about magical links and maps. And you look like you need a drink. Blaze?" she called over to the bar, not taking her eyes off me as she hastily made neat stacks of all her books and papers, closed her laptop, and pushed it all to the end of the table.

"Already making 'em, Petey," came his response, and she nodded.

"All right, let's hear it."

I had barely opened my mouth when Blaze slid drinks onto the table for us. "You two ready for Trivia Night?" Without even waiting for us to answer, Blaze turned to his cousin, Nimue. "Dev said she'd be here to partner with you in a few, and if you didn't wait for her, you were as good as dead to her."

Nimue chuckled, and I shook my head. Even after almost 30 years of being their friends, it was still shocking to see how close the friendliest demon and the surliest witch were. But they were inseparable.

"I really shouldn't stay. I'll have to drive us back soon." I tried to push the drink away.

"I think your patient is settling in for the long haul, so you might as well relax for a bit." Blaze shrugged before heading off. As one, Petra, Nimue, and I turned to see Ryker twist off the cap of a bottle of vodka and take a long swig straight from the container, ignoring the glass Blaze had set out in front of him. Maia stood behind the bar, shaking her head, but didn't seem inclined to stop him.

I sighed, not willing to take on the responsibility of cutting him off, but also as his doctor, I needed to pretend I wasn't seeing this. Sure, his pain meds were gone from his system, but it still wasn't a good idea.

"Ryker may be the most difficult patient I've ever had to work with." I pulled my focus back to my two best friends. Petra sipped at her drink, studying me over the glass. She circled her hand in the air in a *go on* gesture while Nimue leaned her elbows on the table, and I slumped back in my seat.

"Not only is he a typical male that thinks he's being as tough as nails, while really whining more than any female patient I have ever attended, but he's just so…" I trailed off, searching for the word.

"Hot?" Petra answered for me, then shrugged innocently when I glared at her.

"I can't contribute to this conversation since Kit is by the bar and can still hear me, but," Nimue paused, her eyes wide as her nose scrunched, offering the teeniest nod of agreement.

"I mean, yes. That too." Without any conscious thought, my eyes moved towards where Ryker sat at the bar, and snagged on the way he chatted with Maia.

The platinum blonde bartender was a new hire since I'd left town, so I didn't know much about the girl beyond her name. She wore an oversized navy blue hoodie with the hood pulled up over her face, casting most of her appearance in shadows. A long braid, almost white in the low lighting of the bar, hung over one shoulder, trailing down almost to her waist. The few times I'd been in here before, I'd never seen her interact very much with the patrons, but Blaze seemed happy with her.

Maia was busy polishing a glass while talking with Ryker, and I caught myself glancing back and forth between her and the annoying dragon.

"Earth to Selene." Petra waved her hand in front of my face, pulling my attention back.

"Sorry," I mumbled as I took a long swig of my drink. Blaze was by far the best bartender I'd ever encountered — his mixed drinks were as smooth as they were potent. "What is this?"

"I don't ask questions anymore." Petra smiled as she took another sip.

In a blur of black clothes and blue hair, Devanna slid into the booth next to Petra. I couldn't help but chuckle at her shirt, reading Not All Witches Live In Salem as she reached across the table, her fingers snaking around my glass, and she took a long swig of the drink before blowing out a breath.

"I just spent three hours dotting every *I* and crossing every *T* on my new permit request, and I swear to the goddess, if that overgrown Zazu doesn't authorize this one, I'm going to pluck out all his feathers and light them on fire."

Before any of us had time to process *that*, Blaze walked to the table at the front of the dining room, picking up a sparkling pink rhinestone microphone. "You ready to get started?" he asked the crowded room, and everyone began chatting. "The first rule of Trivia Night: You do not talk about Trivia Night."

I waited for the low laughter from the audience, but was slightly taken aback by how solemn everyone's expressions were. After living in Boston for the last 13 years, I sometimes forgot how seriously everyone in the Cove took... well, *everything.*

Looking around the bar, I noticed several of the tables filled, the young witch Aurora sitting with her demon boyfriend, Nox, at one; Lysander and a handful of guys I vaguely recognized as his band-mates at another. Zaphiel, an angel, sat at a high-top with one of Dev's witch friends, Castor, and at the table next to them were a few of the local wolf shifters whom I recognized by sight, if not name. Kit stood at the bar next to Nadir, with a few others from their skulk, watching over the crowd as they sipped at their pints.

"Topics are drawn out of the hat at random, so we don't know what it is yet. Choose your partner wisely — no switching once the topic has been announced, even if you know you're already done for with the partner you've chosen."

"What do you say, Nims?" Dev whispered, locking eyes with Nimue across the table from her as she pulled her bright blue hair up into a knot on her head, cracking her neck to loosen up like this was a physical task she was taking on.

"Tonight's our night, Devvie." Nimue smiled back, winking at me as Dev scowled at the nickname.

"And that is two rules too many, so here we go!" Blaze stuck his hand into a large fishbowl filled with folded white paper slips, swishing his hand around dramatically as he squeezed his eyes shut. With flourish, he withdrew a paper, holding it up as he opened his eyes, delight shining brightly as he read it. "And tonight's topic is Sandra Bullock movies!"

Dev cackled, the sound fit for an evil villain. "We've got this in the *bag*."

Nim rubbed her hands together excitedly. "Been studying for this since '95."

"Do you have buzzers or something?" I asked Petra, and all three of my friends gaped at me.

"Fuck, sometimes I forget how long you've been gone, Leens," Dev said, her eyes and mouth a flat line. "No buzzers. You shout your favorite swear word, and Blaze chooses by speed first, originality second if it's a tie."

"Oh," I shrugged, glancing at Petra as I tried to catalog every curse word I'd ever learned. "Well, okay."

"Ready for the first question?" Blaze asked, and everyone lifted their drinks, cheersing loudly before he continued.

"In 1995, Sandra Bullock played the role of a token collector in the movie *While You Were Sleeping*. Her character's name was Lucy, which was also her character's in another movie she later starred in. What was the second movie?"

"Fucktrumpet!" Dev yelled at the same time Maia called, *"Pissflaps!"*

My mind hardly had time to register the question, let alone think of the answer as I looked from one woman to the other. Petra choked on her drink, spraying liquid across the table. "Sorry, I'm not going to be much use here, but this is always hilarious to watch."

"Damn, that was fast," Zaph said, slightly frustrated.

"Damn is not the least bit original and you were too late.

Fucktrumpet takes the cake here, so Dev, what's the answer?"

"Her character's name was Lucy in both *While You Were Sleeping* and *Two Weeks Notice*."

Not even waiting for Blaze to confirm her answer, Dev and Nimue high-fived, letting out a loud *whoop* of excitement. With a flick of his hand, Blaze marked a 1 under their names on the chalkboard behind him, then looked down at the next question.

"In the movie *Miss Congeniality*, Cheryl is asked to describe her perfect date. What —"

"*Twatwaffle!*" Maia called out, and Dev threw up her hands.

"Isn't that illegal? She didn't even let you finish the question?"

Blaze scoffed, his dark hair falling down over one eye. "You should know by now that I'm the *last* one to enforce rules. So, no, it's not illegal. Maia?"

"April 25." I couldn't help but glance at the bartender, noticing the way her eyes sparkled with delight. Ryker sat in front of her at the bar with his back to me, sipping out of a glass now, which I guessed was a relief, though he didn't seem to be participating. But just as I was about to turn back to Blaze, I noticed Maia's hand sneak across the bar, knocking knuckles with Ryker.

Blaze added a 1 under Maia and Ryker's names and continued. "Sandie starred alongside Ryan Reynolds in —"

"*Kumquat!*" Nimue yelled, and the bar went silent. All eyes turned to focus on our table, but no one more serious than Dev.

"*Kumquat?*" Dev asked, her voice full of disdain. "Really? That was the best you could do? A *fruit?*"

Nimue cringed, pink tinting her cheeks, but Blaze cut in before she could defend herself. "That doesn't count as a swear, so I will be disqualifying you from this question. Also, Nimmie, I've never been more embarrassed for you. Really need to work on your shitty vocabulary. Kit, help her out with this." Blaze gestured helplessly at Nim, but Kit only threw a hand up with a shrug.

"My wife can swear when the occasion calls for it, right, mate?" From across the room where he stood with Nadir, Kit gave her a look that could've had a nun ripping off her habit, and Nim went from pink to fuschia.

"Get a room," Kit's younger sister, Lily, jeered from her booth. She was paired with Julian, his arm slung around her shoulders.

"I think we have to forfeit this question," Blaze said. "In which two movies did Sandie play doctors?"

This time, I *knew* I saw Ryker lean over the bar to whisper something to Maia before she called out, *"Thundercunt!"*

"What spells have you tried on him?" Devanna asked after trivia had wrapped up, nodding her head towards the bar. She and Nimue had ended up neck and neck with Ryker and Maia, of all people, though the girls managed to win on the final question.

I half-turned to look at Ryker again, and was surprised to see a chessboard in front of him; he seemed to be playing against Maia every time she walked by his perch. The bar had quieted down after trivia, but apparently we weren't leaving yet.

"Mo gave me one to test for his iron poisoning." I turned back to her. "But as far as healing spells, I tried the day after he was injured but it, um, didn't work." Dev's brown eyes caught mine, no doubt sensing there was more to it. Even if I didn't particularly want to talk about it, I had to admit she might be able to help. "I haven't used much magic in the past couple years. I wasn't able to access it."

Understanding dawned in her eyes, but it was Petra who spoke up. "Since your mom died?" She winced sympathetically, and I nodded.

The last time I'd even tried to access my magic was right before I'd gone to Boston, just a few months before Petra and I were assigned as roommates in college. Even though I couldn't tell Petra everything about my supernatural life at the time, she'd been there for me in a way no one else had, offering me comfort or distraction in that especially hard first year alone.

Dev hummed in thought while she swirled the whiskey in her glass, ice clinking. "Maybe you need another witch to help you reach your magic again; unlock it."

"Are you offering?"

"No," Dev scoffed, but it wasn't in rudeness, more like self-awareness. "You need someone who will be patient and understanding." The three of us chorused *Oh* and nodded knowingly, which she met with a flat stare, but otherwise ignored. "Someone who can tap into other witches' magic, work with them, and amplify their power. A Harmonic witch." She paused, no doubt running through the witches in town. "Try Lysander."

My surprise must have shown on my face, because Dev laughed. The last person I expected to be one of the most sought after Harmonic witches would be the band frontman pretty-boy Lys, even if he was the son of our Coven leader.

"Ostara has made sure he's trained in every discipline," she explained. "But I've seen him work with other blocked witches before. He's good. Why do you think he's such a good musician?"

I shrugged. "All right, send me his info."

As Dev pulled out her phone to do just that, I chanced a look back at the bar. Again, I experienced a twinge of something in my gut at the sight of Ryker chatting with Maia, her leaning forward over the bar with an enigmatic grin while she moved a chess piece.

My phone dinged, and I saw the text from Dev with Lys's contact info, resolved to contact him as soon as I could. Anything to get Ryker healed up and me out of his life before we both did something else we would regret.

Chapter Sixteen

RYKER

Chess with Maia had been a welcome surprise. She'd set the board down in front of me soundlessly after trivia wrapped up and most of the other patrons filtered out of the bar, and she actually gave me a run for my money.

Unusual, given my many years of practice.

I especially liked that Maia wasn't overly chatty, asking pointed questions and discussing the game, but not once had she asked about my injury.

It hadn't hurt that I'd felt Selene's eyes on us now and again while Maia and I played. I knew Selene wouldn't admit it to herself, but damn it, we had a score to settle ever since she'd claimed our one-night stand was *nothing special*. If I needed to make her a little jealous first, then I would. Eventually, she'd give in, I'd earn my repeat performance, and then we'd see if she could still deny that I was the best lay of her life.

When the snow started coming down so hard we couldn't see the street from the bar, Blaze kicked everyone out, saying he wanted to take Petra home.

"You going to make it home okay?" I asked Maia as she cleared the chess board and returned it back to the shelf with the other board games.

With a smirk, she turned back to me, eyeing my leg where my cast rested on the barstool next to me. "Not like you'd be much help if I couldn't." She raised a brow, challenging me, then glanced back to where the girls still sat in their booth. "Besides, you've got bigger problems to worry about than me getting home safely."

I didn't even bother to turn — I could feel Selene's eyes boring a hole through the back of my head as I finished the last of the vodka in my bottle.

"Til next time, Pearl." I winked as I pushed the bottle across the counter, and Maia jerked back in surprise. Before she had time to form a response, I swiveled around on the stool, Selene now standing right behind me.

I noted with a glimmer of satisfaction how her eyes flicked between me and Maia, questions swimming.

"Do you need help?" was all she said though, and I shook my head with a grunt before following her out to the truck.

The truck barely made it up my driveway, tires spinning until we slid back down the hill a few yards several times over, but eventually, we reached the top. I leaned over and clicked the garage opener on the mirror, but nothing happened.

Clicked it again.

"Power must be out."

Selene sighed deeply, but shut off the engine. "Don't suppose you have a generator for times like this?"

"Not usually here enough to bother."

She swung the door open, hopping down adorably like she was dismounting from a horse, the truck was so tall for her. I heard her mutter *Great* under her breath before the door slammed behind her.

By the time I'd made my own way out of the truck, Selene was by my side to help. I almost shook her off, almost told her I didn't need her, but the snow was several inches deep already and the crutches kept slipping on hidden ice. So I allowed her to spot me back to the door.

When we got inside, it became apparent that it wasn't just the power that was out, but the furnace as well.

"Ryker," Selene swung on me once she, too, realized how cold it was inside, breath fogging in the air already. "We can't stay here like this."

"Heat rises. And we can use the stove."

She furrowed her brow, and I nodded at her to continue up the stairs to the loft.

I wasn't surprised she hadn't noticed the stove before — there hadn't been a need to have it going while she'd been here, and it had become something of a spare shelf in its downtime, covered in books and whatever else needed to get off the ground. Considering my entire house was one large open room, even to down below in the garage, the heat from a wood-burning stove wasn't functional most days. The nostalgia of it was what drew me to it — it reminded me of a hearth from home.

Now, as I hobbled up the last few stairs, she went over to where it sat off to the side of the television and began to clear it off. Luckily, even though the power was out, the clouds and white snow diffused the light from outside enough that, with the wall of windows in front of us, we had enough light to see by, at least here in the main space. I'd need to find a flashlight for the bathroom eventually, but heat first.

"Where's the wood?" Selene finished clearing off the stove and looked around the space.

So many jokes, so little time. She must have sensed my train of thought, for her tawny cheeks darkened as I smirked at her, then jerked my head back downstairs.

"Back of the garage."

She nodded, pressing her lips together, and her brown eyes scanned my leg. "Guess this is my workout for today."

"Don't tell me you're afraid of a little manual labor?" She narrowed her eyes, unable to tell if I was making another insinuation, and I refused to confirm or deny. "I'll light it and keep it going, fair enough?"

As Selene went back downstairs to locate the logs, I settled in front of the stove, making sure it was cleaned out and ready for a new fire. I hadn't spent winters in the Cove in years, but I'd still insisted on it being installed when I'd built this place. There was something inherently… well, not *comforting*, that sounded absurd, but *familiar*, maybe, about fire. I'd grown up in a time when it was the only source of heat, after all.

She came back up a few minutes later and dumped the logs at my feet.

"How much will we need?"

I looked at the handful of logs she'd managed to bring up in one trip. She was not going to like my answer. "Hel of a lot more than that." As predicted, her eyes widened in that way like she was resisting rolling them, before she turned and stomped off to get more. To her credit, she wasn't complaining.

By the time she'd returned again, I had a small bunch of kindling lit and was getting the first log to catch. A few more trips, and we had a decent enough pile that might see us through the night.

Even after the stove was up and running, it would take a while for the heat to permeate the space, and it would probably never get to a temperature Selene would consider *warm*.

"We should plan on sleeping down here," I said as she finally took off her coat and gloves, draping her coat on the back of a chair and her gloves on the table to dry out. "For the heat."

"*We?*" she asked. "I wouldn't have thought the cold would bother you. Aren't you part-reptile with fire roaring in your veins?"

You won't be warm enough without me, I wanted to say, but then she'd think I cared. So I just shrugged. Let her read into that whatever she wanted.

Chapter Seventeen

SELENE

Even with the stove going, the loft was freezing. I would never admit it to the male, because he was insufferable, but he was right. I'd have to sleep in front of the stove if I wanted any hope of rest at all, and his warmth would help considerably.

I grabbed all the blankets I could find and brought them over to the living room, dragging the thin rug along as well. Ryker only watched with his piercing green eyes as I also grabbed all the pillows and cushions to make a little nest to sleep in. Lying on the floor wasn't going to be comfortable no matter what, but I could try to make it bearable. If only that airbed hadn't been a dud.

Changing into dry clothes — most of the ones I'd been wearing were varying degrees of damp just from walking through the snow from the bar to the truck, then the truck to the house — I dropped a kettle on the stove, making myself a cup of tea to warm up and slipped my jacket back on. I offered one to Ryker, but he waved it off, staring into the flames.

"Do you miss it?" I settled into my pillow nest next to him, careful not to spill my tea as I leaned back and tugged a blanket over myself.

He pulled his eyes from the stove to me. "Fire?"

"Fire, scorching stuff, terrorizing villagers, whatever you dragons do in your free time."

The corner of his mouth twitched as he turned back to the stove. "I'll have you know I haven't terrorized any villagers in quite some time."

"Oh, my mistake."

We settled into a surprisingly comfortable silence, the only sounds the crackling logs in the stove and the wind and snow against the wall of windows. I finished my tea and set it aside, reclining even farther and pulling the blanket up to my chin.

Suddenly a hand reached across my torso, gripping my waist as I was hauled into Ryker's chest, and I nearly cricked my neck whipping it around so fast to shoot a questioning stare at Ryker.

"You're shivering."

Was I? "I'm fine."

"Your lips are blue."

That was an exaggeration. I knew — medically — that it wasn't cold enough in here to give me hypothermia, not with the stove going, but I had to admit his extra warmth felt nice. Maybe I was just being weak. I allowed him to nestle us together, my side into his chest, and had to press my eyes shut as I inhaled the scent of sparks and steel and leather this male always seemed to carry.

Goddess, I'd forgotten what a giant he was until he was wrapped around me like this, and the way we fit so perfectly was enough to twist my brain into mush. Ryker reclined on his side, head resting on one hand, pulling me into him, and had his cast propped up on a pillow. I lay on my back against the soft rug with my ear pressed practically against his heart, and I could have sworn it was beating a little bit too fast.

Just then, my phone buzzed from the floor beside me where I'd placed it, saving me from the ridiculous train of thought I'd nearly started down.

I extricated my arm from the mountain of blankets and pillows to reach over and lift it up, tapping the screen to make a text show.

Lysander: Hey, happy to help. Want to meet tomorrow?

I sensed Ryker reading over my shoulder — nosy dragon — and felt him stiffen beside me as I swiped open my phone to text Lys back. Dev must have given him the heads-up that I might want his help with the spell.

"Problem?" I asked sweetly, not taking my eyes off my phone as I texted back *Sure, thanks.*

When Lysander's response of *Looking forward to it* with a smiley face came back, I could have sworn I heard a low rumble.

"What does that little punk think he can help you with?" I'd never heard Ryker's voice so husky.

Well, maybe *once* before.

"Witch business." I set my phone back down and tried to find the same comfortable position as before, but it was difficult now that my heat-sharing buddy had gone still as stone.

"Flores." I couldn't help lifting my eyes to his, the green gone as bright as I'd ever seen them where his face loomed over mine. "You got needs, you come to me."

I tried to stop any reaction to his words, but something must have shown across my face, because his pupils flared. "He's going to help me with a spell to help *you*. That's all." Why was my voice so shaky?

Time stretched out between us, static charging the room as he studied me. Under the weight of his gaze, I suddenly felt acutely aware of his arm resting across my torso, every place where our bodies touched, even though we were both fully clothed. Somehow, he'd scooped me until my knees were bent and tucked against him, his own bent and pressing against my shins as he lay facing me.

I could practically see the smoke that would be drifting out of his nostrils if he were in dragon form, waiting for me to have a response to the rest of his insinuation.

"I can take care of myself perfectly well, should the need arise." What the *hell* was I saying? I blinked in surprise at my own innuendo, wishing I could run away from the intensity of his stare, but his arms and body had me locked in place.

"But not better than I can."

My breath hitched as his hand found the inside of my knee under the blankets, tracing patterns with his fingers, but not inching any higher. Did I want him to? I should have been pushing his hand away. Right?

"I don't remember anything special."

His eyes narrowed, pupils flashing vertical for a heartbeat. "Is that a challenge?"

No. Yes. Maybe?

His hand started to trail up the inside of my thigh, slow enough I could have stopped him, but every nerve in my body was lighting up. I held my breath, waiting to see what he would do, knowing every moment that I should put a stop to it. Whatever this was.

I was here in a medical capacity. It was unprofessional.

It was *glorious*.

His hand reached the top of my thigh, but instead of moving where I needed it, he switched to my other leg, moving down with the same tantalizing slowness.

It was so *hot* in here. Why were we on the floor in front of the stove? I was melting. I couldn't even think straight, as focused as I was on his hand.

His lips grazed the sensitive skin behind my ear, and a shiver ran down my spine. "Do I need to remind you what I can do to you, Flores? What I can make you feel?"

I might have whimpered something in response, but I couldn't be sure, and the next moment I inhaled sharply as his hand slipped under my shirt, whisper-soft against my skin until he reached my breast. His thumb skated across my skin, wildly sensitive even through the fabric of my bra. I clenched my thighs together, and a smug glint entered his eye, no doubt scenting exactly what he was doing to me.

"I don't even need to get you naked, and this is how you respond to me." His teeth grazed the lobe of my ear.

"Ryker," I breathed, but I didn't know what it meant. Did I want him to stop? Or hurry up?

A soft chuckle rumbled in his chest, like he knew what I wanted even if I didn't.

My heart pounded furiously as his hand snaked down again, and it took everything in me not to push my hips up and try to guide him where I wanted him, but I couldn't give him the satisfaction of appearing so needy. Even if I was.

His fingers finally found the top of my pants, sliding

back and forth across my stomach, toying with me. I breathed out a huff of impatience, and he chuckled again.

"Need something, Flores?"

His eyes locked with mine as his warm hand stilled, laying flat across my abdomen between my hips, so close and not nearly close enough. My thoughts drifted back to that night after Blaze's Halloween party — the night I'd spent months trying to forget, mostly because the male in front of me? He was unavailable, and I knew it. Why else would I have put myself through the endless torture of all of those awful first dates? I needed to forget him, and move on. But that was easier said than done when his hands traced circles over my navel.

"Yes," I finally whispered, giving in to what my body was aching for, heart and mind be damned.

"What's that?"

"You," I breathed, and his pupils flared again. "I need you."

"I thought so." His eyes flicked to my lips, but he didn't lean in to kiss me. I didn't care, because he finally slid his hand under my clothes, down between my legs, and a moan escaped me as a finger finally pressed in the right place.

He chuckled again as he toyed with me, sliding back and forth but not inside. I couldn't resist anymore, and moved my hips with him, heat flushing my cheeks, but I was too far gone to care.

"You get this wet on your own, Flores?" He nibbled my neck where it met my shoulder, his voice raspy against my skin. "Or is this only for me?"

"I —" Just then, a finger slid into me, and I whimpered, unable to form coherent speech anymore. He shifted at the sound, and I felt his own need pressed against the side of my thigh.

A moment later, a second finger joined, and then I was pushing my hips up into his hand as he thrust them inside me, the heel of his palm hitting me just right.

"Gods, Flores," he growled, letting his head hang down until it pressed against my shoulder, the sound of his hand suddenly drowning out any others in the loft. "You're going to come for me."

It was a statement, not a question, but its soft command sent me hurtling over the edge. I breathed out his name against his chest as he pressed his hand against me, working me through it, my lungs heaving as stars swam in my vision.

His own breathing was heavy, and I could feel how hard he was against my leg, but he didn't make a move to do anything else. Instead, he slowly withdrew his hand, bringing it outside of the blankets and held it up. Our eyes met again, his expression full of smug satisfaction as he brought his fingers to his lips, sucking the moisture off of them.

Ryker: 1, Selene: 0.

Chapter Eighteen

RYKER

Selene fell asleep shortly after our little escapade, curling her body into me for warmth. I left my arm draped around her waist, pulling her into me, offering her every bit of my heat as her cheek rested on my chest. Without realizing what I was doing, I traced small patterns over her back, just enjoying the feel of her next to me.

Sleep didn't find me as easily, what with the dull ache in my leg that never left, and now the raging hormones that still fought for release. But tonight hadn't been about me. I'd had enough of Selene's comments that our time together was mediocre — she just needed a reminder.

No one was better than me.

With that same thought, my hand stilled.

Guilt surfaced as I looked down at her, knowing that I shouldn't lead her on like this. Maybe I'd been wrong to push this tonight. Selene would get attached — would think this meant something it didn't. And then I'd hurt her.

My life was far from conducive for relationships of any kind. Hel, I had enough of a time maintaining friendships, let alone romantic relationships. The life I'd chosen meant I was never in one place for long, and attachments were a bad idea.

I didn't want to hurt her.

But gods, she was gorgeous.

I brushed the hair from her face, placing a gentle kiss on her forehead, and closed my eyes.

Sometime in the night, the power was restored, and I woke to the house flooded with heat. The stove had died down, but still had the red glow of burning embers within. I pushed to sit up, reclining with my back against the couch, casted leg outstretched in front of me while I waited for Selene to wake up.

"Morning," she said with a lazy smile as she rolled towards me.

I nodded, then turned to the window, checking the storm.

A silent beat passed that seemed loaded and awkward, but I said nothing. With a huff, Selene stood, walked to where her bag lay on the floor, then into the bathroom, the door slamming behind her.

I winced at the sound, but knew I'd done the right thing. What happened last night? It was amazing, but it was also the last time anything could happen between us, even if that made me a bastard.

Selene spent just short of an hour in the bathroom, the sound of running water switching to that of a hair dryer, then to the sound of Shania Twain's *That Don't Impress Me Much* playing loudly. I'd never spent much time around women, so I had no idea if this was normal or not, but I had a bad feeling.

Finally, she emerged, and I was already kicking myself for my earlier promise. Wearing a pair of perfectly fitted jeans, and a pale pink sweater that hugged her curves just right, Selene looked radiant. Her curls were bouncy and fresh, so much so I wanted to reach out and touch them, but that would be stupid. I tucked my hands in the pockets of my sweat shorts — I had changed, but ended up wearing a clean version of what I'd worn the day before — to keep my hands from moving on their own.

"Breakfast?" Selene asked as she circled the kitchen island, and began pulling out eggs, bacon, tortillas, and a skillet. "I'm making myself a burrito, but I can leave out the ingredients if you'd like to cook something for yourself after I'm done."

She cut her eyes my way in challenge, then focused on the task in front of her. Guess I wasn't the only one writing off what happened yesterday then.

I watched as she made her breakfast, then bit into her burrito. The contented hum she released sounded a bit exaggerated and forced, especially since I knew exactly how her moans sounded when they *weren't*, but I let it slide. After she ate, she gestured to me, then left all of the pots and dishes scattered over the stove and countertop.

"I need to get ready for Lys," Selene said as she stood next to the kitchen table, hands on hips.

My eyes darted to the side, trying to follow her train of thought, until she pointed at the table. A laugh caught in my throat when I realized her meaning — she was kicking me out of my own kitchen.

"And where exactly do you want me to go?" I held my hand out, reminding her that it was all one open room up here.

"The couch. Your bed. Downstairs. I don't care." She shrugged, piling up all of the stray medical supplies still out on the table. "He texted me this morning that we'd need space to work."

I grunted, which she took to mean agreement. What it actually meant was I needed to destroy Lysander's phone and ensure he permanently lost Selene's number while he was here.

Chapter Nineteen

SELENE

Lysander showed up almost a half-hour later than he mentioned he'd be there, which was slightly annoying, but I chose not to dwell on it.

"Selene," he said in a smooth, deep voice that betrayed just how good of a singer he was. "It's so good to see you again after all these years."

Lysander bent to kiss my cheek, then went European on me and kissed the other as well. While it took me by surprise, I didn't pull away from the male's attention.

At 36, — four years older than me — Lysander had always been around in the periphery of the Coven, but unattainable. With his dark, coiled hair offset by his light tan skin and shockingly pale green eyes, Lysander was a knock-out, and he knew it. While he was quite a bit taller than me at six feet, he was nowhere near as large as Ryker.

"You too, Lys." I smiled up at him. "Thanks again for agreeing to help."

"Of course, of course." The grin he aimed back at me

sent butterflies through my stomach. "Always happy to help a friend."

From somewhere behind me, Ryker grunted, and it was as if I could *hear* his eye roll. The sound drew Lys's attention as well, his gaze sliding over to the surly dragon with something like amusement.

"Ryker, I didn't even see you there. Glad you could make it."

"To my own house?" Ryker scoffed. "Despite the revolving door around here lately, my home is far from a fucking conference center."

"Ignore him," I said as I pulled Lys towards the kitchen table I'd cleared for us. "Toothless cold-turkey quit his meds yesterday and is a joy to be around."

Lys laughed, a deep rumbling sound that was all sex appeal, and I'd be lying if I said it didn't make my insides do another little dance. "I don't know," he smirked, "I've always found Ryker to be quite pleasant."

"I'm right here," Ryker mumbled, shaking his head at our sarcasm. I ignored him completely.

"So, Devanna mentioned that you're trained as a Harmonic witch." I changed the subject as I pulled out a chair to sit in. Lys took the one directly across from me, gently placing his crossbody bag on the table next to him. Then, he laid his hands across the table, palms up, reaching out for mine.

"I am." He smiled, his eyes scanning my face. "And a Healer. But surely not as good as you, Doctor." He winked, and I blinked rapidly. Feeling the weight of *all* of his attention, I glanced down at my own hands in my lap, suddenly feeling self-conscious about my abilities as a witch, even though I had the utmost confidence in myself as a doctor. But Lys reached across the table, open palms in front of me. "Here, place your hands in mine, and let's see if our magic can resonate."

Steeling my nerves, I did as he said. Lys took a slow, deep breath as my palms touched down on his, encouraging me to do the same, the sound soothing and almost hypnotic as we exhaled together. I closed my eyes, trying to focus, but the sound of Ryker grumbling from the couch made it hard to stay present.

"Can you be quiet, please?" I cracked an eye open, shooting a glare Ryker's way. He flung his hands up in frustration, but did as I asked.

"It's odd," Lysander said as he pulled his hands from mine, eyes narrowing at me in confusion. "Your magic feels off — far away, somehow." His full lips puckered as he took a moment to think. "But here, I have an idea. Music always helps me focus, so let's find something to set the tone."

"Oh, my gods," Ryker mumbled again.

"What kind of music do you like?" Lys went on, completely ignoring Ryker's running commentary, as he pulled out his phone and swiped to unlock it.

"I'm not too picky." I shrugged, following his lead and ignoring the dragon.

"*Not too picky*?" Lys raised a brow, an enticing grin playing across lips. "What does that even mean?"

"Oh, I don't know." I pulled my gaze from his mouth, a smile twitching at my own as I met his eyes again, a knowing glint in them. "Anything with a fun beat that I can move to."

"Ah," Lys nodded with a teasing wince, "you're a *pop* girl."

"Yeah, I guess." I nodded. "What's your favorite?"

"I like the classics," Lys said as he flicked his thumb repeatedly across his phone screen, searching for something. "Van Halen. Hendrix. Pink Floyd. Zeppelin."

His hand stopped, and he set his phone down as the sound of Van Halen's *You Really Got Me* came through the speaker on his phone. Lys immediately began to thumb out the beat of the song on the table. I'd never been *cool* enough to hang with Lys and his group growing up, but in that moment I could picture him onstage, guitar slung low in front of his hips. The grin he sent me as he encouraged me to enjoy the song was contagious, and I found myself smiling back.

"Just makes you want to dance along, doesn't it?" he said as the song ended.

I laughed, maybe a little breathily. "Not my usual, but yeah, I guess," I agreed, though I couldn't really see how this would help with my magic.

"You *guess?* Selene. Girl. Come on. You've been gone from the Cove too long. You really should come to one of our shows while you're up here. We have a great time. I could get you VIP access, free drinks all night — you'd love it."

"Is there a point to all of this?" Ryker interrupted us yet again. "What does music have to do with magic?"

Lys's white teeth glistened as he smiled, his eyes crinkling at the sides in amusement at Ryker's reaction. As he removed several crystals from his bag and laid them across the table, he said, "You've clearly never experienced true witch magic. First of all, Selene here is a bit wound up. Can you not see the tension radiating off her?" I squirmed in my seat, not needing a reminder of how I'd let myself slip last night, succumbing to the release Ryker had worked from my body. But then this morning happened, and the tension was back, thick as ever. Lys went on, clueless to how close he'd really hit to the issue. "Music is *everything*. It helps the connection to our deeper soul, the root of our magic. It just takes the right tune to draw it out from deep within."

"So what's your soul song? *MMMBop*?" Ryker retorted, and I bit my cheeks to keep from laughing over the fact that Ryker even knew *MMMBop*.

Lys was back to flicking his phone screen, searching for the perfect song. "Right now isn't about me, Ryker," he said, then nodded at me. "It's about Selene here. She's the one who needs to get reacquainted with her magic. Who needs to relax and let her power flow freely."

The opening chords of The Eagles' *Witchy Woman* played, and the song caught my attention as much as Lys's words. He stood from the table, circling around to stand beside my chair. Leaning onto one palm in a way that brought my attention to his toned forearm, he began arranging the crystals on the table.

"These will form a pentagram, with you as one of the points," he explained, and handed me a piece of chalk. "Sketch it out, starting at yourself."

I began sketching, but his eyes squinted as I drew, and I stopped halfway through, sensing something was wrong. He hummed in thought as his eyes flitted between me and the table before they lifted back to me.

"May I?" he asked, though I wasn't entirely sure what he meant. He gestured to the table. "Something seems off."

I'd barely nodded when suddenly he was behind me, and leaning down over my shoulder. He shifted the crystals slightly, re-aligning them to some mental image he must have had of how they needed to look. Meanwhile, I was suddenly overwhelmed with the scent of him, all citrus and vetiver, a flush rising to my cheeks at the feel of his warmth at my back, my shoulders, at his arms lightly brushing mine as they adjusted the stones.

"Okay." He rested his hands on the table, and I found myself hoping he wouldn't pull any further away, wrapped up in the charisma and charm that was so different from the angry, hot-and-cold dragon behind us. "Try the sketch again."

I did as he said, the lines slightly shifted from before, and I felt him nodding over my shoulder, pleased with the align-ment. I set down the chalk when I was done, eyeing the pentagram now before me and willing my breath to remain steady, even with his presence at my back.

"Close your eyes, Selene," he whispered next to my ear, so close I could almost feel his permanent five-o'clock shadow against my skin. How a male's voice could be so sensual was a strange thing — I almost could have believed him part selkie or even vampire, but of course, those were only imaginary creatures. He slid another crystal in front of me. "Hold this crystal here, between your palms, anchoring the pentagram. Feel the music. Breathe to the beat."

I took a breath, concentrating on the beat of the music, the sharp, cool planes of the crystal between my palms, and focused.

"That's it," he murmured, and I squirmed in my seat, a

shiver racing down my spine. "Feel your magic. Let it run through your fingers and into the crystal. Charge it with your healing power."

In my mind's eye, my magic appeared like a well deep within me, full of glistening water. Upon his instructions, I let my hand glide over it, feeling the cool surface beneath my skin as if it were real.

"You're doing great," Lys said. "Keep breathing."

I nodded and kept going, so caught up in the feel of my magic. I'd been in the human world for so long, it had been ages since I'd explored my power like this. Had I ever been this *aware* of my magic, almost as if I could physically reach out and touch it?

"Ready for more?" Lys whispered as his hands touched down on mine, his body caging me in from behind against the table. "I'm going to add my magic to help you draw yours out even more. Just lean into it, let it power yours."

Between the magic and the music, my body felt ignited, energy humming within me in a way that it never had before.

"That's right," Lys said, his voice anchoring me to the present as magic rose up through my body and into my fingertips, coming back to me with an effortless accessibility I hadn't felt in years. He pulled back, his hands leaving mine to rest on the back of my chair, and part of me hated to lose his nearness. "Perfect."

Marveling at the feel of my magic, I hardly heard him. I hadn't realized how much I'd missed this. I'd spent years proving to myself that I wasn't *only* a witch — that I was just as strong and useful without my magic as I was with it. But when had I last let myself truly be a *witch*, too?

I hummed in contentment, feeling more self-confident than I had in years, and felt my power rise out of the well, drifting into my hands, ready to use.

Chapter Twenty

RYKER

The more I watched this terrible reenactment of the pottery scene from *Ghost* at my kitchen table, the more my blood boiled.

As Lysander purred into Selene's ear, passing off instructions for how he wanted her to manipulate her magic, touching her casually, my eyes flashed green, sending out a wash of my own, far superior power over the room.

Selene gasped, her eyes flying open as she turned to where I still sat on the couch.

"Was that you?" she asked, eyes wide as she pushed around Lysander and strode towards the couch.

She dropped to her knees in front of me, and gods, my imagination went *wild* at the sight. Her hands laid gently on my leg, fingers tracing over where the stitches from her emergency surgery had been only minutes ago then trailed down to the black cast covering my calf.

"What changed?" she asked, her mouth slightly ajar as she glanced up at me through her lashes.

My nostrils flared, something rising inside me that I

couldn't quite explain, but Lysander shifting his weight broke the silence of the room, reminding me of his completely unnecessary presence.

"Leave."

With a shake of his head and a soft chuckle, Lysander grabbed the rest of his belongings. Selene chewed on her lip as she eyed the crystal she'd just charged with so much magic, I could feel its pulse from across the room.

"She wants the crystal." I nodded at the stone sitting on the table, and Lysander smirked.

"You speak for her now?"

Selene scoffed, then rose to her feet, dusting off the knees of her jeans, and turned to Lysander. "No. He absolutely does not."

Why did her words bother me? I didn't have time to think too much on that before she went on.

"I would like the stone though, if that's okay with you. Just to borrow it." Selene smiled up at Lys, and I rolled my eyes for the hundredth time since he walked into my house. "I can't tell if his power surge was enough to heal the bones and internal injuries, or only the surface wounds."

I glared at her back. "I'm fine."

She spun on me then, meeting my glare head-on. "I'll be the judge of that, as your *doctor*."

"The crystal is yours." Lysander smiled, pulling his *purse* back up onto his shoulder. "Plenty more where that came from."

"Thank you." Selene grabbed Lysander's hand, holding it gently in her own. "I think I needed this today."

Lysander's eyes flashed to mine before looking back down at Selene. "Anytime. I'd still love to have you join me at one of my shows." Selene opened her mouth to answer, but Lysander cut her off. "You have my number now. Just think about it."

Selene nodded, crossing her arms over her chest as she followed him towards the stairs.

"Ryker." Lysander raised a brow at me, then saw himself out.

My jaw ticked, but I couldn't bring myself to voice a response. A moment later, Selene reappeared beside me on the couch, frowning down at my leg.

I hissed through my teeth as she poked and prodded it, and she nodded to herself.

"Not fully healed, then," she concluded. "But maybe we can try switching you to a boot instead of a cast. You should be able to put some weight on it now without risking further damage to your tibia." Withdrawing her hand from my leg, she pulled back, bringing her attention to my face, which I tried to school into complete neutrality. "What was that power surge?"

I honestly didn't know — maybe I had an *idea*, but that wasn't the same — so I shrugged.

"Do you seriously dislike Lys so much you had to show him up, blasting through the iron in your system?" She was holding back a smile, apparently amused at my childishness. "He really helped me, so —"

"Are you going to go to his stupid show?" Okay, yes. I sounded like a child. I didn't give a shit.

A glint of something I couldn't read entered her eye, and I blinked, pinpricks of darkness edging into my vision.

"Maybe," she hummed. "He's never looked twice at me before — though it's been a good thirteen years since I was really around — but he seems nice." I grunted. "Friendly." I narrowed my eyes. "Warm and open. *Fun*."

My teeth ground together. Why was the room spinning? "You mean, he's a total tool."

"Well." She patted my arm patronizingly, and I clenched my hands into fists to stop myself from reaching out and grabbing her. "I'm sure you'd see it that way."

"Flores." She smiled in that saccharine way of hers. "He's probably fucked every supe from Portland to Saint John."

Her eyes widened briefly. With intrigue? No. Disgust, *surely*.

Acid pooled in my stomach, and not the good, *light it up* variety that preceded my flames. The pinpricks of darkness were closing in as I fought to stay sitting upright, vertigo twisting the couch beneath me like I was losing control of my wings in the middle of a storm. Static rushed through my ears, but even as my chin bounced against my chest, I thought I heard Selene whisper, "Then he'll *definitely* know what he's doing."

Darkness consumed me.

When I woke up, it was morning again. I'd slept through a whole day and night? That couldn't be good.

The couch beside me was empty, and turning, I saw Selene asleep on the bed. Of course, she hadn't been able to move me — though she was plenty in shape, I was easily double her weight. I rolled my neck, stiff from its many hours at an awkward angle, and pulled myself gingerly to my feet.

In the bathroom, I stared in the mirror.

No.

I leaned in closer, brow furrowed, eyes widening.

My long hair — which had been a golden blond for as long as I'd been able to shift — was streaked with white.

Chapter Twenty-One

SELENE

Ryker passed out mid-sentence, scaring the shit out of me. That was *not* normal. For anyone. But especially not a supernatural dragon.

Checking his stats all night did nothing to comfort me — his temperature was elevated even for a dragon, and his pulse pounded a wild rhythm, far too fast for anyone asleep. The only thing I could come up with was that the burst of magic wore him out, even if it had only partially healed his wound.

I considered texting Orion, or Devanna, or *someone* to let them know things were getting weirder here — magic-wise — but what could they do? We were all in the same boat.

After the fifth vitals-check with no changes, exhaustion pulled at me, and I finally allowed myself to get some sleep, hoping he just needed to rest.

Sun peeked through the clouds as I allowed myself a moment to wake up, listening to the shower running — a relieving sign that Ryker was alive and functional. Just as I rolled over to go check on him, the bathroom door opened, and my jaw dropped.

His hair.

Ryker had buzzed it.

Gone were his shoulder-length blond strands he usually wore tied in a knot on the top of his head.

"What did you do?" I lurched into a seated position.

As I searched his face for an explanation for this seemingly rash behavior, he rubbed a tattooed hand over his hair, but only offered a shrug in response before swinging on his crutches over to the closet to grab clothes.

I opened my mouth to question him again — the male was as vain as any I'd ever met, so this seemed like a big deal — but my phone buzzed.

Devanna: *Coven meeting this afternoon. Morgaine's house.*

Suddenly the rest of the room faded away, all my focus centered on those words.

Coven meeting. I swallowed. I hadn't been to a Coven meeting since —

"I need you out of the house."

I shook my head, trying to pull myself back to the present and to focus on the dragon who was staring me down. He'd managed to get himself into a pair of shorts, but nothing else — all those intricate tattoos across his muscled chest were on full display. Not that I noticed.

"What?" I coughed out, not sure what he'd even said.

"This afternoon, I need you out of the house."

"Why —"

"It's not personal."

It *felt* personal with how he was avoiding my gaze, but I wasn't about to tell him that. I raised my phone and wiggled it. "I have a Coven meeting, anyway."

He nodded sharply, then made his way to the kitchen and began making coffee.

Apparently, I was going to a Coven meeting.

Pulling off my winter gloves, I made my way through Mo's kitchen later that afternoon, having borrowed Ryker's truck again to get into town. I started when I saw Petra at Mo's kitchen table, laptop and books spread around her as always.

"Hey," she said, scribbling one last note before setting her pen down and smiling at me. "Was Lysander able to help with your magic?"

I slid my coat off and draped it over a chair. "I think so. While he was there, yes, but I haven't tried to access it since." I could hear other witches settling into Mo's living room, and an image from the last time I'd been in there flashed through my mind. I winced, hoping I wouldn't walk in on another reverse harem reenactment this time, and tilted my head. "You're working in here instead of the carriage house today?"

Petra shrugged. "Heat went out. Orion has been in a tizzy over everyone's heat and power outages lately, trying to fix it himself rather than wait for Sergio. He was practically spitting like a cat when I was at the cottage last, so I'm avoiding their house, too. Thought about going to Scally-wags, but Blaze is setting up for Bingo, and you know how loud it gets in there."

I raised a brow at Mo as she swept through the room with Ruby, humming to herself and ignoring us, but my suspicions were all but confirmed by the mischievous glint in her eye. She was up to something.

"Hey, thanks for the air bed," I called after her, and Mo stopped, turning back to me.

"Glad it worked for you!" She smiled broadly, blatantly ignoring my sarcasm, and I rolled my eyes. "It's so nice to have you back in town for a Coven meeting. It's been too long."

Ruby was assembling a plate of cookies for the meeting and gave me a glance of curiosity. "Are you also an Aura witch?"

I chuckled, shaking my head. "No, I'm not."

"Selene is a Healer," Mo said with a sigh, "but I could have made an excellent Aura witch out of her if she'd shown an interest. Her mother was one of the best Aura witches I've ever met, and a Seer, to boot."

My spine stiffened at the mention of my mother, but the sound of Ostara calling from the living room kept me from responding.

I followed Mo down the hall to the big living room, and found it filling up with many of the witches from town, most of whom I hadn't seen or spoken to in years. Peg Fernsby and Eva Watford greeted me as I passed, Lysander flashed me a grin, and I took a seat next to Devanna, her friend Castor on her other side.

Dev turned, studying me for a moment, and I fidgeted in

my seat under her inspection. Memories of sitting in these meetings with my mom at my side flooded my mind, and I could almost hear her voice, her lilting laugh.

"This won't take long," Dev whispered as she nudged my shoulder in support.

I nodded, willing my heart to cease the marathon it insisted on running, focusing on the room around me. There were several people I didn't recognize, either because they were younger than me and I'd never paid them any attention, or perhaps they were new to town since I'd left. So much had changed.

"Did you jump the dragon yet or what?"

A laugh escaped me before I could stop it, turning to see a glint in Dev's eye I might have expected from an altogether *different* witch. I couldn't help but wonder how much she was curious, or if she was trying to distract me. "Is that some new euphemism the kids are using?"

Dev rolled her eyes at my attempt to side-step the question, but luckily Ostara was about to start the meeting, saving me from further interrogation.

Ostara perched in an armchair so regally she made it look like a throne, her hands resting elegantly on its armrests and her legs crossed. The white streaks in her hair caught the light as she turned and assessed the room, her penetrating gaze landing on me before moving on.

Once we were all settled, Mo took a seat across the coffee table from Ostara, and the head witch narrowed her eyes.

"Morgaine," Ostara began in a tone that brooked no argument. "I must insist the human leave. This is Coven business."

Mo blinked, her eyes slightly oversized behind her thick teal glasses. "Oh, Petra?" She waved a hand. "She can't hear a thing from the kitchen. And even if she could, she's good at keeping secrets. Pretend she isn't even there."

Ostara seemed inclined to protest, but it was Mo's house, after all, so after pressing her lips together, she moved on.

"Why are we meeting here and not Ostara's fortress?" I whispered to Dev as Ostara recounted for the others who weren't at the town meeting all that had been discussed about the magic in town, to several gasps and many expressions of alarm.

"Bat infestation," Dev answered. "That Victorian house is so old, it takes a whole staff to run the place. She would have gotten rid of them magically, but —"

"I must caution all of you," Ostara raised her voice, meeting eyes around the room. "Errakal will seek out new witches to work for him, if he hasn't already. As we don't know where he is, we can't rule out the possibility he won't return here. Don't forget he is half-demon, and therefore far more powerful than any of you." She let that sink in, and I couldn't help but notice she hadn't included herself in that assessment of weakness, even though it applied to her, too. "If he approaches you, be very careful. Don't anger him, but don't agree to anything either. Then report it to me immediately."

People nodded and murmured to each other. A cat hissed, and I turned to see Mrs. Farrington wrangling her black cat, Bagheera, back into a bubble backpack. The cat pawed at the clear plastic separating him from the room desperately as Mrs. Farrington tried to calm him. "So sorry."

"What we're finding," Ostara tapped her fingers against the floral patterned arm of the chair, all but ignoring the eccentricities of this Coven, "is that, while we still have access to our magic, we are unable to *replenish* that magic once it has been used. Reports from Orion say that other towns across the country are experiencing the same problems as well."

"Shit," Dev muttered under her breath. Worry twisted my insides as I thought of the burst of magic Ryker had used last night — how much power had it taken to heal that wound?

"For that reason, Orion and I are sending someone who doesn't rely on magic to seek Errakal out — to find him and see what we can glean of his motives and next steps."

An ominous thundering filled my ears as her eyes swung to me, quickly followed by every other gaze in the room.

"Um." I shifted in my seat. "You want *me* to take on a half-demon-half-witch with…" I trailed off, because I honestly couldn't wrap my head around what she was asking of me.

"Not take him on." Ostara shook her head. "Find him, assess him." She tilted her head. "Though if you have an opportunity to shoot him, by all means, don't waste it."

I tried not to laugh. *Shoot him?* I'd never shot *anything*.

"Even Ryker hasn't been able to find him, though, so —"

"About that."

The room turned as one when Petra entered the room, a

map held open between her hands that she set down on the coffee table.

"I must insist —" Ostara glared angrily, but Morgaine waved her off.

"Yes, dear? Did you find something?" She scooted her own chair closer to look over the map.

Petra took a seat on the couch as we all craned to see the map, covered in drawn, criss-crossing lines. The ley lines.

"Orion gave me all the coordinates for where Ryker just missed Errakal, along with the dates," she explained, pointing to stars across the map. "It's subtle, but it does make a pattern."

"None that I can see," Ostara huffed.

"Not a witch mark," Petra agreed. "Not a pentagram or anything like he tried here in the Cove. Looking at the ley lines as a whole, this is more like a watershed, only instead of water, the medium is power." She traced the map, stopping at certain points. Then she pulled a piece of thin tracing paper from underneath and placed it on top, showing the map underneath while adding another level of information. "If you trace the ley lines like a watershed, tracking the high and low points, I believe these would be the contours. It's similar to how archeologists search for ancient civilizations — follow the water, but in this case, power."

Petra sat back, letting the rest of us crowd around the map. The sound of a crash at the back of the room had us all turning towards where Ruby now sat on the floor, blushing furiously. The floral wingback she'd been in now sat in pieces around her as if it had exploded.

"I didn't mean to," she squeaked, eyes wide as she stared

at Mo with a crystal in her hand. "It seemed so fragile, and there's a little power left in this crystal. I thought it'd be enough to reinforce it."

Ostara puckered her lips in annoyance, but Lys and the male sitting next to him stooped to help her. Quickly, Lys had the pieces cleaned up and carried out of the room.

"No harm done, dear," Mo said with a smile at her young student. "That was only my *third* favorite floral wing-back. I don't mind. But let's not use more magic right now, hmm?"

Ruby nodded vigorously, and I loved Mo all the more for how she'd handled that. The girl was plenty embarrassed enough on her own, without being scolded in front of the entire Coven.

"Assuming this is accurate," Ostara's voice rang out, bringing us all back to attention. She merely glanced over the map before leaning back. "How do you propose this would help Selene find Errakal?"

Petra cleared her throat, taking on her *professor* voice easily. "Everywhere he's attacked has been somewhere the power pools, where ley lines cross, and there's a dip in the magical contours." She indicated with a wave the stars she'd marked. "Like water, it all flows somewhere, moving continuously, pulled towards —"

"The heart," I cut in, understanding sparking within me. Petra met my gaze with a nod, relieved *someone* was catching on, and I continued. "You're saying magic works like the circulatory system. The greatest force of it concentrated at the heart, wellspring of it all." I moved forward so I could lean over the map, scanning for the wellspring of magic that should exist, if Petra had mapped the contours accurately. Which was a huge *if,* given this was all conjecture.

Then I saw it, and my gaze shot up to meet Petra's.

"Colorado."

"I think so," Petra nodded. "Yeah."

The witches spent the next hour debating the map Petra had presented, but I was convinced. Not that I was thrilled to have to go to the Rocky Mountains and find Errakal, but it was a step in the right direction to fix everyone's magic. Hopefully.

"Lucky you were here, Petra," Mo said just loud enough to be heard by Ostara across the room. She winked at the two of us as we moved from the living room back to the kitchen as the meeting broke up.

If I hadn't already known she'd meddled with the heat in Petra's carriage house, I did now.

I didn't have long to ponder that, because just then, an almighty roar coming from outside rattled the windows. Two dozen witches pulled on coats and ran out the door, following the sound down to the bay a block from Mo's house.

Emerging from the water came a giant of a man, easily as large as Ryker, bare-chested and wearing only linen pants, despite the frigid temperatures that frosted our breath on the air. His long golden hair flowed behind him as he carried a small girl in his arms, water dripping off him as he moved towards us up the rocky shore. Still in her sea nymph form, the girl had a beautiful, long, scaled tail encapsulating her legs and torso. A mermaid, straight out of every little girl's dreams.

"Ronan?" Ostara pushed to the front of the crowd outside, Lys at her side. "What's going on?"

The king of the sea nymphs. I'd never met him in person — wasn't sure he'd even come onto the mainland in my lifetime, to be honest.

His glacier-blue eyes pierced us, darting from one to another, as he gently brushed white-blonde hair away from the girl's face. "You have to help me."

I pushed to the front of the crowd, worry eating at me as I glanced between Ronan and the girl.

Something was very wrong.

Chapter Twenty-Two

RYKER

Orion and Blaze arrived in the living room only moments after Selene headed out — driving *my* truck, again — to her Coven meeting. White wings ruffling behind him, Orion smoothed out his grey button-down as he took in my space before finding me seated at the kitchen table.

His brow lowered. "Ryker, what —"

"Holy shit." Pushing his black hood off his head, Blaze hurried forward, black eyes wide, until he leaned against the table from the other side, palms flat on its surface. "What the hell did you do to yourself?" He gestured vaguely at my hair.

I gritted my teeth. "That's what I needed to talk to *Orion* about."

Orion raised a palm. "You said it was urgent, and Blaze was in my car, so I didn't stop to drop him off first."

As Orion was talking, Blaze helped himself to a seat at the table and one of *my* strips of bacon, clearly intent on sticking around to hear what was going on. I'd called *Orion* because he was one of the few supernaturals in the area that

I trusted not to blab to the whole town about my predicament. The same could not be said for the gleeful-eyed demon to his right.

"Fine." I rubbed a hand absent-mindedly over my newly-shorn hair. I'd never had it short like this, not all of it — usually only the sides were buzzed — and it felt strange.

Orion settled in beside Blaze, and I told them what had happened: the surge of magic, how my injury had healed but not completely, how I'd passed out, how I'd woken up to streaks of white in my hair, then chopped it in a panic.

"What do you think it means?" I asked after we'd sat in an uneasy silence for a few minutes. I had my own suspicions, but I was hoping Orion would have different ideas. Ones that weren't so disturbing.

The angel's piercing grey eyes assessed me clinically, from my cropped hair down over my arms. He wasn't nearly as old as I was — nobody in the Cove was — but he'd seen a thing or two in his day and had actual training in magical disruptions. I tried to keep the desperate hope from my expression, schooling it to be as flat as usual.

"I think you're aging." His tone was straightforward. Emotionless. This was why I could sometimes tolerate the male. "Ostara called this morning about their Coven meeting today. Their theory is that magic isn't replenishing, like a battery that can't be recharged. Could be the same for you."

"That could be bad," Blaze interjected helpfully with a strip of bacon hanging forgotten from his fingers in mid-air, his delight from earlier turning serious. "I mean, how old *are* you?" He glanced between me and Orion. "If this keeps up, could he age to death?"

"That will not be happening," I scoffed, but my stomach soured when Orion didn't agree with me right away.

"We can't know for sure," Orion shrugged, eyes narrowing slightly. "It sounds like you used a lot of magic — whatever you had access to around the iron poisoning — to heal the wound, and since magic isn't replenishing and it's what keeps you from aging…" he trailed off, letting my imagination fill in the rest. "I'd strongly recommend you don't use any more power if you can help it."

"You *think*?" I snapped, then pressed my lips together. It wasn't Orion's fault — he was merely stating the facts I'd already suspected.

But shit, this was bad.

"You'll be glad to know the witches are making a move forward, then," Orion continued, pulling me from my thoughts. I waved a hand at him to elaborate. "Since we can't restore magic right now, they've decided to send someone who *doesn't* use magic to go after Errakal and see what she can learn."

A witch that didn't rely on magic? Wait, did he mean —

"*Selene?*" I coughed, incredulous, and Orion nodded.

Oh, Hel, no.

"No gods-damned way," I shot at him, already struggling to stand even though I didn't know where I thought I was going. It wasn't like I could hobble all the way down my hill on my crutches or drive a vehicle like this, and Selene hadn't yet switched me to a walking boot. I leaned forward on my palms, splayed out on the table. "First of all, if even *I* couldn't find the bastard —"

"Petey's been working on that." Blaze beamed, pride radiating off him in waves. "She's had all these maps up around the living room for days now, hopping between them with her notebook."

"How you convinced that human to be with you is beyond me," Orion muttered.

"So, now we trust the —" I waved a hand vaguely to indicate Blaze's information, "— cartographic skills of a human who's only known about our kind for a few *months* to be able to find someone that even *I* —"

"You don't have to trust it," Orion said simply, standing. "Ostara has made her decision. Selene is probably finding out about it right now."

Suddenly, I was seething. Blood pounding, chest heaving. That *witch* wanted to send my — send Selene out into the world *alone*, unable to even use her magic to defend herself if shit went sideways?

I struggled to stay calm, to stay rational. Orion would respond best to cool, well-reasoned arguments — I knew the male well enough to know that by now.

"This is a half-assed plan, at *best*," I bit out, doing a piss-poor job at the calm thing. Not my style anyway. "She's going to need help, and she's going to need an actual strat-egy. We need to slow down and figure this out before an unarmed, untrained witch goes out to hunt down your half-demon *brother*," Blaze flinched at the way I spat the word at him, but I didn't stop, "who has no qualms about killing people to get what he wants. Or did everyone forget about the sacrifices? I remember saving your little *human* from becoming one."

"No one's forgotten." Orion crossed his arms. "But what choice do we have? Without being able to use magic —"

"So we just send him another witch to sacrifice? Because that's what will happen here."

Orion and Blaze continued to talk strategy, but my mind was seething now. No way would I let Selene out of my sight. Not a chance.

I tried to rationalize to myself that I'd feel this strongly about anyone heading off after Errakal, because he was *my* target, but I wasn't sure that was true. The thought of her in harm's way set my teeth on edge.

My skin itched as I tried to listen in to whatever the males were saying, wanting to pull my phone out and text Selene immediately. To tell her to come home now.

But I'd fucked it up between us, hadn't I? We were back to weirdly distant after I'd panicked when she woke up in my arms in front of the fire. More than anything, I'd wanted her to be happy and feel good, and yet the thought of growing attached to her — to anyone — had me putting as much distance as possible between us.

I stared down at my phone, contemplating stooping so low as to fake an injury to call her back to me, when Blaze's hand swung in front of my face.

"Hey," he said as he leaned in, drawing my eyes up to his. "Lost you there for a minute."

The anger that boiled just under the surface of my skin fought to erupt, to slam my fist into the demon's face and blame him for the trouble his brother was causing, but instead, I let out a deep sigh.

"Tell me you idiots have a plan other than using Selene as bait?" Orion and Blaze exchanged looks, some unspoken conversation happening between them, before Blaze shrugged.

"Well, Plan A got shot to hell when, you know," he gestured at my leg, "you got shot to hell. Selene is only Plan B. Not really the go-to option, but a hell of a lot better than nothing."

Instantly, I dropped my crutches and slammed Blaze against the wall, holding him off the ground with my forearm pinned under his neck.

Orion pinched his thumb and forefinger over the bridge of his nose. "Put him down, Ryker. That's not the plan. Blaze, knock it off."

My eyes shifted to slits as I stared at Blaze, meeting his own black gaze head on. "Tell me every fucking thing I could ever need to know about your brother. And demons while you're at it. All of it. Don't even think about trying to work around my command. Figure out how to spill your secrets so you don't have your girlfriend's best friend's death on your conscience."

Blaze glanced sideways at Orion, but turned back to me when smoke seeped out of my nostrils, my dragon riding so close under my skin I fought to control it, trying to prevent the shift to conserve my magic.

"Oh, shit," Blaze whispered as he glanced down at my chin. "Your beard just turned white."

I dropped him instantly, hopped to the bathroom, and slammed the door.

Chapter Twenty-Three

SELENE

"She won't wake." Ronan's gaze kept shifting around until it finally locked on Ostara. "She was out at — " he broke off, eyeing the rest of us and seemingly unwilling to divulge sea nymph secrets, as was their way. "— She was swimming. It was only luck one of her sisters found her floating in the current. I don't know what happened, but she won't wake up. We tried everything —" he broke off, clasping the girl's tiny hand in his large one, though it might have been to hide how his own was shaking.

"Who is this?" Mo said gently as she approached, placing a hand on the girl's forehead with a concerned frown. Small iridescent scales lined the ridges of her eyebrows and along the sides of her neck, flashing turquoise and purple in the sunlight.

"My daughter." His voice broke. "Corissa. My youngest daughter."

"Give us some room to work," Ostara said, then she spotted me lingering and waved me up. I nodded, understanding what she wanted, and stepped up to address Ronan, terrifying as he was.

"Can you place her on the bench?" I indicated one of the several benches that ringed the small, stony beach. He complied, setting her down gently, then kneeling down in the snow at her side, her small hand completely enveloped by his.

Doing my best to check her vitals without any of my usual equipment, I bit my lip. "She seems to be asleep," I said. "But I can't see anything externally wrong. No injuries or lacerations. No —"

"She's not just *asleep*," Ronan growled at me, and I nearly keeled over with his ferocity, which was saying something considering I'd faced down an injured dragon days before. "She was fine this morning, and now she *won't wake*." He half-turned, still on his knees, and found Ostara again. "Help her."

Ostara, Lys, and Mo piled into the back seat of Ryker's truck, while Ronan took the front seat, still clutching his daughter to his chest. As soon as everyone was in, I jumped into the driver's seat, and turned over the ignition. As quickly as I could, we were on the road, headed directly for Ryker's.

"All of my stuff is there," I told Ronan for the third time, feeling the need to explain myself yet again. "With magic on the fritz, I need my medical supplies."

"Just hurry," he bit out between clenched teeth.

I nodded, going as fast as I was comfortable, but also conscious of the slick roads left from the storm. As we parked in the garage, I hopped out of the truck, hitting the ground hard and hurrying towards the doors to the loft above. Everyone followed me wordlessly, and we rushed up the steps.

"Flor —" Ryker started from his position at the table, then noticed the audience at my back. His eyes flicked up to Ronan, then down at the child in his arms.

"Put her on the couch." I pointed, and Ronan followed my instructions as I rushed to the table, gathering what little supplies I had. I shot an apologetic glance at Ryker — I knew he didn't like people in his space, but Corissa was more important. Meanwhile, Lys crouched next to the small girl, hovering his hands over her as he sought out the source of the problem magically. We might not be able to *use* our magic, but just tuning into it like Lys was doing wouldn't draw any power — it was more like focusing on one of our senses. Why hadn't I thought of it?

I internally slapped myself for the oversight, and knelt at her side with my stethoscope. Everyone was talking around me, but my hearing was laser-focused on the sound of her steady heartbeat. Like I'd done with the music, I breathed deeply, letting the sound of her whooshing pulse send me into a trance.

My eyes drifted up as I tried to focus on my hearing and my magical insight, until suddenly my eyes snagged on Ryker across the sofa, watching me intently with his bright green eyes. Then I saw his beard. "Ryker," I paused, "Why is your beard suddenly white?"

His gaze met mine, but Lys cleared his throat from

behind me, and I snapped out of it, glancing back down to Corissa.

"Let's try the crystal," Lys said, and I turned to him with wide eyes.

"Oh." I nodded, trying to let my mind and body sync back up after the weird moment with Ryker. "Yes. Okay. Right. I was going to use it on Ryker's leg, but —"

"Use it." Ryker's words were clipped, but he stood back up, leaning on his crutches, and moved away to make space around the couch.

Lys brought the charged crystal over, laying it gently in my hand. Instantly, the power radiating off it prickled my palm. I sucked in a breath as I let it wash over me; my hands tingled with energy, and I moved my fingers over Corissa's prone form, hovering just above her skin.

My heart was pounding as sweat beaded on my brow, feeling the well of magic in the crystal just like I'd felt in myself. The power was there, I just needed to use it. To direct it. To point it towards Corissa, and ask it to help her. Anxiety flooded me, and my hands began to shake as tears gathered in my eyes.

What if I didn't remember how to do this? What if I did something wrong? What if the magic didn't answer to me, and didn't heal her? What if I made her *worse?*

"Let the magic go," Lys spoke calmly above me, trying to help me through this next step. "The crystal answers to you now, so only you can do this. Let it flow from the crystal, into you, and onto Corissa. You can do this, Selene."

Without realizing it, I was shaking my head. Barely above a whisper, the words, *"I can't"* slipped out of my lips.

Warmth settled in along my back as a low growl

snapped me from my hysteria. Large, pale, tattooed hands settled on top of mine around the crystal, Ryker perched behind me on the coffee table.

"Yes, you can," he whispered for only me, breathing in my ear, his frame effectively blocking out the rest of the room. "You can do anything. You heal people every day the *hard* way — with no magic — and are confident in your abilities. You cook like a gods-damned Michelin-star chef. You fix cars." He paused, chewing on his lip. "Well, maybe let's not use that as an example right now."

A laugh stuttered out of me as I wiped away an errant tear that dripped down my cheek at his words.

"You performed surgery with no equipment, no machines, no nothing, on an angry dragon, and we all lived to tell the tale." His voice was gruff with pride, and I realized it was for me. Whatever had happened between us last night, or hadn't happened this morning, I could feel the emotion in his words. I could hear something in his voice that I could only describe as awe. "All of us here would be lost without your help, and Corissa needs it now more than ever. Do you think you can help her too, Selene?"

The sound of my name from his lips sent a shiver down my spine, but his words were everything I needed to hear. I sucked in a large breath and held it, letting the magic run its course yet again. Ryker's large hands left mine, and my hair lifted off the back of my neck as the power surged from the crystal, into me, and then passed through to Corissa.

My awareness drifted over the girl with the power of the crystal, like I'd been granted magical x-ray vision. Her heart pumped blood normally, lungs expanding with each breath, but where I'd felt a well of power in Ryker while his hands were on mine, in Corissa there was… nothing. Emptiness. The charge surged into her, slowly filling the well where her own magic should be. I let out a shaky breath as I checked her over again but found no physical injuries.

"What is it? What's wrong with her?" Ronan barked.

"She'll be fine." I continued to let the crystal's power flow into her, pouring every drop of Lys's and my combined power in the stone into the girl. "Her magic was completely drained, but this is giving her some."

"When will she wake up?"

I bit my lip. He wasn't going to like my answer. "I'm not sure. Her magic was *gone*. This is giving her enough to hold onto, but it might not be enough to wake her up until she can replenish more on her own. Or, she just might need to rest. We'll have to wait and see."

"That's not good enough," Ronan snarled, his worry transforming into frustration. "Ostara, surely you have another healer in your Coven to take a look at her. One who is actually *competent*. Unlike this one, who hardly seems to know what she's doing and needs a crystal to do the actual work for her."

Before I could even respond, Ryker was up, standing at his full height as he stared down the king of the sea nymphs.

"Careful, Ronan. If the next words out of your mouth are another insult to Selene, I'll rip out your tongue and use it for shark bait."

My eyes expanded in shock as I looked between the two posturing men, the tension so palpable I could practically taste it. Nervous energy hummed in my veins, a combination of the testosterone oozing off of both Ryker and

Ronan, and also at the rush of my own hormones from Ryker defending me.

As if I needed another reason to feel anything for him.

"All right, well." Mo clapped her hands together from somewhere to our left. She and Ostara had been nearly silent the entire time, or maybe I'd been so focused on what I was doing that I'd forgotten they were here. "I always do love some misplaced male aggression. Particularly in movies, not so much in real life. You're all a bit whinier in person, I find."

Her words broke Ronan and Ryker's stare off, and my eyes caught on Lys shaking with laughter behind Mo. Ostara smacked him on the arm, and pushed him towards the door.

"Show's over, everyone," Mo said as she ducked down to where Corissa still lay on the couch, rubbing a soothing hand across her forehead again. "Her aura is much clearer, and she'll recover. Ronan, time for you two to head back underwater to Gungan City."

Ronan's brow creased in confusion as he stared at Mo, obviously missing the *Star Wars* reference. He leaned down, scooped his daughter up into his arms, and made his way back towards the stairs to the garage.

"I'll drive them back to town," I mumbled as I stood, brushing off my pants to give my hands something to do. Avoiding Ryker's gaze, I followed the rest of the party down the stairs.

Chapter Twenty-Four

RYKER

My chest still heaved with emotion as I watched Selene sprint down the stairs away from me and the room emptied. Anger surged in my veins, my dragon roiling under my skin, aching to break free. But even the smallest magic seemed to pull more power from me than I could control, and my body was already feeling the effects of it.

Pushing aside the pain and anger, I stood, and slowly made my way down to the garage. Selene had already left with Ronan, his daughter, and the others, taking my truck back into town, so the garage was quiet as the doors slid open for me. I headed towards the back wall, past the Aston Martin I bought after it was used as a Bond car, and the Lamborghini I could hardly look at after Selene had pointed out how Hollywood they were. She wasn't wrong, and I'd never been a fan of driving it anyway. Too hard for a male like me to fit in there.

Aside from my cars, my next favorite thing to collect was much more practical for my line of work. My crutches clicked as I pushed myself across the space, and stopped at a seemingly empty black wall. There, mounted to the side, was a touchscreen that showed lighting controls, speaker and music selections, and other home automation services. But as I placed my palm flat on the surface of the monitor, another screen opened up and began scanning.

Red lights made several passes over my hand, reading each fingerprint as I waited patiently. Security was of the utmost importance to me, and what was behind this wall mattered more than anything else I owned.

With a pleasant chime, the lights on the screen blinked green, and a seam appeared in the center of the wall, splitting in two as the partitions slid to the side.

Bright white LED lights flicked on overhead and in the shelves, illuminating my most treasured possessions. I took stock of my collection, mentally cataloguing what I would take with us when we left. I lost track of time as I inspected and double-checked the key items I wanted to bring, falling into my familiar pre-job rhythm of cleaning and assembling.

"Whoa," Selene's voice came from behind me, and I damn-near jumped at the sound. The fact that she was able to sneak up on me was far more alarming than any white hair on my head. I quickly scanned the room, making sure we were alone, adrenaline pumping in my system with this new-found weakness.

Magic hummed in my veins, wanting to do a sweep of the space to ensure we really *were* alone, but it was too late now, and I couldn't afford to be any weaker.

Selene's jaw hung loose as she walked towards me, drawn to the items illuminated within like she was inspecting works of art in the world's finest museum. I tapped several buttons on the touch screen, ensuring the garage doors were all closed, and all of the windows and doors were locked tight before I allowed myself to follow her gaze.

Hanging on the walls and in display racks around me was every weapon I'd ever owned.

Selene's eyes were wide as she walked around the room, staring at everything. Some of them were active weapons — both magical and ordinary — and some were priceless artifacts, collected over centuries for their history and beauty.

"Are these all yours?" she asked as her eyes swung to me. I nodded, watching her reaction more than anything else, and her gaze moved back to the weapons.

"You've fought with all of them?" Her fingers traced delicately over the handle of a katana I'd received after locating a kidnapped tiger shifter cub in Japan.

"Most. Some were gifts."

Selene moved on, circling the room as she examined the history of my life, whether she knew it or not. Her feet stopped in the center of the room, standing in front of a large marble pedestal I'd been waiting for her to notice.

On it sat a hammer that was as old as I was, from my homeland. I'd had it encased in bulletproof, unbreakable glass, and treasured it more than any item I'd ever owned.

Selene didn't blink as she ogled it, her gaze flicking between the runes covering every surface of the weapon and me multiple times before she got up the courage to ask the question I knew she wanted to ask.

"Is that..." she pointed at it.

"A Viking war hammer? Yes." I nodded, cutting her off before she could ask more specific questions I knew would follow. Even through the thick glass, I could feel the power coursing off the ancient weapon, ready to be wielded once again, and was sure she could too.

I moved past her, the sound of my crutches on the metal floor drawing her eyes away from the hammer, and back to me.

"But we don't need the hammer for what we'll be doing," I said as I stopped in front of a row of guns, some practically the size of Selene, others so small she could fit them in her back pocket.

Her brows flew up at my words as I lifted a smaller gun that fit easily in my palm off the hooks on the wall. I raised it, sighting the garage doors, before laying it flat in my hand and flicking open the chamber to double-check it.

"What is it that *we'll* be doing, then?" she asked as she turned to face me, arms crossed over her chest. The sight of her challenging pose as she stood confidently in a room full of the most dangerous weapons in North America was so far beyond hot, I needed a new word to describe it.

"We're hunting demons, of course," I answered as I spun the chamber, listening to it whir loudly before snapping it closed. Grabbing the barrel, I held it out to her, grip first. Her eyes flicked down to the weapon as two small creases formed between her brows, confusion and apprehension warring in her expression.

"I'm not taking that," she shook her head.

Our argument over whether or not I was joining her on her new mission to hunt down Errakal was very brief — I was going, whether she wanted me to or not. Finally, she threw up her hands, shook her head, and marched up the stairs towards the loft above.

The sound of pots and pans clanging together reached me while I spent a few moments alone in my weapons room, putting everything back in its perfect place. The false wall slid back until not even a seam was left to show it was there, and I made for the stairs.

Something was sizzling in a pan, already smelling delicious as I entered the loft. Leaning my crutches against the wall, I hopped to a stool in front of the kitchen island and sat down, facing her.

Selene's brown curls were wild, messy from where she must have quickly slapped her hair into a bun on the top of her head while she cooked.

"Avoiding eye contact with me isn't going to make me stay behind, you know," I said after several minutes ticked by of her silent treatment.

"I'm not avoiding you. I just have nothing left to say." The glare she shot me seemed contrary to that fact, but I let it slide.

She worked in silence for several more minutes, and I eyed the fried rice she was making. Everything Selene had cooked so far was fantastic, and I was eager to try it.

"So your magic isn't replenishing then, correct?" Selene asked, and I slid my gaze back up to hers, pondering her question. "You tried to heal yourself, and then you passed out from magic use. I'm guessing you shaved your head because your hair came in white, like your beard is now. Right? So you're aging?"

Her inflection changed as she neared the end of her

little speech, worry filling her tone. But was it worry for her patient? Or worry for a… friend?

"You can't come with me, Ryker." She shook her head while she sliced up a pineapple. "If you get hurt again, I can't heal you magically, and you can't use more magic. You need to stay here."

I leaned forward across the counter, waiting silently until she felt the intensity of my gaze as I stared her down. When her eyes finally met mine, her breath caught in her throat.

"I need *you* to understand something, and I refuse to repeat myself, so make sure you're listening, Flores." She paused, holding the knife in her hand as she stared at me. "I am a mercenary. I have been a mercenary for so long it's laughable. There is no one better equipped to take down a demon who has no qualms about murdering innocents than me, whether I have magic or not.

"And under no circumstances will I repay the kindness that you've shown me — even when I didn't want or deserve it — by sending you out alone to find a murderer. Do not bring it up again." My words came out a little more growly than I intended, but I continued. "I'm going with you, and if I'm injured, how fortunate that I have a very capable doctor traveling with me. Now finish cooking that. I could hear your stomach grumbling from downstairs."

Several minutes later, she scooped the fried rice into two bowls, topped each with a handful of chopped pineapple and scallions and a dash of soy sauce, then pushed one across the counter to me.

"Eat," she said as she stabbed her chopsticks into the bowl. "Your body needs all the strength it can get for what's coming next. Then, after dinner, I'll switch you to a walking boot."

Taking that as a begrudging acceptance, I stabbed a piece of perfectly seared chicken with my fork, and took a bite, letting a victorious smile spread across my face.

The moment she bit into her own food, she moaned, and my mind slid directly into the gutter. I paused, fork in midair, as I watched her chew, the sight more seductive than any I'd ever seen before.

When her heavily lidded gaze slid up to mine, I knew she'd done it on purpose. She might be willing to let me accompany her on this trip, but she wasn't about to make this easy on me, either.

SELENE

The sound of a phone vibrating jolted me awake. I blinked rapidly, adjusting to the dim light before my gaze settled on the sight of the very naked, very tattooed chest next to me. I wish I could say I hadn't been plastered to his side, but the mere centimeters between us led me to believe that was too much to ask for.

Ryker's arm lifted as he rolled over, picking up his phone. With a swipe, the screen lit up, casting a harsh glare into the dark room. The sudden change was enough to have me scooting away from his warmth and dropping my feet off the bed. Quickly, I stood, rushing into the bathroom and closing the door behind me.

Standing in front of the mirror, I took a deep inhale, counting to four before exhaling and willing myself to pull it together. I couldn't pretend I was unaffected by the way he'd defended me in front of Ronan yesterday, even if I was still annoyed with his hot and cold behavior. Something inside me shifted when his hands laced around mine, instilling not power, but confidence and support, right when I'd needed it most.

Yes, Ryker was one of the most annoying, prideful males I'd ever met. But that moment… that had been different. And I couldn't seem to piece together this new side of him with the same arrogant asshole I'd come to know. It didn't help that he never seemed to wear shirts at home, either.

The heavy fall of his walking boot had me turning my head towards the door, listening before a small rap sounded. "That was Orion. He convinced Endymion to open the General Store for us to get supplies before we leave."

"Okay." My reflection in the mirror showed my hair wild from sleep, frizz sticking up in a halo around my head, and mascara slightly smeared beneath my eyes. Exactly the image I wanted to portray to the Norse god on the other side of the door. "Give me 15 minutes and I'll be ready to go."

"No hurry," he answered before he shuffled away from the door.

With a heavy sigh, I flipped on the sink and began washing my face. "Be professional, Selene." I scrubbed at my skin, willing my heart to get in line. "Just a patient like any other."

Even I didn't believe my own pep talk.

Ryker stood in front of the coffeemaker, still wearing the black shorts he'd slept in and nothing else. I'd managed to tame my hair, braiding it back beneath a turquoise baseball hat.

Trading the scrubs I'd slept in for a pair of black leggings and a fitted grey quarter-zip sweater, I felt slightly more human. At the last minute, I'd decided to leave the zipper undone, showing just the sliver of the top of my pink sports bra.

He turned to me as I entered the kitchen, nostrils flaring slightly as his eyes hovered over my chest, staring intently at the zipper. I had to fight the urge not to tug it up, cheeks heating under his inspection, but I just smiled, snagging the other cup he had sitting out on the counter for me.

"What do we need to get from the store?" I asked as I sipped at the warm coffee. I was pleasantly surprised to taste the hint of vanilla in my drink, glancing down at it before my eyes tracked back up to him. "Did you make me a vanilla latte?"

Ryker grabbed the back of his neck, limping to the fridge to pull out some eggs. I was glad to see he'd taken my advice to put as little pressure on the foot as he could, even in his walking boot. "Seemed like your type of drink."

"It is," I said, voice clogged with emotions I didn't want to feel. "Thank you."

Ryker grunted, and I smiled, glad to feel some of the weird tension between us dissipate with just that one sound.

I pulled out my phone and found the website I'd loaded earlier. "With everyone's magic on the fritz, I figured we can't ask Blaze to flicker us out to Colorado. I was looking at flights leaving from Boston, but wasn't sure where to book the flight *to*. What airport is closest to Timber Creek?"

Ryker's deep rumble of a laugh drew my attention up from my phone screen to his face. I'd heard him laugh so few times, the sound was still surprising, even distracting when paired with the dimple on his cheek.

"We're not flying out of Boston," he shook his head.

"Ok, well, we can leave from Portland then, I guess, and just deal with connections."

"No."

I squinted at the male in frustration. "Then you plan it."

"I have."

"Great." I rolled my eyes. "So what's the plan?"

"I'll fly us." He took a sip of his coffee, his eyes never leaving mine above the mug.

"News flash, Norbert, you're *also* out of commission. Plus, I'm not signing up to ride *you* for a cross-country flight."

The moment the words left my mouth, I instantly regretted them. The heat in his gaze told me he knew exactly where my mind had gone, and I could have slapped myself for the double entendre.

"Not like that," I shook my head, trying to recover. Why was it so damn hot in this room? "You know what I meant."

Ryker cleared his throat, shifting his posture slightly where he leaned against the counter still shirtless, damn him, and took another sip of his coffee.

"As enjoyable as that image is," he raised a brow at me, "I'm the only *pilot* I trust. I will fly us — in a plane. *My* plane."

"Why on *earth* would a dragon need a plane?"

Ryker didn't bother answering me as he set his mug in the sink, then hobbled to his closet, pulling down a bag.

I followed him, leaning against the doorway to the closet, still confused by this sudden turn of events. "Do you know how to fly this plane? I can't imagine that a dragon —

who can fly with his own wings — would have much experience in a cockpit."

Ryker's hands stilled with a shirt in the bag, his heavy green gaze swinging back to me as he leaned in. "Trust me, Flores," a sly grin spread across his face, that stupid dimple showing up yet again, "I'm far more experienced than anyone you've ever been with. I know exactly how to handle all of the buttons and gears to make your ride as smooth and satisfying as possible. You'll never forget it. After this, any other *pilots* you might have, any *flight* you take, all you'll be able to think about is me. Nothing else will ever compare."

I wasn't totally sure we were still talking about planes, and if I was being honest with myself, I already knew just how smooth Ryker's *ride* was, too. Halloween had been unforgettable, and that was the problem, wasn't it?

Not missing a beat, Ryker went on. "We're heading deep into the mountains tomorrow, so you need to pack every piece of cold winter gear you own."

"Oh." I shook my head, trying to clear the naughty imagery that *just wouldn't fade.* "Okay. Sure."

"There aren't any stores nearby, so we'll be taking food and supplies with us."

"Makes sense. What are we bringing?"

Ryker smirked at me as he threw several black shirts in the bag. "Well, figured I'd let you handle the food since this seems to be your love language."

I couldn't help but laugh even as my cheeks heated. But he wasn't wrong. I loved taking care of people, hence the whole doctor thing. "I think I can handle food."

"Good."

"Anything else we need?"

Ryker gripped the edge of the dresser, and I shamelessly watched as his naked torso contracted, muscles in his arms flexing. Pulling my coffee to my lips, I prayed to the goddess that any drool fighting to escape went into my cup and not down my chin. No matter how many times I'd seen Ryker's bare chest and arms, he still took my breath away.

"Pack medical supplies. Just in case."

My gaze snapped up, settling on his face, but he refused to meet my eyes, turning instead to head into the bathroom.

Chapter Twenty-Six

SELENE

I drove us into town in the truck later that morning, headed for the General Store. It had been years since I'd been inside — Endymion, the demon who owned it, never kept regular hours, only opening when he felt like it. Sometimes that meant it was closed for weeks at a time, others only during the thunderstorms the male seemed to love so much.

"Go around the block and park behind the store," Ryker said as we neared it. I side-eyed him, hearing the unspoken challenge. The closest parking spots to the store were the parallel ones in front of the gazebo, directly across the street from the General Store. Even partially healed, Ryker was still in a walking boot, and didn't need to take any extra steps. So I took that challenge head-on.

"What are you doing?" he asked hesitantly as I flipped on my turn signal, tuning him out. Ryker sucked in a breath when I stopped in front of the gazebo, threw the truck in reverse, and placed my hand on the back of the passenger headrest.

I couldn't lie. Parallel parking in the lifted truck was

more difficult than I was prepared for, but I breathed deeply, ignoring the way Ryker eyed me. Like prepping before surgery, muscle memory took over, and I executed it flawlessly. Ryker shifted in his seat as I put the truck in park, swinging my smug gaze over to him. "Like a glove."

Ryker's jaw worked as he gripped the door handle, pushing it open. I dropped out of the driver's side, falling a few feet to the ground, and circled the truck to help him across the street. Fortunately, the streets were mostly clean after the last snowstorm, and I'd insisted Ryker wrap his new boot in a plastic sleeve to keep it dry before we left the house.

As I stepped up to Ryker's side to cross the street, my eyes snagged on the gazebo. The white wood blended in with the snow on the ground, but there was a bright spot of rainbow color huddled on one of the benches inside. I leaned forward, squinting as I tried to make out what the pile of hideous patterns was. Then it hit me.

"Mo?" A moan rose from the pile of fabric, shifting slightly as I neared. An inkling of worry shot up my spine as I changed directions, rushing through the snow to her side. "Mo. Talk to me. Are you okay? What's wrong?"

"My head," the ancient witch I'd known my whole life mumbled.

I began ripping back the ponchos — plural — she was wearing, ignoring the kaleidoscope of color each layer revealed.

"What happened?" Ryker asked as he limped to my side.

"I'm dying," she groaned, and I pulled off my gloves, placing my hands on her pale face.

"I can't smell any blood on her," Ryker whispered, his

eyes roving her body for injuries. I nodded, agreeing with him. Nothing noticeable stood out to me either.

"What hurts?"

"Everything."

"Can you tell me what happened?" I asked, trying not to panic at the thought of losing Mo, the closest I had to a mother figure. This hit too close to home. "Did you fall?"

"Fall?" Mo pinched my hand. "Just how old do you think I am, young lady?"

I met Ryker's gaze silently. I was *not* going to respond to that.

"I was at Scallywags last night."

"Did you use your magic?" My hands hovered over her, but I didn't feel the same depleted state as I had with the sea nymph. There didn't seem to be anything at all wrong with her. "What happened at Scallywags? Or after?"

"Nothing." Mo shook her head lightly, then moaned again. "Just an ordinary night, like any other."

A laugh rumbled through Ryker's chest at my back as he stood.

Ryker bit back a smile, eyes alight with amusement. "I cannot tell you how much joy this brings me, Morgaine. Might be the happiest day of my life."

"What is *wrong* with you?" I asked, fury lighting in my veins for the dragon. No matter how much Mo loved to push his buttons, who would wish ill on someone like this? She was clearly in pain.

But Ryker's smile didn't fade, not even as he leaned down to hover right above Mo. "Welcome to your first hangover, Mo. You deserve this more than anyone I've ever met."

I glanced up at him, then back down to Mo. "Mo. How much did you drink last night?"

"Same as usual, I suppose."

"Ah, well," I said, biting my cheeks, "that explains it."

"Am I dying?" Mo asked, laying the back of her hand over her eyes like she was a fainting damsel. "Is this the end for me?"

"Probably not," Ryker said as he rolled his eyes, moving to exit the gazebo and heading across the street to the General Store. I could have sworn I heard a mumbled, *"Unfortunately."*

Turning back to Mo, I held in the laugh. Mo's magical hangover cure was her closest-guarded secret, only given to those she felt most worthy. Petra always seemed to get some, whether she asked for it or not. Devanna almost never did.

"Think you can walk home?" I asked, hand rubbing over Mo's arm.

"I could if I still had legs, but I'm pretty sure they're gone."

Her legs, still very much there, were covered in the most obnoxious floral pattern I'd ever seen. "All right, well, let me go get Blaze. He can carry you home."

"No, no, don't trouble Blaze." She patted my hand, and I got the impression she didn't want Blaze, who would most definitely give her shit for the rest of her life, to know about this. "Noxie." Mo mumbled, eyes closed but lifting a hand to point across the green. I followed her finger, noticing the new store in town for the first time. *Pop Nox*, the sign on the window said, the letters painted in red and white stripes. Flames licked up from the bottom frame of the glass, giving the building a strange vibe.

"He'll be up?" I asked, noting on my watch it was only 10 a.m. "Seems early for a demon, especially a young one."

"Young love will do that to you." A slow smile spread over Mo's face before her nose scrunched again, another low moan erupting from her. "Move back, dear, I'm going to be sick."

I gently rolled her to her side, facing out from the gazebo, and hurried across the yard to fetch Nox.

Pushing open the door, the aroma of chocolate and popcorn immediately enveloped me, but nothing compared to the sight on the walls.

"What in the ever-loving fuck?" I whispered, eyes wide as I took in the shelves covering every available inch of wall space, housing *hundreds* of Beanie Babies, this little shop the epitome of the town's obsession with the stuffed animals. Little plastic beady eyes stared back at me, all somehow focused on the door where I stood, and I reeled back from the sight. Trying to focus anywhere but the stuffed animals on the wall, I glanced down at the glass counter in front of me, eyeing the multiple flavors of popcorn to the left, and the neat rows of fudge to the right.

"Oh, hey!" Aurora called as she pushed through the saloon-style doors between the shop and the kitchen. "Welcome!"

I didn't know the young witch well, but I'd seen her at the Coven meeting, and knew Dev had taken her under her wing since she'd arrived in town. Tortoise-shell glasses perched on her pale, lightly freckled nose, highlighting her heart-shaped face. Brown hair was pulled back in a high ponytail, curled lightly on the ends as she moved towards the counter. After noticing the Beanie Babies, I'd expected a wild outfit to match the insane decor taste, but she wore a navy pencil skirt over pink tights, a pretty floral sweater matching the exact shade of the pink tights.

Remembering why I was here, I asked, "Is Nox here? I could use some help."

Aurora's head tilted as she eyed me. "Sure, I can get him. Everything okay?"

"Yes." I smiled. "All good. Mo asked me to fetch him for her."

"Oh, okay." Aurora grinned in return, then turned back to the kitchen. Moments later, Nox came out, black beanie over his messy blonde hair. Seeing his grunge style next to Aurora's bright florals was jarring, but it worked for them. Something about it seemed… familiar. But I shook the thought free, grabbing Nox by the hand without a word and dragging him out of the store.

"Uh, hey," Nox said, offering very little resistance as we trudged through the snow towards the gazebo.

"Long time, no see, Nox," I replied, realizing how little the young demon knew me. "Mo needs your help getting home."

"Oh shit," he nodded, steps getting quicker. "Is she okay? What happened?"

We heard Mo moan as we neared the gazebo. "Forgive me goddess, I've sinned *so* many times. If you let me live through this, I swear I'll never meddle in the love lives of those I love *ever again*."

"Even the goddess wouldn't believe that," I said as I held back a smirk.

"Okay, only on the weekends," Mo amended. "Maybe every other day."

"Is she," Nox paused, eyes darting to mc then back to Mo where she lay curled in the fetal position on the bench of the gazebo, "Is she drunk?"

"Probably, yeah," I chuckled. "Hungover, at least. But probably still drunk. Think you can carry her home?"

Nox pursed his lips. "If you puke on me, I'll never forgive you."

"I can't make any promises, dear," Mo groaned, but Nox bent down to lift the elderly woman, cradling her in his arms as he stood upright and moved across the lawn. Mo threw her arms around his neck, head resting lightly on his chest.

"You smell like burnt popcorn," she gagged, and Nox rolled his eyes.

I watched as they crossed the street, heading to her house on the other side of the green.

"Is she okay?" Aurora asked, and I turned to see the young witch in front of me. She'd pulled on a purple knee-length parka and a matching beanie with a fur pom-pom now, and I grinned.

"Nursing your first hangover at… however old she is has got to be an eye-opener."

Aurora's eyes widened in understanding before she pressed her lips together to stifle a laugh. "Poor Mo," she murmured, as we watched Nox walk off with her.

"Will you check on her later?" I didn't know the young witch very well, but she seemed kind enough and I knew she'd be just around the block from Mo's with her shop here on the square. "I have to head out of town, or I'd do it."

Aurora nodded. "Of course. I'll ask Dev for help to make her something."

I thanked her again before I made my way over to the

General Store. I didn't have the heart to tell Aurora that those two witches weren't exactly on the best terms — then again, if anyone could get Dev to help Mo, somehow I'd bet Aurora could.

Rejoining Ryker in front of the General Store, we pushed open the door and were greeted by darkness. Then, a loud crash.

"Hello?" I called out. "Endymion?"

"Coming!" a muffled voice reached us a moment before Endymion emerged from the backroom, his grey hair fanned and wild about his head like Einstein.

"Did you lose power?" I indicated the lack of lights.

"No, it's — I've never actually had to use the light switch and I can't find the blasted thing." The older demon tripped over something behind the counter and muttered a curse as he righted himself. "I usually just magic them on."

"Gods' sakes," Ryker growled under his breath while I scanned the one-room shop and spotted a set of switches half-hidden behind a row of lava lamps.

"Found them!" I flicked them on, and Endymion let out a sigh of relief, thanking me profusely.

"You're wel — oh." Now that we could actually see the shop, I almost wished the lights had stayed off.

Above the row of lava lamps was a row of what appeared to be vintage erotica photographs. Below the lamps, an assortment of pantry staples. There were a few rows of what one might consider normal items for a general store — a small refrigerated section, toiletries, cleaning supplies. But on the far wall was a selection of what seemed to be homemade ceramic fantasy creatures — each more bizarre than the last. In the middle of the shop was a large fish tank. I approached it tentatively, expecting the worst, and had to hide my grimace as I gazed at possibly the ugliest fish I'd ever seen.

"Oh, you want to meet Belphegor?" Endymion beamed as he came around the counter, his eyes softening as he took in the horrifying creature.

"Um —"

But he was already waving me closer, shaking a cup of small shrimp into the tank that Belphegor snatched up quickly.

"Belphie loves his shrimpies," Endymion chuckled proudly. "He's a goblin shark. Beverly said she had him in her shop for five years, and nobody wanted him. Can you believe that? Well, I took one look at that little face and just couldn't say no."

Before I had a moment to process that, Ryker's voice reached us from where he'd wandered to the back of the room. "Endymion, please tell me these aren't what I think they are." We both turned to him where he held up what could only be described as —

"Ah, yes, I'm afraid they are," Endymion nodded, and Ryker made a disgusted noise in the back of his throat as he placed the item back on the shelf. "Some of the gang got a bit carried away at a Sip'n'Sculpt one Sunday and, well — you know how it is after a cocktail or two. One minute you're making a clay pot, the next, it's become a dildo." He shrugged casually, as though that sort of thing happened to everyone. "Two for one, if you're interested," he added hopefully.

Ryker merely leveled a look at him, and Endymion sighed.

"What can I help you guys with, then?"

We left not long later with a first aid kit and a bare minimum of food supplies for a few days in Colorado. Ryker explained we didn't want to add too much weight to the small plane, but we wanted to have a few meals with us in case we weren't able to stop anywhere else right away.

We were just heading out the door when I thought of something and tugged Ryker next door to Dev's shop.

She looked up from behind the counter as we entered, scowling the moment she saw me.

"As I already told Aurora, no, I'm not making Morgaine a tea. It would do that witch some good to experience a hangover now and again. Maybe she'll think twice about restricting that hangover cure of hers next time."

"One," I leaned my hip into the counter, "ever heard the phrase, *you catch more flies with honey*?" She rolled her eyes, but I continued. "Two, you *will* make her that tea, or I'll tell her exactly what you were doing on Halloween." She leveled her steeliest stare at me, but I'd looked into Belphegor's cold eyes and there was nothing left for me to fear. "And three, that's not why I'm here. Do you have any *ferrouscide* on hand?"

That seemed to snag her attention, and she sat up straighter. "I'll see how much I can find." She rose without another word of protest and slipped into the backroom.

"Any what?" Ryker turned to me the moment she was gone.

"*Ferrouscide*," I said. "It can help stop iron poisoning from spreading beyond the wound site. It can't remove it or act as an antidote, but it can keep the spread localized if applied immediately. It wouldn't have worked on you because the bullet had been in your leg for too long already, so I didn't try it. Unfortunately, it's incredibly difficult to make, but I figure any little bit could help."

Ryker nodded in understanding as Dev re-emerged, holding a tiny vial in her hands that she passed over to me.

"This is it, so I hope you won't need it," she said. "No more than two drops, or it'll do more harm than good, and if you have more than two points of injury, you're out of luck."

I reached for my wallet, opening my mouth to ask how much the vial was, but Dev shut me down.

"Your money's no good here, Leens. Just catch that bastard and get us our magic back. If I have to hear Blaze complain about doing the dishes or counting the till manually one more time, I won't be responsible for my actions. Besides, I'll just bill Orion instead."

We were hopping back in the truck when a series of grumbling curses reached us, and I turned to see Nox struggling to shovel a foot of frozen-solid snow in front of a small duplex. He took a break, leaning on the shovel and panting, before he spied us watching him from across the square and gave a half-hearted wave.

"Catch that bastard and get our magic back, will you? I can't do this shit manually like a human forever."

Well, at least we had our motivation.

Chapter Twenty-Seven

RYKER

We spent the rest of the afternoon packing and preparing to leave for Timber Creek. Selene turned in early, but my mind was restless, working through all of the preparations we'd need for our trip.

Everything was different this time with Selene accompanying me. Safety was a much larger concern than it usually was. Not only did I not have my magic at my disposal, but I also had to cover for Selene, all while still being stuck in the awkward walking boot for my calf, even if it was better than the full-cast.

I stared at the walls of my weapons room, running through every scenario I could imagine.

We were headed deep into the mountains, so I might need a grappling hook. I pulled it off the wall and placed it in the duffel on the black table in the middle of the room.

Definitely needed Striker, my favorite sniper rifle I'd procured from a magical arms dealer a few years ago. Reaching across the shelf, I grabbed every box of the magic-laced bullets made especially for Striker. Encased in an iron alloy, these rounds were made to stop magical beings in their tracks. The reminder that the same type of bullet had been used on me had me grinding my teeth together, but I shoved the memory aside.

Several other guns made it into the bag, including the smaller handgun I offered to Selene the day before. When the time came, it was the perfect size for her. Maybe I should have her practice with it once we got to Colorado — just to see her using it; her surgeon's hands steady on its grip, the way her hair would cascade as she tilted her head to sight her shot. I blinked out of the fantasy, adjusted my pants, and snagged another box of the same magical ammunition fit for the smaller guns to add it to the cache.

Light glinted off the back wall as a pulse of power hummed through the room.

"I haven't forgotten you," I said aloud as I zipped up the duffel on the floor. Standing, I turned, pacing towards the back wall where an ancient sword hung. Pulling the scabbard from the hook next to it, I stared at the blade that I'd carried into every battle.

Gram, named after the weapon that Sigurd had fought Fafnir with in Norse legend. The irony was not lost on me that that blade was famous for *slaying* a dragon, and yet, this one had answered to a dragon for a millennium.

The magical blade was damn-near sentient, the runes engraved along the sharp edges glowing a bright green that matched my eyes when in battle. Even after all these years, I didn't fully understand its magic, but together, we had never lost a battle.

If ever there was a fight I was determined to win, it was

this one. Nothing could happen to Selene. I had to find Errakal, and I had to recover my magic.

My hand settled on the duffel handle, and I set the bag into the backseat of my truck, ready to go for tomorrow. I flicked the lights off in the garage, waiting for the weapons' room doors to snick shut, then made my way upstairs to bed.

Selene was breathing evenly as I settled in next to her. My fingers itched to reach across the mattress, to pull her towards me, to feel her safe and whole as danger loomed ever closer. But it wasn't my job to provide her with comfort. It was my job to protect her, and that was something I could do.

Selene's small blue rolling suitcase sat against the wheel of my truck the next morning, waiting to be loaded. She was quiet as she drove us out of town following my directions towards the hangar. I called ahead this morning, so the plane would be ready by the time we arrived. The sun was up, peeking out between the clouds. Conditions were perfect for a flight, and I was excited by the idea of returning to the sky once more, even if I had to be encased in a metal tube to do it.

The gate in the chain-link fence surrounding the airport slid open as we approached, and Selene's jaw dropped as she took in the small plane parked on the runway, waiting for us. While I could have opted for a larger, fancier jet, I'd always loved flying the little Maule M-7-235B, and it was the perfect size to fly alone.

"You *own* that plane?" she asked, her eyes sliding to mine as we rolled through the gate and towards it.

"Park here. They'll move my truck into the hangar once we're gone."

She did as I asked, unbuckling her seat belt as I did the same. I greeted the attendant who took the keys from Selene. After I'd retrieved our bags from the back, we hopped up the stairs to the plane, and I slid into the cockpit.

It was a tight fit for a male my size, but looking over all the controls and gauges made me feel at home.

"Can I sit up here with you?" Selene asked as she plopped down into the co-pilot seat, not waiting for a response. I turned, my eyes settling on the three seats behind me, then back at her, but she didn't answer my silent request.

With a slight grumble, I slid my headphones on and began the takeoff protocol. Selene's eyes lit with excitement as she followed my lead, donning her own headset. The hydraulics pulled the doors shut, and within minutes, we were moving down the runway, ready for takeoff.

The wheels of the plane touched down on the runway in Colorado, and I breathed a sigh of relief. Weather conditions were rough — not uncommon here in Timber Creek — but the turbulence on the way down was always more challenging.

"Okay over there?" I asked Selene as I pulled my headphones off, resting them on the hook below the dash. We'd

188

had to make several stops to refuel, but hadn't lingered more than an hour anywhere.

She nodded, but said nothing, probably feeling the effects of the landing. I unbuckled my seatbelt, and stooped in the cockpit, glad to be standing on two feet again, albeit in this clunky boot. She followed me out of the plane and down the steps onto the runway.

"Great to see you again, Ryker," Gio called as he greeted us, noting with a blink my booted leg, then my shorn hair. "Nice landing, as always. I have your Jeep waiting for you with the heater on."

I shook his outstretched hand, glad he'd kept the rest of his thoughts to himself, and took the keys from him. As I stared down at the keys, I realized I'd forgotten something important.

"Hey, Selene," I turned to her, already politely chatting with Gio, about what, I had no clue.

"Yeah?" she asked, eyebrow raised in question.

"Do you know how to drive a stick?"

Gio's head whipped in my direction, then quickly back to Selene, appraising her differently now. It had been years before I'd let him inside my cars, even to pull them up to the hangar for me. The fact that I was willing to let Selene drive one of my vehicles was huge, and he knew it.

Selene sauntered over, hips swinging even in her turquoise puffy coat, as a smile spread across her face, and swiped the keys from my outstretched palm. My jaw worked, both from the idea of her driving my Jeep, and at how undeniably sexy she was at all times, even dressed down in her workout gear and winter coat.

"The boot would be cumbersome for both a clutch and

a brake," she nodded as she turned the corner around the hangar, walking confidently like she knew where she was going. "Good thing I *do* know how to drive a stick."

Her voice was laced with excitement, and it was catching. She loved driving like I did, and that was about the most attractive thing I'd ever seen.

The moment she spotted my Jeep, she sucked in a breath, and stopped in her tracks. I understood the feeling — this car was one of my favorites. All black, like all of my cars, this Wrangler was fitted out for the winter conditions here. Lifted tires, light bar, winch — you name it. As long as Selene actually knew how to drive manual, we would have no problem making it to my cabin tonight.

"The smiley-face light bar really screams *This is Ryker's Jeep* to me," Selene said with a chuckle as she pointed at the spotlight covers above the windshield, and I only shook my head.

"You'll be happy I have that light bar in a few hours when the sun sets and you realize where you're driving."

Rather than seeming intimidated, Selene's grin spread wider in excitement. Fuck me, I was in over my head with this witch.

We hit the road, and I was content with Selene's driving, even if it was gods-damn uncomfortable for me to sit the passenger seat of any vehicle. Not because I didn't have enough room — I'd had the second row removed from the two-door Jeep, and the seats shifted back to accommodate my large stature easily — but because I was never the passenger in any vehicle. *Ever*.

"We need some road trip tunes," Selene said as she puckered her lips. "I doubt I can stream anything up here though."

I fought back a smirk as I watched the snow-covered mountains around us. It was at least an hour drive from the airstrip to my cabin, and every mile of it was remote switchbacks deeper into the wilderness with nothing and no one around. No cell service out here, just the way I liked it.

"Got any music on your phone you can play?"

"I don't listen to music."

"At all?" she scoffed. "That can't be true. You mentioned *MMMBop* to Lys, even if it was a diss, so I *know* you know Hanson, at the very least. Or is it all 90s boy bands that you're into? You can be honest with me, you know. I won't judge."

I grunted, because what was I supposed to say to that? Before I could stop her, she reached across the dash, flipped on the stereo, and was pushing buttons, searching for radio stations. Static greeted us.

"Nothing works out here," I stated the obvious, right as she pushed the CD button. Immediately, the beginning piano lines of Evanescence's *Bring Me To Life* played through the speakers on the roll bar over our heads, and Selene let out a high-pitched laugh.

"No music, huh?"

Selene's lips curled into her mouth, pinched between her teeth as she fought back a smile, or a laugh. Either way, I shifted in my seat uncomfortably as the song continued on. I reached down to turn it off, but she gasped and slapped my hand out of the way.

"Don't you dare!"

I sat back in silence, looking out the window at the passing snow-covered pines, fighting to control my emotions. I could count the number of times I'd been embarrassed on one hand, and this was one of them.

She skipped a few songs, but tapped the steering wheel to the beat of several, shaking her head along with the music, obviously enjoying it, and I eventually relaxed. "You'll turn at the next break in the trees a quarter mile up," I pointed to the right, indicating for her to pay attention, and she nodded in understanding.

The CD paused before looping, then began to play again. My breath caught in my chest as Selene sang along to *Going Under,* mirroring the raspy voice of Amy Lee perfectly. Her eyes sparkled with mischief as she continued to belt out the words. By the time the chorus came on, she leaned down, turning it up louder, and banged imaginary drums on the steering wheel. Whether I wanted to or not, I smiled.

"Good goddess, you're hot," Selene sighed. "Don't smile like that. I can't take it."

"I wouldn't have picked Evanescense as your type of music," I chuckled, shaking off her last comment and turning down the next song.

She laughed, down-shifting as we descended a steep grade. "What millennial girl didn't have an emo phase as a teen? Evanescence was an anthem for our whole generation, and also apparently for ancient angsty dragons."

"I can't imagine you as an angry teen."

"Yes, well, combine some heavy abandonment issues

over the fact that I had zero family growing up other than my mom, and teenage girl hormones, and an Evanescence fan was born."

Her tone was full of resentment at the comment, so I sat in silence, waiting to see if she wanted to elaborate. I admired how open Selene usually was — a trait I didn't have in common with her.

As expected, she went on. "It was always me and Mom." Her voice was laced with sadness, and I turned towards her to show I was listening. "I don't know why that wasn't enough, but teenage-me got it in my head that my family didn't know I existed, and that's why they weren't involved."

"Did you find them?" I asked, following her train of thought.

A bitter laugh escaped her as we slid on the ice. She focused, righting the wheel perfectly, and shifted down to first. The way she handled cars had me at half-mast — I didn't even need to offer any pointers to her. She knew what she was doing, and it was hot.

"Yes," she whispered. "I found them. Turns out they knew about me all along. Mom made the right choice moving us as far as possible from them, but it took me a long time to understand that. Then it was too late, and Mom was gone."

"I'm sorry for your loss," I said automatically, feeling my own grief well within me at her story, however brief.

"It's history," she nodded, seeming to need her own reassurance. A moment of silence ticked by between us, but I let it, giving her time to process.

"Turn right up here."

"What about your family?" she asked as she slowed,

prepping to turn, and my heart plummeted in my chest. "Anyone in your life?"

"No."

"That's lonely." She frowned at me as she turned, bringing the car to a stop. She ducked down to peer through the windshield, taking in the tall pines on either side of us, the road barely wide enough for my Jeep. "We're going up here?"

"Think you can handle it?" I raised a brow, waiting for her to chicken out. Leaning down, I brushed her thigh as I reached across and flicked on the light bar, illuminating the path in front of us. A jolt of electricity shot through my veins at the brief touch, and she sucked in a breath. My words were challenge enough, though, as the wheels crunched forward across the packed snow.

Chapter Twenty-Eight

SELENE

My heart raced in my chest, bruising my ribs as I drove up the winding, snow-packed path. I couldn't even bring myself to call it a road, it was so narrow.

"Can you keep talking?" I asked after several moments of silence went by. I was glad I'd ditched my bulky coat before getting behind the wheel — my nerves were enough to raise my temperature already, even without the heat in the car. "I realize that's asking a hell of a lot of you since you've got the whole strong-silent-type thing down pat, but it keeps me calm. And I feel like we both want me to be calm while I'm driving right now."

Ryker grunted, hopefully in understanding, but eventually broke the silence.

"How many dragons do you know of in our world?"

My eyebrows shot up as he opened this line of conversation. I thought he'd start talking about cars, or the weather, or something inconsequential, not about *himself*.

"Um," I thought about it, trying to think through if I'd

ever heard of *any* dragons other than him. He'd been the first I'd ever met. "Not many. Why, how many are there?"

"Five."

His answer was so blunt, my eyebrows shot up in surprise. "That's not very many."

"Even when I was born, we were already rare," Ryker sighed, staring out the window, his mind far away. "That was over a thousand years ago, by the way. When I was born."

"Holy shit," I muttered before I could keep my reaction in. "Sorry."

"Nothing to be sorry about." He shook his head. "Supernaturals — even the long-lived angels and demons — don't usually live *that* long. Hel, even most dragons don't live that long," he muttered the last part, almost to himself. When his bright green eyes met mine, I suddenly understood.

"You've seen a lot of people in your life die." My heart broke for him as I sensed the weight on his shoulders. Imagining my own grief for my mother multiplied by the infinite number of people Ryker had lost over the last millennium was gut-wrenching. Tears welled in my eyes in sympathy for him. "I'm so sorry, Ryker."

"Don't be." He turned to the window again. "It's much easier to be alone. I prefer it this way."

But something had changed in his voice with his words. Something that betrayed that while he spoke the truth, maybe he didn't quite believe it.

Words were lost on me as I thought through what else I could say. Nothing. So I didn't. Instead, I reached across the console, slipping my small hand in his. Ryker glanced down to where my tawny fingers laced with his pale ones, then over at me.

"You're not alone right now though." I offered him a tentative smile before I let his hand go, returning it to the wheel. "You have me, and Orion, and... Blaze, maybe? Mo?"

Ryker shook his head with a mumbled *I don't count Blaze* that bubbled a laugh out of me.

"Dragons are incredibly rare," he went on. "I never knew my parents, but orphans were pretty common in those days, what between the harsh conditions and the violent life-style. Fortunately, I lived with other supernaturals, but it was still a Hel of a surprise when I realized I was the only one with wings."

"Did you know *any* other dragons?" I asked in shock. "Just you?"

"Just me."

"That sucks." I shook my head, trying to wrap my mind around being that isolated even as a child as we continued to creep up the hill at a turtle's pace, though the road was starting to level out.

"Well, there was one other dragon for a while, but," he paused, rubbing his free hand over his buzzed head, "we didn't exactly see eye to eye. Fortunately for me, it was Viking times, and dragons were highly revered. God-like, almost."

"So that's where the ego comes from." I nodded in understanding, and Ryker chuckled. "Add in the bone structure, that damn dimple, and um —" I choked my next words back, *the size of what's hiding in your pants*, but I feared the glance down at his crotch might have given me away. I cleared my throat. "— Well, it makes for a killer combo."

The deep rumble was so out of character, I stepped on the brake, gaping at him. His almost neon green eyes were locked on me, dancing with mirth as he stared me down.

"You continue to surprise me, Flores." His voice was raspier than it was a moment before, and the heated look in his eyes was almost predatory as he took me in. "Park here."

"What?" My brow drew down in confusion at the sudden shift in topic. I turned, trying to see anything through the thick trees. "Here?"

He pulled the parking brake, and I swung my gaze back in his direction. As his arms reached across the console, gripping my face and yanking me towards him, my eyes expanded in shock.

The feel of his lips touching down on mine was so jarring, so unexpected, that I forgot to close my eyes, still wide-eyed as I fought to focus on what was happening.

He pulled back from the kiss too soon, leaning back in his seat, and my hand drifted up to my lips as if I needed to confirm that out of body experience had just happened.

"We get out here," Ryker said as he reached for the door handle, and my hand shot out to stop him, landing a hard smack to the middle of his chest.

"Hang on just one minute." I fought to regain my breath, my heart beating so fast I could hardly hear around its heavy thump. "What the hell was that?"

Ryker smirked as he turned in his seat, eyes meeting mine. "A kiss."

I involuntarily rolled my eyes at his stupid comment, and

he chuckled. "So we're back to the *hot* side of your hot and cold attitude towards me, then."

"I've never told anyone much of my history before," Ryker went on, and my mind worked to understand the words he was saying. "It was a powerful moment for me, and I wanted to kiss you, so I did.

"The problem is," he went on, his voice dropping lower into a near growl that sent heat pooling low in my abdomen, "now my mind is less worried about hunting demon-witches and how to navigate snowmobiles with this dumb boot, and more focused on how I can fuck you right here in this Jeep."

A shocked laugh escaped me, but damn if his dirty words didn't have me contemplating the same thing.

"I don't know if that's a good idea." My brain forced the words out of my mouth, even though my body was screaming in opposition. Ryker and I had been skirting a repeat of last Halloween for days now, the momentary fling in front of the fire not nearly enough to quell the fire in my veins.

"No?" Ryker unbuckled his seat belt, lacing a hand around the back of my neck and hauling me towards him again. "You sure?"

His voice rumbled across my skin as he grazed his nose across my sensitive neck. The incoherent sound that squeaked out of me was not a no.

"See," he whispered into my ear, "the problem with being a shifter — a *dragon* — is that I can tell when you're lying to me. Your heart rate changes, your breathing hitches, your eyes dilate. So many tells. I don't recommend it."

"No poker with dragons," I managed to mutter. "Got it."

Ryker's deep laugh sounded again, and the sound combined with the way his breath tickled my skin had me shivering.

"The other thing you're forgetting," he whispered again before sucking my earlobe into his mouth, running his teeth over the sensitive flesh. I gasped, eyes slamming shut as I shifted in my seat. "I can smell exactly how much you like this idea."

Ah, damn.

When he turned my face back towards his, I didn't hesitate. My lips slammed down on his, my hand reaching up to his jaw to pull him to me as fiercely as he held the back of my neck. Before I could completely understand what had happened, the seatbelt clicked, releasing me from its hold, and I shrugged out of it. Ryker's hands settled on my waist as he hauled me up and over the center console, sliding me down his lap.

We didn't skip a beat, tongues tangling as the thin fabric of my yoga pants brushed against the rough denim of his jeans, and I gasped at the hard length I felt there. Our breathing heightened, his teeth nipping my bottom lip, a whimper escaping me as his hips shifted. I didn't know whether it was the small space of the car or the emotional conversation before, but either way, neither of us held back now, fog quickly filling the windows.

Ryker's calloused palms slid under my sweatshirt across my skin, tracing the underside of my sports bra, and I squirmed at the touch, accidentally — or maybe not — grinding down into the hardness beneath me.

"*Fuck*," Ryker growled, hands slipping back down to my

hips as he pulled me flush against him. "You still have your IUD?"

I nodded aggressively, words lost to me as heat flooded my body. I wanted his hands on every part of me, my skin practically trembling, and it had nothing to do with the snow outside the vehicle.

"Grab the roll bars above you."

As soon as I did, Ryker reclined his chair flat, then yanked on my leggings, pulling them and my underwear down to my bent knees in one swipe. He lifted my right leg, yanking off my boot and the pant leg as he bared me to him, then released me to straddle him once more. Instantly, his hand rubbed across my skin right where I needed him, and I damn-near purred at the contact.

While his fingers worked me, Ryker undid his belt, shimmying down his own pants, and freeing himself. My hands still fought for purchase on the roll-bars above as he lined up correctly, and slammed his hips up into me.

The movement was so jarring, and so fantastic, my weight shifted, sinking me even further down on him.

"Shit, Selene," he tipped his head back against the seat as I rose up slightly on my knees, then sank back down again. As if I unleashed the beast within him, Ryker's eyes glowed a bright neon green, and his hands gripped my hips so hard, I'd sport hand prints later.

"Hold on."

The words were my only warning, and I tightened my fingers in the padding on the roll bar above me as he pulled me slightly off him, then slammed back into me, fucking me from beneath.

I moaned as my head fell forward, overcome with sensation. Ryker didn't stop, his movements frenzied as if he'd felt the same need I had in our close proximity these past few weeks. Needing to feel him, I dropped one of my hands from the bar, resting it on his chest, the muscles of his abdomen flexing with his movements even through his shirt.

A shot of boldness drifted through me, and I lifted my eyes to his, letting him see the way he was making me feel. My eyes were only on his for a moment before he reached up, grabbed me by the neck and hauled me down on his chest, kissing me fiercely as his hips continued to work beneath me.

"You can deny that last Halloween wasn't the best sex of your life all you want," he growled as he hit something deep inside me. My body hummed as heat pooled in my belly, working me towards the edge quickly. "But there is no denying *this*, Selene. No one has ever made you feel the way I do, made you purr the way I do, made you come the way I do. And you're going to come for me, aren't you?"

Even if I had wanted to deny him, my body wouldn't allow it. I exploded, stars bursting behind my closed eyes as the sensations washed over me. My muscles turned to mush, but Ryker still moved beneath me, his movements becoming wild and irregular.

With a roar, Ryker's hips stilled, and he pulsed beneath me. My head fell down on his chest, resting against his shoulder as I fought for air.

Chapter Twenty-Nine

RYKER

This Jeep had now become my favorite car I'd ever owned. That was saying something, considering the collection of vehicles I'd amassed over my very long life. But damn, what had just happened in here… even if I lived another millennium, I'd never forget it.

Cleanup in the small space was difficult, but we managed to get ourselves dressed and returned back to our semi-composed states. The windows of the Jeep were fogged over, and I rubbed my elbow across the glass to clear it, wishing I could clear the haze that hung over my heart as easily. So instead, I focused on the task at hand.

"In the back is a set of snowshoes you'll need to grab," I instructed Selene. "Put those on, and you've got about a two-minute walk through the snow to a small shed. There's a padlock on the door, and the code is 007."

Selene barked a laugh, then realized I was serious, and mumbled a *sorry*.

"As my doctor, I'm assuming that you would balk at the idea of me trudging through the snow with my boot," my teeth ground together at my next words, "so I guess I'll wait here while you go fetch the snowmobile. Have you ever driven one?"

She tilted her head to the side. "No, but I've driven WaveRunners dozens of times. Same thing, right? Just on the snow instead of the water?"

In my best impression of Orion, I pinched the bridge of my nose between my forefinger and thumb, rubbing the tension away. I hated not being in control, but if I was going to give that control up to anyone, it'd be Selene.

"Pull the choke like you would on a WaveRunner to start the engine, yes."

Selene nodded, then reached to grab the snowshoes from the back seat. The move brought her chest level with my eyes, and I fought back the temptation to pull her back into my lap for round two. That would wait for later in the cabin, when we had more room.

Quickly, Selene had her jacket back on, hat pulled low over her ears, and gloves secured. She opened the Jeep door, and a blast of cold air broke the moment, snapping me back into the present. I tossed her a flashlight and she buckled into her snowshoes, then jumped down from the Jeep, landing in a puff of snow.

"Be back soon!" she grinned, slamming the door, then flicked on the flashlight and hopped through the snow in the direction I'd pointed out.

Minutes ticked by and worry ate at me. When I couldn't stand it any longer, I opened the door, dangling my feet down out of the car as I watched. Waited. Listened.

The roar of the engine broke the stillness of the forest around us, and warmth spread in my chest as the headlight of the snowmobile popped into view through the trees, making its way towards me.

Never had I met anyone as capable as Selene. It was a major turn-on, and for the first time, I regretted situating the cabin so far off into the woods, and the extra time it would add between our escapades.

"Ready when you are, big guy," Selene called out as she stopped near the Jeep and climbed off to help me. In a matter of minutes, we had our luggage strapped to the sled behind the snowmobile, and she helped me hop one-legged through the snow to reach the snowmobile.

"I'm driving this time," I said as I threw my leg over the seat, settling in. She didn't argue, climbing on behind me, and lacing her arms around my torso.

Without meaning to, I dropped my hand on hers, holding on to her as I revved the engine. A high, joyous laugh escaped Selene as we shot through the woods, snow spraying up behind us.

She snuggled into my back as we ate up the distance between the Jeep and my cabin, heading straight up through the trees. If anyone was nearby, they'd know we were here, but that wasn't a concern since there were no other houses within several miles.

I rarely brought anyone else to my cabin, and suddenly I was excited to share it with her. Soon enough, we pulled up to the cabin, and I slowed. Selene's hands loosened around my waist, and she gasped as she took in the sight.

My house was situated in a clearing, several pines around, but not much else. The walls were mostly windows, planned intentionally to overlook the meadow at the front of the house, with a porch off the master bedroom on the second floor. In the summer, the field filled with bright, colorful wildflowers, but now, everything was covered in a blanket of untouched snow. Behind us was a stunning view of the two tallest peaks in Colorado, framed perfectly from the living room.

I stopped the snowmobile as close to the front steps as I could. Selene slid off the seat, jumped down and efficiently grabbed each of the bags from the sled, carrying them up onto the porch.

"What the hell did you pack in this thing?" she asked as she began to drag my duffel full of weapons towards the steps, metal clanking from within. I hopped my way to the bottom step, then took it from her, lifting it easily up onto my shoulder.

Her eyes laser focused on my forearms for some reason, and I glanced down at them, trying to figure out what had snagged her attention.

"What's the matter?" I looked at my arms, wondering if I'd torn a sleeve on something, but saw nothing amiss.

"Nothing." Selene shrugged, but the glint in her eye and the change in her scent told me she was lying. Whatever had caused the more salacious direction of her thoughts, I couldn't help but support.

We headed into the cabin, left the bags by the door, and I bee-lined for the wood stove to get it going. Selene made herself at home, finding her way to the kitchen and then heading up the stairs to explore. I hadn't changed much about the place in years, but I'd paid a witch a hefty sum in the 70s to cast a spell over the whole place to keep it from gathering dust in my absence.

The furniture was much more rustic and homey than

my loft in Deadlights Cove. There, everything was cast in shades of black and grey, as modern and sleek as the sports cars parked below.

Here, browns and earthy greens dominated the space. The timber walls reminded me of my childhood, although the modern insulation was much preferable than the drafty feel of a Viking longhouse. Furs draped over the back of the couch, and the entire space felt like home.

Once the stove was going, I slipped out the sliding door onto the back deck while Selene was still upstairs. I pulled back the canvas cover to the hot tub and turned it on to start warming it up for later. *After.*

Selene was coming down the stairs again as I pulled the glass door shut behind me, brushing the snow off my boots on the doormat.

"Look what I found — were you outside?" Selene was holding a *Scorch the Dragon* Beanie Baby, which I could only assume Blaze had left here as a joke.

I narrowed my eyes at the offending toy, regretting bringing Blaze and Orion out here that one weekend. "Just checking on the house." Selene moved over to a bookcase below the TV and set Scorch right on top, watching us, and I rolled my eyes. "Hungry?"

"Not really." Despite the chill that still filled the cabin, Selene slipped off her coat and hung it on a hook at the door, then turned her attention back on me.

"You'll need to drink more water here than you're used to."

"Really?" She stepped closer, amusement in her eyes.

"The altitude." I cleared my throat.

"*Oh*, sure," she hummed.

Damn it, I was trying to take care of her before we started round two, but she was making it nearly impossible to hold myself back.

"More water. Got it. What else do I need to do up here, in the mountains, all alone… with you?" By the time she spoke the last words, she'd reached me, placing a hand on my chest as she leaned her body against mine, glancing up at me.

"*I'm* hungry," I said as I ducked my head down to her level, meeting her gaze. Her scent changed instantly as she understood my meaning, then turned and slowly walked back up the stairs.

She paused several steps up, turning to look back over her shoulder at me with a wicked smile. "Well, come on then."

Chapter Thirty

SELENE

"Oh, my goddess."

My jaw hit the floor the next morning when I got my first real look out the sliding glass doors off the kitchen.

It had been too dark to see much the night before, but now the bright morning light glinted off the snow in the meadow around the house, snow-capped mountains ringing us in the distance, and tall pines as far as the eye could see. The cabin was far enough up the slope that I could also see rolling hills off to one side until another mountain slanted up through them.

I was still taking in the view when I heard Ryker moving in the kitchen.

"You better bring me here in the summer sometime." I turned and took a stool at the kitchen peninsula. "I bet the wildflowers are amazing."

He took a sip of water, something unreadable in his expression. "They are."

I noticed he dodged my request, but he was a male of few words. "So, what's the plan for today?"

Setting the glass down, Ryker leaned his palms on the counter, his muscles bunching under his black t-shirt. "We need to go into town, and see what Larkin knows. Then we'll go from there."

"Larkin?"

"West Larkin. Alpha of the wolf pack out here, more or less runs the town. They're so remote, their angel only checks in a few times a year."

"Okay, got it." I nodded. "Anything I should know before we get down there? The Cove is the only supe town I've been to."

He shrugged, crossing his arms. "There are more shifters here than in the Cove. It's mostly shifters and witches, as far as I know. Just don't insult the Alpha and you'll be fine."

I rolled my eyes, because every supernatural alive already knew that kernel of wisdom, and went to go get dressed.

Backtracking down to the town took less time than I'd thought — the darkness and nerves had made the drive seem longer the night before, or maybe my excitement made it seem shorter today. Now that I was here, I couldn't help but wonder *why* I'd never visited another supernatural town. The scenery was stunning — several feet of snow covered everything, but I could easily imagine the flowing rivers, waterfalls and meadows around every curving bend in the road that summer would reveal. No wonder Nimue had set up her photography work out here for so many years.

As we neared the town, buildings started to pop up and the road narrowed, a mostly frozen creek running parallel to the street. Reaching downtown, two- and three-story buildings bordered the road, a mix of brick and wood siding, and the flat roofs gave the whole town a distinctly Western vibe.

"Was this a mining town?" I stopped at a light, glad for the opportunity to look around while a few wolves trotted across the street. Even though the place was covered in snow, it was lively, people bustling around, walking and some even cross-country skiing down the street. Definitely not something we would see at the Cove.

"It's Colorado," Ryker stated. "They were all mining towns."

"Are they not worried about humans?" I gestured at the wolves acting distinctly non-wolfish right in front of us as they waited at the crosswalk.

"They keep the road closed and put out press once in a while about lead and arsenic in the water table. Keeps most of them away."

Right. "Well, we're here. Where's the pack house?"

He pointed down the road. "It's up the hill at the far end of town. Can't miss it."

As we drove down Main Street, the pack house came into view, and Ryker was right. We could not have missed it.

A giant lodge-style mountain cabin with huge windows overlooked the town and the mountain range behind us. Built with a mix of log and stonework, the pack had spared no expense on the home, if it could be called that.

"Does the whole pack live here?" Pulling up to the wrought-iron gate at the base of the hill the house sat on, I suddenly felt nervous. This was much different than the

Sayana's humble farmhouse, or even Darius' red-brick Colonial back in the Cove.

"Nah, just the Alpha, the Second, and some of the next tier. Sometimes pack members will stay here if they're wounded or sick. But the rest of the pack is in and out all the time, and this is where they host all main pack events and meetings. Larkin also takes in lone or stray wolves while he helps get them situated into the pack, so there are a lot of guest rooms."

I slowed the Jeep as we approached the empty guard station, rolling down the window to buzz the intercom.

"Scales, that you?" came the staticky voice through the speaker.

Ryker leaned over. "It's me, Fluffy, let us in."

I pressed my lips together to stifle a laugh as the gate beeped and slid open.

"Don't even start," Ryker grumbled.

"So," I started through a chuckle, leaning down towards the steering wheel so I could look up at the vast structure. "These wolves are rich?"

"The last Alpha owned several mines back in the 1800s and left it all to the pack."

Edging through the gate, I drove up the winding drive to the house, parking where a large male pointed us to the side of the main stairs. Several other SUVs and trucks were parked here, and Ryker's Jeep fit right in.

The male waiting for us had straight but slightly shaggy, dark brown hair and a neat beard. Despite the temperature, he wore only a red flannel and jeans, no coat. His light skin was tanned enough to show how much time he spent outside, even in the winter, and confused amusement shone in his eyes.

"What the hell, man? I'm starting to think you like us." He grinned as Ryker got out of the Jeep. "Two visits in a month?" Then he noticed Ryker's new footwear, and he paused.

"Shit," he cursed. "I heard what happened, but hardly believed it. You were really shot?"

Ryker grunted something in response as I hopped out of the car and made my way around to the front. The male's eyes immediately shot to me and gave me a once over. His nostrils flared as he stared, and I shifted my weight, remembering at the last minute to duck my eyes in a show of respect.

"Who's your witch?"

"Dr. Selene Flores," I introduced myself, smiling at him even though his demeanor had turned more guarded. Standing next to both of them, I felt every inch of my five-foot, two-inches. As big as this guy was, Ryker still had several inches on him. Despite that, the male exuded the authority and dominance all head shifters did, the natural confidence of predators at the top of their pack.

"This is Terran, pack Second," Ryker supplied, brow furrowed as he glanced between me and Terran. "Terran, we need to speak with Larkin. Is he in?"

"About what?" Terran crossed his arms, eyes moving from me back to Ryker.

Ryker's gaze flitted up to the huge deck behind Terran that stretched almost the entire length of the second story. A few pack members lingered there, some of them listening in, leaning over the railing, and others chatting with each other.

But even with the distance, any one of them would be able to hear us with their sensitive ears.

"Same reason I was here a month ago."

Terran nodded slowly, then jerked his head back at the house. "Come on in. I'll track him down." He led the way to the main door, calling out as soon as we were inside, "Leif!"

Stomping the snow from my boots, I saw an expansive entryway, a giant winding staircase off to the right, and a doorway into what looked like a massive, state-of-the-art kitchen underneath its curve to the left. Slate tiles gave it a rustic vibe, even while the huge pewter-dipped antler chandelier glistened with elegance.

A blond kid in a grey hoodie and jeans came jogging in from another doorway off to the right, his blue eyes scanning us quickly before he turned to Terran. "Here, boss."

"Get our guests settled in the living room." Terran took off down a hallway, leaving us with Leif.

Leif smiled and pointed to the hallway towards the kitchen, walking only slightly in front of us. "This way. Anyone need coffee or something? Tea? Water?"

"Coffee, black, for me."

Leif nodded and turned to me expectantly.

"Green tea would be great, please, if you have it. Thank you." Ryker chuckled to himself, and Leif's eyes widened slightly a second before his grin did as well. "What did I say?"

"Oh, nothing," Leif headed off towards the kitchen as we passed through the doorway, indicating we should head left to the living room. "You're just — you're nice." I could have sworn the kid's cheeks were turning pink.

"Not a lot of *please* and *thank yous* from Alphas and

Seconds," Ryker said under his breath, hand on the small of my back as we rounded a large grey sectional and took our seats.

The living room was big enough to seat at least twenty people across a range of couches, armchairs, and even a few bean-bag chairs. Above a stone fireplace was a giant television, and along the back of the room ran a row of windows with another spectacular Colorado view. The room opened up into a rec room — a wall of books and board games behind a pool table, ping pong table, air hockey table, dart board, and another, smaller lounge area.

Leif joined us again a few minutes later, setting our drinks down on a coffee table made of a large slab of wood, raw edge and all.

"Anything else I can get you?"

"We're good." Ryker's tone was meant to dismiss him, but instead, the kid took a seat in one of the armchairs.

"Great. You're the dragon, right?" Leif leaned forward eagerly.

Ryker took a long sip of his steaming hot coffee to avoid answering him.

"Yes, he's the dragon." I ignored the rumbled warning from my left and tried to shift Leif's focus. "And what's your role around here, Leif?"

He shrugged. "Whatever they need. We take turns helping out, at least until we come into our full powers."

"What happens then?"

"Well, then sometimes it's harder to —"

"— harder to take orders, depending on your wolf's rank," a smooth, deep voice finished for him.

Leif shrugged and nodded, ducking his head.

A male nearly the size of Ryker strolled around the edge of the sectional, his hair darker than Terran's beside him but their skin nearly the same suntanned shade that was highlighted by his white t-shirt. Everything about him exuded raw power and control, each movement calculated and lithe — clearly this was the Alpha, West Larkin. Hazel eyes raked over both of us, catching on Ryker's boot as he stood to shake hands.

"Ryker," West said in greeting.

"See if Nova needs help in the garage," Terran shot at Leif as the Second took a seat, and the boy leapt up and dashed out of the room.

West took another armchair next to Terran.

"Should we start getting used to you?" West leaned back, his elbows resting on the arms of the chair, hands hanging off the ends in a picture of ease, though I knew any shifter was always ready to leap into action, if needed. Ryker scoffed, but it seemed West hadn't expected an answer anyway, as he continued, "And you've brought your female." His eyes slid to mine. "Showing her around?"

"Oh, I'm not —" I started, the same second Ryker blurted, "She's not —" but then we both stopped. What were we?

"No?" Amusement entered West's expression, and he shared a glance with Terran. "She smells like you."

"*She* has a name, actually," I said, honey-sweet with a smile to match. West's head tilted. "Dr. Selene Flores."

"Well, Dr. Selene Flores," he stretched his legs out, crossing at the ankle. "West Larkin. Glad to meet you. What's a witch doing with a dragon way out here?" He shot a glance at Ryker's boot again. "And why are *you* walking around with an injury?"

Chapter Thirty-One

RYKER

Larkin grilled me, asking question after question once we shared the news about magic not replenishing. With clipped words, he sent Terran off to make phone calls, summoning the local Coven for a chat as well.

"You think Errakal is hiding somewhere around here?" Larkin asked, brow furrowed in thought as he leaned back in his chair.

Selene pulled out her phone, laying it flat on the coffee table between us, and pulled up the map Petra had made.

"My friend Petra mapped out the ley lines, searching for any sort of pattern to Kal's movements so far," Selene said, pulling her hair over one shoulder as she spun the phone for Larkin to see better.

The wolf eyed her carefully, then his eyes flicked to mine. "Blaze's girl?"

I nodded, but said nothing. Larkin's pack had a bit of a history with humans. Under his leadership, the rules were more lenient, and a few wolves had even mated to humans, but that was a relatively new concept out here. The previous

Alpha, Amos Carson, had strong opinions on keeping the lines pure, insisting only wolves join their town, and to intermarry was the same as being banished. Carson was probably rolling over in his grave if he could see the town Larkin had assembled in Timber Creek now, but I much preferred Larkin's new style of leadership, even if it was a bit unorthodox.

"She's brilliant," Selene went on. "If she says this data is correct, then I don't doubt her."

Larkin glanced my way again, seeking out my opinion, and I nodded. As much as the red-headed human annoyed me on the witch hunt last fall, I could admit that Petra was exceptionally bright.

"Could explain why you said some of your shifters on the outskirts were having issues with their powers. My best guess is he's been moving around, testing different nexus points as he was looking for the wellspring."

Larkin steepled his fingers, elbows resting on the armrests as Terran re-entered the room. "Cooper called in yesterday saying his shift was slow again."

Larkin nodded, dropping his hands and leaned forward. "Show me what you have."

The next hour passed quickly as Larkin zoomed in on different spots, calling in different pack members for opinions on anywhere a witch-demon could be hiding that we hadn't checked when I was here last month.

"Whatever spell he's having the witches work with him, it requires some sort of sacrifice," Selene explained as she leaned back in the cushions, her side pressed into mine. "It started off in Deadlights Cove with humans, then last fall they kidnapped a fox shifter."

Larkin's eyes snapped up at her words, flaring a deep amber as his Alpha instincts came to the surface.

"Leif," he said in a deep rumbling voice, the word not much louder than his speaking voice, but energy rippled through the room with the command.

The young wolf skidded across the floor as he entered moments later. "Need something, Alpha?"

"Pull everyone back to the pack house," Larkin's eyes stayed on mine as he spoke to the boy. "Even the lone shifters."

"... Everyone?" Leif stuttered, eyes bulging slightly in surprise.

Larkin didn't bother to answer, pushing to his feet as he rounded the chair and walked down the hallway.

Selene moved on the couch to watch his retreating back, and then glanced my way in confusion.

"I guess we're done here, then?"

A smirk worked its way across my face as I eyed one of my closest friends — which, admittedly, wasn't saying much — then the female next to me who had unintentionally said the one thing that would guarantee Larkin was on our side.

"Have you ever seen a pack hunt together?" I asked, one eyebrow raised.

"No." Selene shrugged nonchalantly. "I mean, I grew up in the Cove, but the shifters were always a world of their own."

I hummed in agreement, and stood to follow Larkin down the hall. Selene hopped up, quickly catching up to me.

"What's going to happen next?"

"It'll take some time for my pack to assemble and the witches to get a lock on him," Larkin said from in front, turning to face us as we reached the front door. "I'll send some hunters out scouting, too, and see what we can sniff out. You two should head home, get some rest, and then tomorrow?" His lips pulled back in a snarl, but it wasn't directed at us. "We'll hunt a demon."

With the sun up, the drive back to my cabin was an easier trek, and I couldn't help but admire how Selene stared with wide-eyed wonder at everything around her.

"New England snow doesn't sparkle like this," she said, and I couldn't help but agree. "There's not a cloud in sight."

"It's like that most days here."

She parked the Jeep next to the snowmobile, and immediately my mind shifted to the memory of yesterday. In fact, I didn't know if I'd ever be able to ride in this damn Jeep again without picturing her hanging from the roll bar, dropping down on me with a moan.

"I can see why you like it here," Selene said, and it took a moment for my mind to recall what we'd been talking about. "It suits you."

I hummed in agreement before pulling the door open and hopping to the snowmobile. Once Selene was on, hands wrapped around my waist, we were off again, headed home.

Selene kicked off her boots once we made it inside, stretching her arms high above her head, then crossing her legs and bending at the waist. "I'm stiff from all of this traveling. Mind if I take a break and do some yoga?"

I shook my head, waving her off, and Selene hopped up the stairs with a smile. Anxious energy clawed at me as I fought the urge to go hunt Errakal down myself, but I knew Larkin and his pack would get the job done faster than I could.

Needing something to do with my hands, I moved to the kitchen and pulled open the fridge doors, hoping that *something* Selene had picked for us I could manage to cook myself. After everything that Selene had done for me, it was time for me to take care of her.

An hour later, Selene came down the stairs, hair high on her head as she strutted into the room barefoot in a bright pink sports bra and matching spandex shorts. She turned into the kitchen, and skidded to a halt when she saw me standing at the stove.

"Did," she paused, eyes dropping to the stove, then moving up to my face, "did you cook for me?"

"Don't get too excited. I'm nowhere near as good as you."

Selene was still locked in place as her mouth hung slightly open, emotions flitting over her face so fast I couldn't read her.

"Just spaghetti and bolognese. Nothing fancy."

"Thank you."

"You hungry now, or should I put it in the oven to stay warm?"

"Well," Selene paused, her scent shifting and I couldn't help but inhale the sultry scent. "I was thinking about getting in the hot tub, if you want to join me."

I didn't even bother to answer as I dropped the pan of spaghetti in the oven and scooped her up, moving towards the door.

Good thing I'd left it on, just in case.

I set her down on the edge of the tub, keeping her bare feet out of the snow as I pulled back the cover, steam immediately wafting up into the brisk winter air. She was already starting to shiver, so I peeled off her pink yoga outfit quickly and set her into the tub.

A contented sigh left her as she settled into the warm water, and I couldn't tear my eyes away from her wriggling into a spot against a jet even as I fumbled with my own clothes and boot. When the metal of my belt clanked to the deck, she turned, her lids growing heavy as she watched me climb into the tub with her.

"Careful with your foot," she said, and I shot her a look, not even bothering to answer. "So, it's usually just you out here in the middle of nowhere in this hot tub all alone?"

I lifted a shoulder as I moved closer to her. "Came with the cabin." Brushing a curl of her brown hair behind her shoulder, I realized the true implication of her words just as I was pressing my lips to the soft skin at the base of her neck. "But no, I've never brought another female out here, if that's what you're asking."

She shivered as my breath tickled her neck, her pupils dilating as my hand curled around her jaw, tilting her head up to mine and pressing my lips to hers.

Something had shifted inside me hearing Larkin call her "your female." Even as I'd opened my mouth to deny it, even as she'd denied it, I'd cut off my own words. Because the truth was, it felt right.

For the first time in a thousand years, this tiny, beautiful witch made me want to make someone mine.

Her mouth opened for me, and I pushed in, stroking her tongue with mine as she let out a soft whine. I groaned at the sound, already hard for her, and ripped my mouth away just long enough to lift her onto my lap, her legs straddling me. She ground herself against me as her palms ran over my chest, my shoulders, her lips trailing down my neck as I gripped her hips.

It took all my restraint not to lift her up to shove her down onto me, but for once, I found myself holding back. Wanting her to take the lead, to show me just how much she wanted this. Because she'd tried to deny Larkin's statement, too, and as much as I wanted to think I understood what she felt about me, I couldn't be sure.

Her hand trailed lower, grazing across my abdomen, then wrapped around me, and things became a little clearer even as my mind went hazy. I could feel my eyes flicking to dragon and back as she stroked me, and I tangled my fingers in her hair, trying to control my breathing. Selene was practically panting, too, our breaths fogging with the steam from the tub. I pushed up into the grip of her hand as I pulled her head back enough to lean down and nip at her breast.

"Ryker." My name was a whispered prayer on her lips, one I didn't think I'd ever tire of hearing if I lived another dozen lifetimes.

"Yeah, Flores?"

She muttered something incoherent in annoyance at my pretend ignorance, shooting me an exasperated look that lacked heat. Then she was pressing up onto her knees, shifting her weight as she angled me where she wanted me, and, laughing lightly as I shuddered in relief, finally sank down onto me.

"Gods, Selene."

That laugh again. I tried to smack her ass, but the effect was lost in the tub, and it didn't matter anyway. I let her set the pace, and she did it beautifully. Her hands moved to cup the back of my head, tilting me to look at her as she rode me slowly, languorously, like we had all the time in the world and weren't on the clock to hunt down a magic-stealing demon.

I captured her mouth again, tasting every breath and sound she would give me until she was shuddering, clenching around me, and with a few more thrusts, I joined her.

We sat like that, sharing breath, her soft hands around my neck, my hands rubbing her thighs, until our heartbeats returned to normal. Selene rose up on her knees, shifting off me before settling into my side, my arm draped around her shoulders as she rested her head on my chest.

Sun now set, we watched the stars come out, snowflakes swirling through the air, and I wondered if maybe, even after a millennium, a dragon could be capable of unlearning solitude.

The pack house was a flurry of motion the next afternoon, shifters coming and going as Larkin called them all to him, issuing orders quickly and efficiently. We'd not rested *quite* as much as we could have, but between the moonlight, the hot tub, and the gorgeous witch in my cabin, I was a bit distracted. We'd slept in this morning to make up for it, though, and had spent the day lounging in front of the fire as we waited for Larkin to contact us.

This time when we pulled up to the pack house, the driveway was full of cars and trucks, most of them mud-splattered all-wheel drive vehicles fit for the wild terrain. Once inside, I recognized some of his wolves, but also noticed Cooper, a lone cougar I'd met once before.

"Glad you could make it on such short notice," Larkin said as they shook hands.

Cooper said nothing, his eyes glued to Selene at my side. My dragon clawed from within, wanting to hiss and spit fire at him for his lingering gaze, and my jaw ticked with the effort to keep the beast leashed.

"Look away," I hissed, stepping in front of Selene to block his view.

Cooper's sharp eyes rose from her to me, his head tilted sideways as he took my measure. A slow smile spread across his face, and the urge to shift — to show him who the *real* predator was here — was almost unbearable. Selene's hand slid down the back of my shirt, brushing my spine, as if she sensed my inability to maintain control. Instantly, my dragon relaxed into her touch, and I breathed deeply.

"Ryker." Cooper's steady gaze was unnerving, almost as if I could sense his cat's arrogant tail swinging lazily behind him, even now.

Larkin glanced between us, trying to discern this stand-off Cooper and I were engaged in like the gunslingers that filled these same streets years ago. Wisely, Larkin chose to ignore it, clapping his hands together loudly. Everyone gave their attention to the man, and the room silenced.

"Thank you all for coming," Larkin spoke, his deep voice filling the large meeting space we were gathered in. "Most of us have already spoken, and you've received your orders. We have a demon on our lands somewhere, hiding out while he waits to gather power. Across the country, Errakal has been sacrificing humans, and even attempted to use a shifter, in his rituals." A collective gasp filled the space, and several voices began talking over each other at once.

"Silence," I roared, putting just a small drop of magic into the word. Power rippled through the room from me, but instantly I regretted the waste of energy as my knee buckled. Luckily, Selene was still at my side and caught me before I could fall. Her dark eyes were furious, glaring daggers at me.

Everyone waited until I nodded at Larkin to continue. Selene moved from my side as he began to speak again, and I could hardly focus with the loss of her contact. Seconds later, she was back with a barstool she placed behind me.

My chest warmed as my eyes met hers, recognizing her kindness. Placing a finger under her chin, I tilted her face up to mine, making sure she saw my appreciation before I transferred my weight off my aching leg. As soon as I settled, I looped my arm around her, pulling her between my legs to rest against me. The heat of her back against my front was tantalizing, reminding me of how we spent our evening last night. Without thinking, I ran my nose across the nape of her neck, and she stiffened.

"Marking you," I whispered as Larkin continued to talk, outlining the plan for tomorrow.

"Because I don't smell enough like you already?" I watched the way she smirked, her one eyebrow raised in challenge.

"Not enough, no," I answered honestly, wondering where this feral possession I felt for her was coming from. "Males continue to glance in your direction."

Selene's body shook with silent laughter beneath my hands, and my palms slid across her torso as we listened. She didn't shrug out of my embrace, either recognizing she was safer here with me or because she liked the feel of me against her, I wasn't sure. Either way, I'd take it.

My mind wandered, struggling to concentrate as Larkin finished up.

"We need everyone to stay vigilant if there's any chance this demon is in the area and might be targeting shifters. Shields, you have a responsibility to those under you to make sure you know where they are at all times until we figure this out." His gaze slid across the room, meeting nods of agreement from those he singled out. "Trackers, stay behind and I'll tell you what region you're patrolling; the rest of you can head out and make sure your division is accounted for."

Most of the shifters in the room got to their feet, many clapping each other on the back or squeezing shoulders as they made their way out to go check on the other members of the pack. It always struck me as a bit absurd how touchy some of the other types of shifters were — wolves in particular could barely keep their hands off each other.

Once the room had thinned out, only the sharpest hunters and trackers were left, and Larkin motioned them all over to a map on the wall as he began pointing out regions and assigning them. It felt eerily similar to last fall, when we'd all met in Deadlights Cove and had to head out to hunt down the stuck shifters. Hopefully this time, we'd find Errakal before he could take another hostage.

A beeping sounded, and Larkin paused mid-speech to pull out his phone, his lips pulling back in a feral grin as he read the screen. He looked up at the Trackers gathered around him.

"It seems the witches have caught sign of a disturbance out by the old Reynolds Mine. Let's gear up and head out."

Chapter Thirty-Two

SELENE

Faster than I could track, everyone in the house cleared out, heading down to a barn behind the property. Ryker stopped at his Jeep, pulling free the bag of weapons he'd brought with us from the Cove, and lugged it across the yard to the barn. The barn doors were open, and I peeked into the brightly lit space to see rows of snowmobiles.

"You riding with Ryker?" West asked, and I started to answer, but Ryker beat me to it.

"She's with me." His tone was full of gravel. "She's always with me, Larkin."

Heat rose in my cheeks, surely from the crisp air, right? And... *always?* My heart raced in my chest, a mix of the adrenaline of the impending hunt and the giddy feeling in my chest at hearing his words. Did he really mean that?

West threw Ryker a set of keys, pointing at a snowmobile near the front of the barn, and Ryker tugged on my hand, urging me to follow him. Next to the vehicles were helmets, and Ryker handed me one. He slid his over his buzzed hair, showing only his green eyes with the visor up.

My chest felt tight, anxiety warring with emotions I didn't want to give in to, not right now.

Gently prying the helmet from my hands, Ryker lifted it up, and pulled it down over my head. His hands worked to tighten the chin strap, fastening it snugly for me, and my eyes welled with emotions. It had been so long since anyone cared for me like Ryker was doing. Not since my mom had died had I ever felt so looked after.

"You good?" Ryker asked, his gaze focused on my watery eyes.

I nodded, smiling, then realized he couldn't see my mouth behind the helmet. "Yep. I'm good. Let's go find this asshole."

His eyes lit with amusement before he turned to the snowmobile, strapping weapons to the sides. I saw several others, Terran and West included, doing the same. Apparently, we were going in guns-blazing. All that was missing was a stray tumbleweed and swinging saloon doors to make this an old-fashioned showdown.

Throwing his bad leg over the side, Ryker straddled the seat. I settled behind him, and threw my arms around his waist in a position I was growing a little too comfortable in. My gloved hands clasped onto his jacket, gripping tightly, and he flicked on the engine. It roared to life, rumbling beneath me, but Ryker waited for no one, steering out of the barn and into the snow.

Air whooshed around me as we shot through the wintery scene, evergreens draped in heavy snow surrounding us on all sides. Snow sprayed up behind as we drove, and I clung tighter to Ryker's warm back.

Even knowing we were heading into imminent danger,

I'd never felt safer than with my arms wrapped around Ryker. His words rang in my head, over and over — *She's always with me.*

I wanted it to be true.

I wanted this to work.

I wanted to be done with first dates, and devote myself to this male.

I wanted to let myself fall in love with him — to *be* loved by him.

Ryker steered us effortlessly through the forest, and eventually, several other vehicles caught up. The engines roared through the woods on all sides, and I had to wonder how we were going to sneak up on anyone making this much noise.

As if noticing the same thing, a wave of magic spread from Ryker, pouring over the clearing, and silencing all sounds. The engine stuttered, and he slumped slightly in my grip, falling over the handlebars of the snowmobile.

"What the hell are you doing?!" I screamed, hands tugging on his jacket. "Why would you do that?" My voice grew more frantic with each question, heart beating wildly as I thought through every possible way this use of magic could further damage him, deplete him right when he needed it most. "Are you okay?"

"Fine," Ryker grunted, then sat up straighter, gunning the engine, now silent, once more.

But I saw the way his hands trembled on the handlebars, and I didn't buy it for a minute.

After a half-hour, Ryker slowed, the vibration of the engine under us the only sign the snowmobile was still on. The silence spread, almost eerie as the trees thinned, giving way to a large clearing ahead.

We slowed to a crawl, stopping just under the tree cover. Dozens of other snowmobiles did the same. In the clearing below sat rows of abandoned houses, windows long gone in the abandoned mine town. They sat on the edge of a steep cliff over a river rushing hundreds of feet below. My heart raced in my chest as I eyed the area, chills crawling across my skin.

I could *feel* the power in the air. It vibrated, just like the engine, lighting each of my nerve endings on fire.

"What happened to this place?" I whispered, my voice muffled by the helmet.

Ryker undid his chin strap, pulled his helmet free, and turned to me.

"The ley lines here are an excessive wealth of power," he answered as he pulled his gloves free, loosening the straps of my helmet and gently tugging it off. With the visor no longer blocking his face, I could make out the new wrinkles creasing Ryker's skin along the edges of his eyes and lips. The sight hurt my heart, knowing his burst of magic to silence us had caused this. But, damn the man, he was still fine as hell. "Even the humans could tell something was different. While they dug up more silver here than any other mine in Colorado, everything about the place was doomed. Best guess? They hit something vital to the ley lines, and the whole thing blew."

That was jarring. I searched for signs of an explosion,

but everything was so old and buried under feet of snow, I couldn't see anything.

Ryker's hands lifted, resting on my shoulders, and I looked back to him again. "Why are you so pretty?" I asked, then kicked myself for saying it outloud.

Ryker smirked, the creases along his eyes deepening at the movement, and I leaned forward to kiss him before I could stop myself. His hands rested on my shoulders, then slid to the back of my neck, pulling me tighter against him.

"That's enough, lovebirds," West said as he padded through the snow to our side. Ryker pulled back from me, the smirk from before long gone as he scowled at the wolf Alpha. "Scouts reported activity in the main shaft. ATVs parked nearby, and signs of foot traffic in and out. Someone is inside."

I surveyed the abandoned town again, something straight out of a horror movie, and shuddered. This was the definition of a *ghost town*.

Ryker leaned past me, grabbed the guns he'd strapped to either side of us, and tugged them free. Slinging a long-range rifle over his back, he clipped several smaller guns to his belt, as well as several magazines to fill them. Lastly, he withdrew an ancient-looking sword, strapping it to his waist, and I couldn't help but stare. As much as I knew that Ryker was a supernatural bounty hunter and mercenary, I'd never seen him in action like this.

"You think all that will be necessary?" I asked as I eyed the weapons wearily.

"Better safe than sorry, Flores."

I pursed my lips, but couldn't come up with an argument. Still, the whole thing didn't sit well with me.

When he handed me the small gun I'd held in his garage, I stared down at it, head shaking slightly. "I can't take this."

Ryker's fingers closed over mine, forcing me to grip the weapon. "You can, and you *will*."

"Ryker, I'm a *doctor*." I returned his glare. "I *save* lives. I don't *take* them."

"Then aim for their knees," Ryker answered bluntly. "I refuse to send you into this fight undefended. I can't —" he stopped himself, throat working as he broke eye contact.

I waited silently, wanting him to continue, even though the temptation to prompt him was killing me.

"You can't die."

"I don't plan on it." I forced a smile, but knew it didn't reach my eyes. "But I'm not taking this gun. You'll just have to defend me yourself, Drogon."

With a heavy sigh and an eye roll, Ryker hopped off the snowmobile and began working his way through the snow to the others. I drew in a deep breath, trying to calm my racing heart before I followed behind.

Chapter Thirty-Three

RYKER

Snow covered the rail tracks leading into the mine, but footprints marred the snow everywhere. From the opposite side of the mine entrance, Cooper gave the hand signal that all was clear. Selene stood mere steps behind me, and I fought to even my breathing with the thought of her going in practically unprotected.

With the magic in the air, my own power seemed to return to me somewhat, but still felt muted, as if it was there, but inaccessible.

Larkin signaled to Cooper to advance, and he slipped into the darkness of the mine entrance, moving with a silence no ordinary human could have matched. Selene made to step past me after him, snow crunching under her boot, and I winced as I grabbed her arm and halted her, wrapping an arm around her front.

"Cats are best for recon," I whispered as quietly as I could in case Errakal had any shifters with him, and Selene nodded to show she understood.

We all held our breath around the entrance, waiting for

the merest whisper of sound to emerge from the shaft or for Cooper to reappear.

I focused intently, staring into the darkness behind the squared-out entrance. At the far reach of my vision, two blazing yellow eyes blinked, once, twice, three times.

"All clear," I whispered, and stepped into the shaft, Selene at my back. With my favorite Sig Sauer P320 pistol with a suppressor attached in hand, I inched my way forward, scanning constantly for any signs of danger. My boot was awkward, but I took careful steps, and the silencer magic I cast earlier still clung to me, if not everyone else.

Cooper waited at the back of the main entrance, silently pointing to our left. Larkin moved past with several of his wolves, all carrying semi-automatic rifles, reminding me that a lot of them came from a military background. As much as it felt good to be among other predators, I couldn't help but be conscious of the fact that Selene stood mere steps behind me, nowhere near prepared for what most likely lay ahead.

"Stay back," I ordered, meeting her eyes. Fear tinged her brown irises, but she breathed evenly, nodding. Seeing her face this danger head-on made me realize just how much I was coming to care for this female. And that was a scary thought.

Not allowing myself to go down that road, I took the night-vision goggles strapped to her head, and slid them down over her eyes. With a heavy breath, I moved, following behind the others. As shifters, all of us could see clearly in the dark, even with our senses muted, but Selene was at another disadvantage here. Sheered rock rose around us, caging us in on all sides as we moved down the shaft in the darkness. Scorch marks showed in several places, signs of the crumbling remains of the once-active silver mine. Abandoned carts sat on the rails empty of everything but dust.

Selene's heartbeat sounded in my ears, power trickling back into me a little at a time so near the wellspring of the ley lines. Whatever this lid was on my magic, I wanted to rip it off.

Voices sounded ahead of us, and I picked up my pace.

"Shit," Selene muttered, barely above a whisper, but I heard her clearly. I hated that she was here with me. I hated her Coven for putting her in this position. I hated Errakal for causing so much trouble for all of Deadlights Cove.

Then and there, I promised myself that Errakal would be leaving these tunnels either in a body bag or iron chains. No way in Hel would he escape me again.

With my next step, I felt a shimmer of magic wash over me. Power surged in my veins, snapping like a whip against my senses as it ripped down my leg, healing the bone instantly. I drew in a sharp gasp, jolted forward by the feeling.

Selene's cool hands settled on my arm, steadying me. "Did you feel that? What happened? You okay?"

I nodded, rising back up and stalking forward towards the sound of the fight. "Stay behind me."

Selene hovered at my back, peering around my arm as we approached the others, crouched behind boxes and corners above a large chamber below.

At the town meeting last fall, Blaze had described Errakal's set up as a handful of witches plus the demonwitch himself, but what we saw now showed he'd ramped up his operations. Rather than the traditional pentagram that witches often used when they worked together to amplify their power, here there were twelve, a line of white chalk or sand stretching between them to form a twelve-pointed star. But in addition to those twelve witches, several more beings stood around them in an outer circle, at least a handful of which I could sense were demons, which was shit news for us. In the very center, there were also three shifters on their knees, hands bound. More sacrifices.

Larkin's witches were setting up their spell outside the mine entrance, an enchantment to prevent any witches from exiting. But there was no way, even with their combined powers, they'd be able to stop demons. We just had to hope the demons below were either too selfish to take any of their witches with them when they flickered out, or that we were able to get an iron bullet in them first.

In our favor, none of Kal's people were shifters which meant there was a good chance they hadn't heard us coming yet. Two of his would-be sacrifices seemed to have heard us, shooting looks at each other and casting glances around the chamber, but they weren't about to speak up.

Larkin motioned for his people to spread out, and silently, they moved into position around the edges of the chamber, taking what cover they could. We were lucky the space was dark, lit only by a few lanterns held by the witches below and a ball of fire held by one of the demons.

I didn't care what the rest of Larkin's team was doing. For the first time, I had a clear shot to my target, and I wasn't going to miss. Right in the center of the star, Errakal was conducting the whole scene, not that I gave a damn about whatever psycho bullshit he was spewing to these witches.

Making sure Selene was hidden behind a boulder, I

unslung Striker at my back, pulling the rifle into my shoulder, adjusting the suppressor before I leaned my arm across the cart in front of me. I found Larkin's eyes across the room where he crouched behind a crate, and gave a nod to let him know shit was about to get started here. He nodded back, waiting for my signal.

My signal being the bullet I was about to fire into Kal.

Left eye closed, I lined up my sight, Kal right smack in the center. I lifted the safety with a flick, took a deep breath, and fired. With a thundering crack that echoed through the chamber, air rippled around the iron bullet as it soared through the tunnel, sinking into Kal's thigh, right where he'd hit me weeks before.

"Fuck!" the demon growled as he dropped to his knees, blood seeping out of the wound. Shouts went up, and all eyes snapped to where we stood on the ledge. Bullets started flying faster than I could keep track, sinking into the crowd below.

We'd decided that we would shoot to injure, not kill, needing any and all witnesses to gather recon on what was happening. No one here believed this was the end of whatever Errakal had planned, not with the way he kept aiming for larger targets each time.

Still, several witches fell, cries rising up into the cavernous space above. Return fire started coming our way as a few of Kal's witches drew firearms too, and I prayed Selene kept her cover since I had to face forward.

Power surged in a wave as fire licked down the tunnel, two demons materializing out of thin air right in front of me and melting my gun as I gripped it.

I dropped my rifle down into the cart, grabbed my hand

gun and fired, one after the next. Iron sank into the demons' shoulders, crippling them both on impact, as several down below escaped. They both hissed in pain, but still moved towards me. Terran swung a half-melted rifle into the back of one of the demons' heads, taking him down. The other reached me, and I ducked as he swung a punch at my face. I kicked my plastic boot at his ankles, and he went down, but grabbed my arm and pulled me with him, still throwing punches my way. We grappled in the dirt of the mine, the demon still formidable in his strength, even without access to his magic.

With a roar, we flipped, and suddenly I was under him, and his hands went around my neck, cutting off my air as I wrestled to push him off. He gritted his teeth, holding me down, and sounds started to fade as I was deprived of oxygen.

Unable to shake him off, I reached for my magic, willing just enough of my shift to happen, acid pooling in my stomach.

The good kind, this time.

The demon's eyes flared wide the moment he realized what I was about to do, but he couldn't move fast enough.

With an exhale, I shot dragon-fire directly into his face. He screamed, a sound straight out of Hel, his face melting, and his hands finally dropped away from my neck. I lay panting as I shifted fully back to human, taking a minute before rolling to my knees and checking on the rest of the situation.

Bullets flew in every direction, shifters and witches running and dodging for cover, cries and screams echoing through the chamber as people were hit.

We outnumbered them, though, and Larkin's people were good. Within mere minutes, though it felt longer, the thunder of bullets ceased, only the sound of groaning remaining. The rest of Kal's people were now incapacitated by the iron streaking through their veins, finding themselves as useless as I'd been the last few weeks.

Kal lay clutching his leg in the center of the room as I hopped down the rickety steps, feeling lighter on my feet than I had since I'd been shot. I kept an eye out for any firearms pointed my way, but Larkin's people were making quick work of disarming our targets and slapping iron hand-cuffs on them.

"You fucker," Kal seethed between clenched teeth, grasping his leg.

I paced to his side, gun hung loosely at my hip as I couldn't help but smirk down at the demon-witch I'd hunted for so long.

"Caught you."

"Took you long enough," Kal glowered, eyes full of fury. The grin dropped from my face as I glared down at the male. It was unnerving how much he looked like Blaze, the black irises that marked all demons, the same olive skin and dark hair, though Kal kept his longer than his brother. But while Blaze's annoying face was usually grinning with amusement, Kal's expression was all cold cunning. With my booted foot, I nudged his leg, relishing his roar of pain as it echoed through the mine.

"Hurts, doesn't it?"

Errakal's right hand gripped his wound tightly. "This is far from over."

I cocked my head to the side, watching shifters carry

injured witches and demons out through the tunnels towards the exit.

Movement caught my eye, but I was too slow as I looked down at Errakal, noticing for the first time the pistol in his left hand. The gun fired, and I jerked to the left, dodging the bullet as it sailed by me.

I kicked hard at Errakal's hand, sending the gun clattering to the floor, adrenaline coursing through my veins.

A stuttered gasp drew my attention, and I whipped around to see a wide-eyed Selene standing mere steps behind me, clutching her right side.

"Flores." I gasped, closing the distance between us. Her chin tipped up towards me, eyes wide, mouth hanging open. I seized her hand, pulling it away to see the blood already seeping out of the gunshot wound, leaking all over her hand.

Her body began to crumple. My heart lurched to my throat. I reached out, seizing her as I lowered us together to the floor, clutching her tightly. Ripping at her jacket, I pulled it free from her, lifting her shirt to inspect the wound.

"Stay with me," I whispered as I tore my sweatshirt over my head, pressing it to the wound. My hands shook, nowhere near as calm as Selene had been a month ago at my side when I lay wounded in my dragon form. "Don't you die on me."

"Wouldn't dream of it," she whispered, attempting to smile, but it didn't reach her eyes.

"*Larkin!*" I shouted, anxiety roiling through me in waves. "Get your best healing witches down here *right now!*"

"My pocket," Selene whispered, her eyes shutting.

"What's in your pocket?" I asked, not following her

logic. When she closed her eyes, not answering, my heart slammed against my ribs. "Don't you fucking dare, Selene."

I dug through her pockets, hand closing around the tiny vial from Devanna. *Ferrouscide,* the label read. This would keep the iron poisoning from spreading, giving us enough time to heal the bullet wound without worrying about the magical side effects.

Twisting off the top one-handed, I suctioned up a full dropper of the stuff before releasing it over her wound, praying to whatever gods were listening that it worked.

Selene's back arched, rising off the ground as her eyes flew open, mouth wide in a silent scream.

"Move!"

A witch shoved me aside, surprising given her small size compared to me, but I was distraught watching Selene in pain and didn't have time to brace myself. She knelt down, examining Selene's wound, before she cut her eyes to me, then to the bottle in my hand.

"What did you just do?" she snapped, swiping the bottle out of my grasp. "Shit! How much did you give her?"

"I don't know." I shook my head, feeling helpless. "A dropper?"

She turned back towards the entrance to the chamber and barked out, "Dominic!"

A tall, dark haired man with a satchel turned our way and ran over, dropping to kneel beside the woman. She passed him the bottle. "She's going to OD."

Dominic pulled something from his bag, and the two of them got to work while I waited, heart racing and palms sweating, for them to have an update.

I didn't care that the room was clearing out as Larkin's

people took hold of Kal's crew, or that Larkin himself led Kal out limping. I barely heard Terran make a phone call. Somehow, the tiny witch bleeding out on the ground in front of me had become my world, and nothing else mattered anymore, not even my demon quarry.

I couldn't tell how much time was passing. My eyes were glued to Selene, to the rise and fall of her breath, to her hand in mine. I didn't even know when I'd moved around to her other side to take it; I just knew it needed to stay warm. My hearing was honed in on her too-rapid heartbeat, but it was still going, and it was strong.

"C'mon, Flores, you made me a promise, and I know you're not a liar," I murmured, but Selene was beyond hearing me, her eyes fluttering as she fought to maintain consciousness.

The two witches conversed in low voices as they worked quickly in sync which boded well, all things considered. I could only wait.

Eventually, I felt a hand on my shoulder, and I looked up to see Blaze, Orion just beyond him. Both wore grim faces as they saw Selene on the ground, and moved off to confer with Larkin, now that they'd let me know they were here. Hopefully if they'd flickered here, it meant whatever Kal had done to the ley lines was already reversed, or they were confident it was about to be.

Blowing out a breath, the female witch sat back on her heels, Dominic still finishing up bandaging the wound. Sharp dark eyes glared at me from under strong brows as she swung her black hair over her shoulder and pointed an accusatory finger.

"You're an idiot, you know that?" she shot at me. "Too

much *ferrouscide* can poison her magic just as much as the iron itself, only then it'd be permanent."

I swallowed, stomach churning at the thought I could have made her worse. "Is she going to be okay?"

"Of course she is, no thanks to you. We're the best in the fucking west."

With that, she stood and strode off, black hair swaying behind her, leaving me with Selene and Dominic.

Dominic shared a *What can you do?* sort of grimace with me before packing up the rest of his items into the satchel.

"Just ignore Zara," he said in a low voice, a quick glance over his shoulder to make sure she was gone before turning back to me. "Your friend is stable, but we should get her into the care center in town, and she shouldn't move too much until she wakes up on her own." He noticed my boot and asked, "Can you carry her, or —"

"No *or*; I got her."

He met my gaze again and nodded, then headed out after Zara, probably to see who else needed patching up.

My hands shook as I stood and bent to scoop up Selene, and never had she seemed so tiny, so fragile, so practically human as she did then, unconscious in my arms.

Chapter Thirty-Four

RYKER

All night, I sat at Selene's bedside. Timber Creek had an urgent care center that I'd brought her to, demanding she get her own private room as the beds started filling up with others who'd been injured in the showdown. I kept her hand in mine even when Zara came in and attached her to the monitors, needing the reassurance of skin contact.

My thoughts churned through the small hours of the night. What had I been thinking, getting so attached to a mortal like this? Bringing her into my life would only pose a risk for her — look what one day on the job with me had done; she could have died. *I* could have poisoned her.

I *was* a poison to her. Somehow, I'd made her care about me, and to what end? I knew that eventually I'd mess this up, probably sooner than later. I didn't know how to be what she needed, how to take care of her. I looked after myself — *that* was what I was best at. That was what I needed to stick to.

Selene could take care of herself, too — gods knew she'd

done it for her whole adult life before me; she'd do it long after I —

What? Broke her heart? Fuck, was that really what I was considering?

Even as I thought it, a small voice in the back of my head told me I was being arrogant to think I'd had that much of an impact on her. Surely, I didn't really mean that much to her in such a short amount of time.

My skin itched, the need to flee before I hurt her worse riding me hard. My leg bounced as I looked between her helpless form and the door.

She'd see this as the favor it was, right?

I cursed under my breath, running a hand down my face, just as a soft knock came from the open door to her room. I lifted my head from where it hung, my elbows resting on my knees, and saw Orion in the doorway. He tilted his head to indicate he wanted to speak with me, and with one last look at the beautiful, strong witch in the bed, I squeezed her hand and followed him out to the lobby.

"What is it?" I asked, careful to keep my voice down. It was about three in the morning, and the center was full of recovering patients trying to sleep.

"I stayed to oversee the local Coven dismantle Errakal's spellwork, and everyone can already feel the magic pulsing back through the wellspring, though it might take some time until power returns to full strength for everyone. How are you feeling?"

"Fine."

Orion studied me, but didn't ask any more questions. If I was an emotional sort, I might have given him a pat on the shoulder. "We're getting ready to take Kal in for questioning. They asked for you to come along, but I can see if I can delay the Council now that we've caught Errakal."

I raised a brow. "You're taking him to Headquarters?" A silent nod of confirmation. I scoffed. "I didn't think non-angels were ever allowed up there."

Orion crossed his arms. "It's rare but, yes, you'll be allowed in." A muscle in his jaw ticked, which could have been in annoyance or amusement. Judging by his next words, probably both. "Blaze is coming too." His grey eyes slid from mine to the room I'd left. "I know you probably don't want to leave Selene, but Zara said she's stable now. Kal was your target; we could get your hearing and Kal's done all at once. Up to you."

Even asleep, Selene's presence behind me seemed to sear into my back, as though she was glaring daggers at me, but I knew she was still unconscious and it was just my over-whelming awareness of her. I hesitated, guilt weighing on my shoulders at the thought of leaving her, but I'd made up my mind. I knew what I had to do, and drawing it out wouldn't do anyone any favors. No, it was better like this — rip off the Band-Aid.

"She'll be fine," I answered, voice gruffer than I'd intended, and hoped the words were true. But my presence here, in her life, would only do more harm than good. "I'll come."

"Larkin," I called as I entered the pack house, and young Leif came sliding into the entryway a minute later.

"He's in his office, he says you can go back."

I offered the kid a two-fingered salute and headed back to Larkin's office, letting myself in. He was pouring over something on his laptop, and suddenly my stomach seized. I hadn't even given a thought to whether or not he'd lost any pack members, I'd been so preoccupied with Selene.

"Any losses?" I forced myself to ask, bracing my hands on the back of a chair in front of his desk.

"Thankfully, no," he said, looking up from his laptop, but his expression was solemn. "But we have a dozen injured, five with pretty severe wounds, even if they're stable. Demon fire resists healing, as I'm sure you know. The pack is feeling the blow. And we'll take in the three shifters Errakal was planning to sacrifice, at least until they get back on their feet."

I didn't want to offer the male inane platitudes, so I merely nodded in solidarity.

"At least we got the bastard, right?" he added, and I huffed in agreement.

"I'm taking him in now," I said. "Wanted to come up and thank you for your help before we head out."

Larkin stood, coming around and leaning back on the front of his desk. "Glad we were able to help before this got any worse." He glanced down at my leg, nodding at it. I'd switched the plastic boot for a pair of my regular black ones, summoning them from the in-between now that my magic was returned to me. "Were you able to heal up, then?"

"Finally," I grunted, and he chuckled.

"Then let's not see each other for a while, all right? This visit was exciting enough for a couple decades, and we're used to that quiet mountain life up here in the Creek."

A half hour later, after I'd said my goodbyes to Larkin and Orion had somehow found a grey three-piece suit to change into, we headed over to the Creek's police precinct to retrieve Kal. Orion fidgeted the whole way, adjusting his cuff-links — silver angel wings — and straightening his pearly-white tie, more on-edge than usual. Blaze met up with us too, and I hid my amusement at the demon's tuxedo t-shirt, apparently the best he could do in terms of dressing up to visit Headquarters. Orion eyed my own attire — same as always, all black, and still dotted with Selene's blood — but I wasn't about to change for anybody, least of all some jumped-up pigeons who were too big for their britches. In fact, I made sure to step through some particularly muddy puddles, and hoped we had a nice white floor to walk over once we got there.

"Where is Headquarters, anyway?" I asked as we entered the precinct, nodding at the shifter manning the desk as we made our way back to the cells.

"Confidential —" Orion started just as Blaze cut in with, "— Parallel dimension, sort of."

Orion heaved a weary sigh, his lips pursing. "Blaze —"

"Well, it's not like he can ever get there on his own." Blaze threw his hands up, then turned to me. "Only angels can jump through dimensions. It's sort of like flickering, only —"

"Only much, *much* more impressive," Orion finished for him, still glaring at him for revealing angel secrets.

I rolled my eyes and ignored Orion. "You've been there

before?" I asked Blaze, who gave me what would have been a sheepish grin if I thought the male capable of embarrassment.

"Well, maybe one or two of my previous infractions have warranted a little chat with the higher-ups."

I huffed a breath that was almost a chuckle. "I see."

"It's just so great to see Orion in his *element*," Blaze continued, black eyes glittering with mischief as Orion muttered a curse under his breath, making me wonder just what the Hel we were about to walk into. "I can never resist a visit."

We reached the holding cells, finding Kal down in the last one. Despite the fact the entire cell was reinforced with iron, meaning he shouldn't be able to access any of his magic within its walls, they'd kept iron manacles on him in his cell, too.

"I see you've been up to the same old shit, Kal." Blaze approached the bars first, his expression hardening almost instantly from the lighthearted mood he'd been in just a moment ago.

But Kal only stared back at his brother, not rising to the bait. Apparently he was smarter than he seemed. Blaze scoffed and turned away as Orion waved a hand, the cell gate creaking open magically. Kal must have realized the jig was up, because he rose without protest. I grabbed him by the arm as he stepped out of the cell.

"Shall we?" Blaze said and, not sure how this worked, I took a step closer.

There was a clap of thunder I had to assume was Orion's magic, and then the floor dropped out from under us as we swirled through space.

Endless moments later, the world around me stopped spinning and I staggered to maintain my footing.

"Fucking Hel —" I blinked hard, my mind tilting and whirring nauseatingly, but my grip on Kal's arm was still locked tight. He looked a bit green, but remained silent, eyes distant as he heaved a sigh. Blaze shook himself like a dog, and I was glad to see interdimensional travel seemed to affect even demons used to flickering around.

As my mind and vision slowed, I took in our surroundings. We were in a room that seemed to be, for lack of a better term, something of a landing pad; the space wide and empty, the floor clear. Everything was in shades of white and grey, and suddenly Orion's usual wardrobe made a lot more sense. The architecture, if it could be called that, was all sleek and modern, minimalist design. Like a robot had designed it.

"Ah, Purgatory. Wish I could say it was good to be back," Blaze said from my side. I didn't bother turning to him though, instead focusing on the large entryway that read *Lobby*. "Who gave the angels a giant label ma—" Blaze went on, but Orion shushed him, to which he gasped in affront.

"Officer Orion. Late, as usual, I see." A female angel I didn't recognize stepped through the entryway towards us, her thick silver hair in a braid behind her. Wearing pearlescent lipstick that matched her talon-like nails, her heather grey wrap dress was just as formal, if not moreso, than Orion's suit. She raised a brow, appraising Orion's own wardrobe disdainfully before turning to Blaze, lip curling in disgust. "You again."

Blaze grinned. "Dressed up this time, too." He pretended to fix the tie on his t-shirt.

The angel's eyes trailed down to his bright red Converse — a match for his prized cherry-red Mustang Shelby GT500 — her face souring even further.

Her lips pursed as she stared at Kal, but said nothing as she lightly shook her head.

For the first time in my life, I was the last one noticed. She tilted her head to the side, grey eyes trailing slowly from my muddy boots all the way up to my face. My jaw worked as I fought not to react, but couldn't help the eyeroll that snuck out.

"Ryker." She said my name with such precision, there wasn't a hint of question to it. I'd worked for Headquarters off and on over the years, collecting bounties like I'd done with Kal, so it wasn't a total shock she knew who I was, but my patience, or lack thereof, was growing thin.

"I thought we were late."

Orion sighed. "Gabriella, what meeting room are we in?"

She made an annoyed sound but waved us to follow her. We left the lobby and made our way down a wide hallway, just as white and boring as the lobby, Gabriella's clicking heels echoing through the otherwise silent space. A moment later, the hallway opened into an atrium with a large, domed glass ceiling above. We were on a floor roughly in the center of the massive building, glass railings blocking the edges, but missing panels at certain intervals where angels landed gracefully, moving freely from one floor to the next. Dozens

254

of floors rose above and below us, the whole area over-looking an expansive courtyard below. Wings fluttered by, and the whole time, I couldn't shake the resemblance to an oversized birdcage.

Down on the courtyard floor, dozens of angels milled about, more than I'd ever seen in all my years on this world. Though, I supposed we weren't *on* our world anymore, wherever this place existed. Every single angel dressed in whites and grays, their clothes immaculate, starched and ironed to within an inch of their lives. The formal attire made me wonder if they were about to attend a formal dinner or something equally fancy, and yet from the sight of them chatting around water features or reading newspapers on benches, it looked like this might be a typical day for them. Just watching them made me want to crumple my shirt in my hand and intentionally wrinkle it more. Blaze was rubbing off on me.

This was the first time I saw that angels' wings could differ slightly in color — most were a stark white, like Orion's, but they varied to light grey, even a few creams and off-whites. I eyed Blaze's and my own all-black attire, then Kal's dirty and blood-stained clothes, the three of us sticking out like sore thumbs, and wondered what would happen if there was ever an angel born with black wings.

Angels passing us on our floor eyed us curiously, more than one scowling at Blaze and Kal, not to mention the muttering I heard in our wake about the bootprints I was leaving. I made sure to stomp a little harder.

Some greeted Orion formally, and he returned with a nod of recognition, but if I had to guess, I'd say the male seemed nervous.

In the middle of the atrium, Gabriella stopped and pressed a button on what I thought was a plain white wall, a metallic sheen to its whole expanse. A moment later, a bell chimed, and doors slid open from nothingness, revealing an elevator.

"Proceed to Floor Gamma, the Sigma Room," she told Orion breezily, not entering the elevator with us. "They'll be waiting."

The elevator doors slid closed soundlessly as Orion pressed a button on the panel, and silence enveloped us.

"Oo, the *Sigma* Room," Blaze started, the male unable to handle a moment of silence without ruining it. "What's the Sigma Room? Usually they see me in Meeting Room Five."

"That's because your infractions barely matter," Orion offered under his breath. Orion tugged at his sleeves again, straightening his cufflinks for the hundredth time since we left the hospital, and I eyed the male cautiously. No guesswork required: this was, by far, the most nervous I'd ever seen him. "The Sigma room is the Council chambers, and it's for actual, *serious* offenses."

"Oh." Blaze clasped his hands behind his back and nodded. "Well, now I'm offended —"

"Jesus —"

"— *And* I have a new goal in life."

Orion took a deep inhale, closing his eyes as he tried to ignore Blaze, who began humming *Highway to Hell* under his breath. I glanced sideways at Kal, but his eyes were downcast. Still, I could have sworn I saw the hint of a smirk playing on his lips.

The doors slid open, and, as expected, another white, empty hall greeted us. On the far wall stood two large doors, silver handles the only identifier to split them from the rest of the space. Orion stepped forward, shoulders thrown back and head high as he moved in front of us, leading the way, his wings fluttering with each move.

My heart should have raced in my chest at the nervous ticks I noticed in Orion, but I couldn't seem to muster up the energy to care about anything.

Guilt ate at me, remorse threatening to swallow me whole as I palmed my phone in my pocket, wanting to see if there was any word on Selene's status. But what right did I have to check on her when I'd been the one to put her in that hospital?

Pulling my hand out of my pocket and away from temptation, I moved forward to where Orion paused at the doorway, dragging Kal with me.

"Answer them honestly, and try not to sass anyone," Orion said, and I cut my eyes to Blaze, then Kal.

"He talking to Kal or us?"

"All of you," Orion deadpanned, staring blankly at the door handles. "Let's get this over with."

With a tug, he pulled open the doors, and my eyes expanded in shock at the sight before me, but Blaze beat me to a reaction.

"Holy fucking shit."

Chapter Thirty-Five

RYKER

Orion strode through the open doors, but Blaze held back, glancing my way, then to Kal.

My fingers tightened on Kal's arm, practically dragging him towards the doors. For the first time since we'd picked him up from his iron holding cell, the demon-witch seemed to drag his feet. I noted the way his nostrils flared, unease rippling through him.

"Why did you do this, brother?" Blaze whispered, a hint of sadness in his voice as he shook his head.

Kal's black eyes snapped to his younger brother, settling into a deep frown as he studied him. "You're on the wrong side, Sabazios. This doesn't end with me, no matter what happens in there."

"Save your villain monologue for the angels who care," I said as I yanked on his arm, dragging him into the room, iron manacles clanking around his wrists.

We stepped through a narrow corridor, out into the center of a room set up like a lecture hall, five rows of bench seating stacked high in the room. Four angels sat on each one, followed by two on the floor besides Orion. Pascar, I recognized, her black sunglasses perched on her nose even inside. Long black pointed nails tapped on the table in front of her, contrasting sharply against the nearly translucent pallor of her skin. Silver, almost white hair flowed straight down her back to her waist, not a hair out of place. Unlike the other angels all dressed in some form of formal attire, Pascar must have been exempt from the dress code as an Inquisitor, wearing a black leather biker jacket, not so different from my own. She was in conversation with the tall male next to her, but broke off at our entry and gave Orion a smirk before moving to take a seat up in the stands. Voices whispered when Orion stepped up to one of the four chairs waiting for us at the center of the room, but silence washed over the room when the male next to Pascar's eyes met mine.

"It has been a very long time, Ryker," Ezra said, bringing my past back faster than I'd ever prepared for.

"I wish I could say I was glad to see you, Ezra," I ground out. Orion's head snapped to me, eyes wide with unspoken annoyance, but I didn't bother to appear apologetic.

"*Chancellor* Ezra," he retorted with a wicked grin.

It had been 300 years since the last time I saw Ezra, but the sight of the male still sent a wave of pure fury down my spine. I'd heard he'd become Chancellor — the second angel in charge only behind the Premier — three years ago, a term that lasted twenty years for an angel, but had yet to see him since he took on his new, very undeserved, title.

Ezra's white-grey hair was parted slightly off-center and slicked back, its color a product of his species and not his age, as he otherwise appeared like a human in their forties, even while he was several hundred years old. His hands were casually in the pockets of his grey suit with the tiniest of pinstripes in the fabric over a matching vest, muscled chest out as confidence rolled off him in waves. Wings of the purest white were closed tightly on his back, appearing just as perfect as everything else about the male. As I glanced around the space, seeing how these angels deferred to him, I had to wonder… had he fooled them all?

"Sit," Orion nearly barked at us. Blaze paused in front of the chair behind him, then moved to circle the row of chairs, sitting on the far end, not where Orion had indicated. Kal jerked in my hands, needing to disobey just as much as his brother, but I shoved hard on the male, forcing him down into the chair between Orion and me.

"This feels *not great*," Blaze said in a whisper, leaning into my shoulder. I didn't bother responding, only casting a dead stare to the side in answer.

Once we were all settled, Ezra turned to the angels in the rows above us. "Thank you for joining me here today, Councilors. We have gathered today for three infractions."

Blaze leaned forward in his chair, making eye contact with Orion, mouthing, *"Three?"*

I knew they'd wanted to speak to me, and obviously charge Kal, but even I was confused by the third infraction.

Pascar shuffled papers on her lap, handing a file down to Ezra in front of her, who opened it, examined it for a moment, then let a wide, sinister smile span his face when he turned to me.

"Our first order of business is concerning Ryker Odinsson. Ryker, please step forward into the Circle." Ezra pointed to a white circle on the floor I hadn't noticed in my shock at seeing my arch nemesis again.

With a deep breath, I rose, taking the few steps forward to stand in the Circle. A wave of power washed over me as I stepped over the white line, and the fire in my veins winked out. I fought to hold in the gasp that tried to escape me as all magic was sucked from my body, rendering me more human than I'd been even with iron coursing through my blood.

I could feel my dragon reeling inside me, locked tight in an unbreakable cage, panic roaring in his veins, but we were both helpless against the magic.

Not for the first time, the thought of the angels holding this much power over all supernaturals scared me. Knowing that this power was theirs to wield — yanking our magic back as if it never flowed in our veins — was a power no single being should wield. Especially not Ezra.

But now was not the time to fight back.

Glancing down at the folder, then back up to me, Ezra said, "Ryker Odinsson, you are charged with exposing yourself to the humans."

"Ugh, not this again," Blaze muttered behind me. "Surely we can word it better than that." I fought to keep my expression one of bored neutrality.

"On January 25th, news channels through Ohio, New York, Vermont, and New Hampshire reported sightings of a black and gold dragon flying overhead, below the cloud cover. Dozens of accounts showed videos on social media confirming the sightings, which were then shared a collective 2.4 million times. This is in direct violation of the laws of the Paranormal Regulations and Interspecies Council, under section 1.4, regarding the exposure of the supernatural world to humans. How do you plead, Ryker?"

Without missing a beat, I answered. "Guilty."

A shocked wave of voices went through the audience, all eyes focused on me, but I didn't lower my chin.

"You do know the penalty for this violation, yes?" Ezra asked, not bothering to hide the smug grin on his face. In the 600 years we'd known each other, Ezra had been searching for a way to get me here, in this exact situation. And now he was sure he had it. He was going to take my magic.

"If I may interject," Orion said behind me, but Ezra held up his hand. Orion sucked in a breath, and I turned to see him, eyes wide, hand clawing at his throat.

Not once in all my years in the supernatural community had I ever seen an angel turn their power on another angel, and from the growing whispers, I wasn't alone in that thought.

"Let him speak," an angel called from the first row. I turned back, noticing him for the first time. Unlike the others whose hair all seemed to be some form of grey, black streaks wove through his hair, mirroring his wings that seemed to have an almost ombre effect, fading from white at the top to a darker grey, almost charcoal at the tips. "You know the rules as well as I, Ezra."

Facing me with his back to the rest of the angels, Ezra's jaw worked, his eyes focused intently on Orion before he released the magic, and Orion sagged slightly in his chair.

"Apologies, Premier," Ezra said as he turned, a wide smile taking over his features once more. He moved, taking his seat again, and faced us.

"Orion." Ezra tilted his head. "I believe you had something to add."

Orion stood in front of his chair, tugging on his cuffs before he spoke. "Yes. Thank you, Councilors, for hearing me. Ezra is correct, Ryker *was* in direct violation of bylaw 1.4. But in section G, under that same bylaw, it states that a supernatural under the magical influence of another while committing the infraction is due for a reduced sentencing, based on the severity of the infraction."

The dark-haired Premier studied me, then switched his gaze back to Orion. "And is this the case?" he asked, ignoring that Ezra was supposed to lead this meeting. "Was Ryker under the magical influence of another?"

"Yes, Premier Malachi." Orion nodded. I kept my gaze on the angel, Malachi, watching as he leaned over to the female next to him, whispering something into her ear.

Jaw working, Ezra stood once more, standing in front of me, and I couldn't help but smile at him. It wasn't the first time I'd been glad to have Orion at my back, but I made a mental note to do something for the male to show my appreciation. Maybe a new electric, self-driving street-sweeper for the town.

"Start from the beginning. Please detail to us how you, a centuries-old dragon, came to be under the magical influence of another, leading you to shatter bylaw 1.4 in a way our world has never seen before."

So I did.

I began with the story of the human sacrifices last fall, conveniently leaving out that Petra, very much a human, had been with me when I'd spied Kal the first time in Deadlights Cove. Then I told of how Kal hadn't stopped, roping local witches into joining his cause, creating chaos in the shifter world when we were all locked in our forms in November. I painted a broad-stroke picture of what I knew of the showdown at The Last Resort, asking Orion and Blaze to each confirm my story since they'd actually been there, and explained how Kal had escaped once more.

"So I hunted him," I said, tongue running across my teeth as I recalled the fruitless months I'd spent flying across the country searching for the demon-witch. "I did what I do best, as every one of you in this room knows. You've hired me on multiple occasions for just this purpose — I hunted a wanted criminal, intent on serving justice."

You could've heard a pin drop in the expansive room as everyone waited for what came next. Most of the eyes in the room were settled behind me, on what I guessed was Kal. With the story I'd just told, we could all see where this was going.

"As I flew back to Deadlights Cove, I was fully glamoured, as I always am when I fly. Something felt off, so I dipped below the cloud cover, never once removing my glamour. And then," I paused, fighting to rein in my temper at the memory. At everything this male had spurred into action in my life. The feel of my leg shattering on impact, pain shooting through my body like never before. The vision of Selene standing over me on my roof, speaking calmly as I terrified even Blaze and Orion. Then how our relationship had changed, a friendship forming like I hadn't experienced in centuries, a bond tighter than I wanted. Her lifeless form in front of me as I poisoned her. With a deep breath, I continued. "Then he shot me. An iron bullet sank through my thigh, immediately poisoning my bloodstream and rendering me unable to heal or access my magic for two weeks."

"Is this true?" a feminine voice came from next to Malachi, the female beside him looking between me and Kal. "Within the Circle, Ryker is unable to lie, so this is the truth as he sees it. I would like these heavy accusations validated before we make any further decisions as to Ryker's punishment for this infraction. Please bring Errakal Rosewood to the Circle, Chancellor."

Heads nodded in agreement throughout the stands, but Ezra never glanced behind him, his eyes boring holes in my head. With a wave of his hand, the magic around me dropped, and I stepped back, feeling the tidal wave of power sink back under my skin.

I closed my eyes, relief washing through me for only a second before I opened them again, moving to grab Kal's arm where he stood, bringing him forward. I only let go when Kal had stepped into the Circle, his power frozen just as mine had been.

Chapter Thirty-Six

RYKER

"Welcome, Errakal," the female angel said as she stepped down the stairs to stand at Ezra's side. Ezra's jaw tensed as she passed him, to stand between him and the Circle. "My name is Seraphina. I don't think we've met before. Is that correct?"

Kal tilted his head, his shoulder length dark hair shifting slightly with the movement. "Yes. That is correct."

"Excellent." She smiled. "You may not know me, but your father certainly does. I'm the one who put Nergal behind bars seven years ago."

Blaze's head snapped to the side, eyes wide as he stared at Kal, then Orion. From the shocked expression he wore, I had to assume that Nergal's prison sentence was news to Blaze.

"I knew your name rang a bell," Kal said as he appraised her.

I'd heard Seraphina's name before — the Premier's right-hand in almost everything. Her hair was nearly as white as her wings, hanging down her back in loose curls.

The white pantsuit she wore was tailored to her body, painting the picture-perfect image of an angel. But if rumors were to be believed, Seraphina was the most cunning of the angels in the Council, the one called in when all else failed.

Seraphina's bright smile didn't waver as she stepped closer. "Those were some heavy accusations Ryker pinned on you moments before. Are you guilty?"

Within the Circle, Kal couldn't lie, and he could be made to answer, but that didn't mean there weren't other ways he could circumvent the truth. For a demon, this spell would be particularly painful. They struggled to obey.

"I'm sure I'm guilty of lots of things."

A muscle worked in her jaw, but still, she didn't rise to his bait. "Let's try this again. Are you responsible for the bullet that rendered Ryker unable to maintain his glamour?"

He studied her for a beat, the room silent around us. Malachi leaned forward, elbows on his knees as he held his hands clasped in front of his mouth. Ezra was visibly annoyed, leg bouncing under the table as his eyes darted between Kal and Seraphina.

But I couldn't take my eyes off Kal. Something about this seemed off — he was too calm. He'd put up too little of a fight this whole way here. In fact, he'd hardly put up a fight even in the mines.

"I didn't shoot Ryker," came Kal's low voice at last.

The angel's lips pressed together in irritation. "Were you the leader of a group responsible for his injury?" she tried again.

"The leader?" Kal asked, his eyebrows rising as he thought about his answer. "No."

Any hint of friendliness dripped off Seraphina as she stepped closer to the Circle, toeing the line. I could feel the power washing off her as she studied the much taller Kal. He tilted his head down to look at her.

"You're quite beautiful," he said, and the comment threw the angel off for only a moment. A smirk lifted one side of his lips. "It makes sense now, that you were able to convince my father that you loved him, right up until you locked him away for life. I might have been enraptured by you, too, if we're being honest."

She sighed, but didn't step back. "Were you, in any way, involved in the plot or execution of the bullet fired that then tampered with Ryker's magic?"

"Yes."

Seraphina grinned. "How unfortunate for you. Please explain, in detail, how this plot came about."

With a heavy sigh, Kal began his tale.

Kal's story mimicked mine, explaining some of the magical mishaps he'd been a part of for the last five months. None of us had known how far he'd expanded — apparently, Deadlights Cove was not his first target, though he certainly seemed to have a personal vendetta against the town.

I noticed Blaze's face was blanched nearly of all color. He wrung his hands together in his lap as he studied his brother's back, listening to everything Kal admitted to. If Kal were to be believed, which, inside the Circle, he couldn't speak a lie, then there was a wake of bodies he'd left behind across the country.

"And why did your plan include shooting Ryker?"

Seraphina asked, taking all of his many admissions in stride.

"Well, he was on my tail, pissing me off. And humans love dragons." Kal shrugged, seemingly unbothered that he'd just admitted enough crimes to leave him not only magicless for life, but also imprisoned. "He makes a bold statement."

"You son of a bitch," I growled, hand gripping my leg where he'd shot me. All the problems he'd caused for me, for a bold statement?

"You see," Kal said, suddenly breaking free of the iron manacles even inside the Circle. Seraphina stepped back, shock written on her expression. "Some of us are tired of hiding our potential. Our true power."

"How did you do that?" Ezra asked, pointing at Kal's now freed hands. "How did you work magic inside the Circle?"

"Magic is far older than your little Council, Ezra," Kal said, wiggling his fingers in front of his face. With a small jab, he poked at the invisible barrier of the Circle, watching as it cast rippling waves of magic in a cylinder around him. "You want it to obey rules. Your rules. But we demons like to defy rules."

"Who are you working for?" Malachi said, his voice calm but demanding.

"The good of paranormal society."

"I'm sure the shifters you've sacrificed would agree you're looking out for them," I mumbled. Orion shot me a glance, but there was no judgment in it.

"You say you're tired of hiding. Do you intend to reveal supernatural society to the humans?" Malachi pushed on.

A slow, eerie grin crept up Kal's face. "Wouldn't it be so much easier," he mused, almost to himself, "if they knew?" Kal's gaze left Malachi to search out the other angels behind him. "Who decided we should hide, anyway? Angels, surely, a long, long time ago; yet they never asked the rest of us what we thought about that, if we agreed." He shrugged nonchalantly. "Well, maybe some beings out there don't agree."

A tense silence filled the room as the angels took in his words, his implications. The main tenant of supernatural law was to remain hidden from humans. If Kal and any number of his supporters out there were about to start acting against that law… Orion was equally as concerned as I was about that, judging from the tightness in his jaw. There may have been a time many centuries ago when humans could handle some measure of magic in their lives, but in this day and age?

We'd be locked up to be studied and weaponized before we could blink.

Malachi eyed him coolly before asking, voice low, "When was the last time you spoke to your father, Errakal?"

Kal tilted his head. "So hard to keep track of time these days, what with one thing and another. And Seraphina so kindly reminded me that it's been seven years now that he's been in the Iron Keep. Within the last decade, I should think."

Despite the non-answer, Malachi gave a tiny nod as though that confirmed something for him and stood. "With the confessions you've made here today in front of the Paranormal Regulation and Interspecies Council, I, Premier Malachi Russo III, sentence you to life in prison. You will be escorted immediately to the Iron Keep while we continue to gather evidence to support these claims. If you are found guilty of murder and exposing the supernatural world to human society, you and all who have been working with you will have your magic permanently revoked."

Orion sat back on his bench, shoulders back as his wings nearly touched the ground, a small smile tugging on his lips.

"Ryker," Malachi said, and my eyes snapped up to his. "You cannot be left unpunished for your part in this scheme, even if it was unbeknownst to you. As Premier, I determine the extent of your punishment for breaking our Code, and sentence you to three weeks without magic. But seeing as you've already served that sentence for two weeks and have done a number of services for the Council over the years, you are free to leave Headquarters, magic intact."

I breathed a sigh of relief. As much as I knew I wouldn't end up in the Iron Keep for this crime, the PRIC tended to be… well, pricks.

I nodded to the Premier, thanking him silently for the sentencing.

As Malachi began detailing how he wanted his sentencing carried out, Blaze leaned slightly into my side. "Think you can find yourself another pair of iron manacles quickly?" he asked, and my brows dipped.

"I could be wrong. This is pure speculation, but whatever magic Kal has been doing these last several months has been greatly amplifying his demon side. He's gaining power from resisting the angel's magic, even in its purest form in the Circle," he whispered. "But, hundred bucks says when they drop that Circle, you could slap those manacles right back on him."

I wasn't sure I followed Blaze's logic, but demon powers were a well-kept secret, so I couldn't be sure he was wrong either. Hand held out behind my back, I closed my eyes, hoping my magic was fully back. With a thought, I summoned another pair of iron manacles as if I was summoning my clothes, stored in the in-between when I shifted. The heavy metal dropped into my hands, burning lightly where it touched my skin.

I stood, approaching the Circle from behind as Ezra, Pascar, and Seraphina stood around Kal, waiting for Malachi's signal to drop the Circle.

The moment the magic released, Kal leapt back from the angels, preparing to flicker, but his back bumped up against me, right as I slid one iron manacle around his wrist, then snapped the other one in place. "Not again, fucker."

His nostrils flared slightly at the iron locking him in place once more, but the same calm front he'd held in place all day returned.

With one last glance at Blaze, Kal said, "I've warned you. You're on the wrong side, brother. This is far from over." But Pascar and Seraphina flanked him, pulling him towards the angels standing just outside the door, ready to escort him to the Iron Keep.

"Now, as for the third infraction," Ezra's voice boomed out over the space, calling us all back to attention as the doors shut once more. "Orion, please step into the Circle."

There was no mistaking the shock on Orion's face when Ezra called his name, his wings snapping even tighter to his back as he stood stiffly. He didn't look back at us as he forced his feet forward and, with a slow breath to steady himself, stepped into the Circle, his magic leaving him in a wave of energy.

"Officer Orion," Ezra began, sounding far too eager as he read from his folder. "It's come to our attention that you've been lax in your duties as Official Mayor of the Town of Deadlights Cove, Maine, United States of America. Charges include: improper glamouring of the town, allowing magic to be performed by both witches and demons in public spaces, and allowing magical paraphernalia to be displayed in public spaces, namely in a shop known as Carpe Noctem. You allowed a demon," he nodded towards where Kal had just left, "to perform several nefarious spells on lands under your jurisdiction, including the sacrifice of a human, and capture and near-sacrifice of a shifter, which then made all shifters unable to change between their forms for several days."

"I also noted several dress code violations," Pascar added gleefully, handing another paper down to Ezra and Malachi, who frowned at it.

"Orion," Malachi's tone was full of disapproval as he examined it. "Is this you… wearing shorts? And what are these?" He brought the paper closer to his face, squinting hard.

Pascar's grin was anything but warm. "Boat shoes."

There was a sharp intake of breath from all the angels assembled in the room, and I fought not to roll my eyes as Blaze covered a laugh with a cough, even though, apparently, it wasn't a laughing matter. Angels were *such* micromanagers.

"I only ever wore those… garments on personal time," Orion spoke up. "And have you been spying on me, Pascar? You weren't even in town when I wore those."

Pascar *tsk*ed at him, waggling a talon-tipped finger for good measure, and ignored his accusation of spying. "There's no *personal time* for an angel, Orion. You are *always* a representative of the Council. Isn't that right, Premier?"

Malachi put the paper on the table before him, face-down as though he couldn't bear to see it. "That's true, Pascar. However, given the severity of these other charges, we may wish to focus this warning on those."

Orion paled, tugging at his collar. "Warning?"

"Yes." Malachi shuffled through his papers before pulling one out to the top of the stack. "Officer Orion, you are hereby issued your first and only Official Warning by the Council for your lackadaisical leadership of the town of Deadlights Cove, Maine, United States of America. As you know, officers are permitted only one Warning before they face a full Investigation by the Grand Jury and then if, and only if, they are still found to be worthy of a position, they must be re-credentialed and then re-assigned."

With a deadening *thump*, Malachi brought a large red stamp down onto the paper, Orion's jaw working again even as he fought to keep his face clear.

I caught Blaze's eye as Orion accepted his sentencing, and even the demon was too shocked to utter a word.

Chapter Thirty-Seven

SELENE

Everything hurt. That was the first thing I knew even before I opened my eyes. In fact, I wasn't sure opening my eyes wouldn't hurt, too, and I was somewhat scared to try.

I knew by the scent of rubbing alcohol and the soft beeping of machines that I was in a medical facility, which was good. That meant West's people had succeeded at least enough that we got out of the mine. I didn't remember much beyond Kal's dark eyes sliding to mine before he lifted his gun.

I winced at the memory of pain, but as I tried to take stock of my body, realized I couldn't quite feel the wound. I was medicated, then, or maybe a witch had healed me.

With a sigh, I finally cracked my eyes open. The room was dark, but at least I had a private room, and I was hooked up to the monitor beside me. I reached out, wincing slightly with the pain of the movement, to turn the monitor towards me, and blinked to clear the blurriness from my eyes as I read my stats. They looked good, and I let out a breath of relief. I was stable and on the mend, then.

I turned to the other side of my bed, hoping to see —
but there was only an empty chair. Suddenly feeling cold, I
pulled my blanket more tightly around my shoulders. I
needed more information.

"Excuse me?" I called out, hoping whatever night staff
was on duty would be close enough to hear me. I didn't
want to shout and risk waking up anyone else; it was clear it
was the middle of the night by the quiet.

A young woman, maybe a year or two younger than me,
poked her head around the door, black hair swishing behind
her. She had strong eyebrows and wore dark blue scrubs,
entering the room quietly.

"Good to see you awake, Selene," she said, checking my
stats before placing one hand on my forehead and the other
on my ribs, just below my heart.

"You're a witch?" I asked, recognizing that she was using
magic to assess me further.

"Zara, nice to meet you," she nodded, stepping back.
"Well, meet you again. I'm one of the ones who patched
you up in the mine."

"Thank you." I waited a beat so she didn't think I didn't
mean it — because I did — before clearing my throat.
"How long have I been —"

"Brought you in about 8 p.m. last night," Zara glanced
at her watch, "And it's 4 a.m. now. Once we got everyone
here and stable, we've been trying to get everyone healed up.
But hey," Zara laid a hand on my shoulder, meeting my eye
solemnly. "You still have to rest, all right? Your idiot friend
nearly poisoned you. We were able to counteract it, but
that's still going to take its toll on your system."

"I understand. I'm a doctor, actually."

Zara nodded slowly, though her eyes narrowed. "Doctor? Like a human doctor?"

"Yes." I didn't really want to get into my whole life story, so I continued on without elaborating. "Have you seen —"

"The big dude? Your idiot friend? He left with that angel a little while ago." Someone's monitor started beeping from outside my room, and Zara moved towards the door. "Try to get some rest, all right?"

Zara left, and I tried to piece together what she'd said. *That angel* — that had to be Orion, right? If he'd arrived that quickly, then someone must have flickered him out here, and magic was a-go in the Cove again.

I sat up too fast, my head spinning, but looked around the room, trying to see if my clothes were here. On a counter to my side, there was a clear bag with them, and I pulled myself out of bed to grab it before collapsing back down. Zara wasn't kidding when she said that iron did a number on you.

Fishing through the bag, I found my cell phone and searched my favorites before pressing to call.

It rang a few times, and I felt kind of bad, since it was 6 a.m. in Maine and she was a demon, but I knew she might have some idea of what was going on, and more than that, I just needed to hear a familiar voice.

"Selene?" came Nimue's voice, groggy from sleep. Then she cleared her throat. "You're awake!"

"Yeah, I'm awake. Do you know what's going on? What happened here? They said Orion was here, I think, so did Blaze bring him out?"

I heard murmuring in the background, probably Kit beside her asking who was calling her at six in the morning, and then she was back. "Give me ten minutes and I'll come to you."

We hung up, and I slumped back in my bed, some measure of relief seeping through me at the thought of a friend being by my side soon. Tears welled in my eyes as I glanced again at the empty chair, but I refused to let them fall.

True to her word, hardly ten minutes passed before Nimue bustled into my room, her brown hair in a loose knot and dressed in her usual soft pink sweater and leggings under her dark coat, paired with snowboots. I'd managed to get dressed as well, but my shirt had a gaping hole in it, a vivid reminder I'd been shot only a few hours before. Luckily, Ryker had left one of his sweatshirts here, and I pulled it on over my own clothes.

Nimue rushed to my bedside, wrapping me in a warm but gentle hug, her familiar rosewater scent a balm to my soul, then pulled back and sat on the edge of my bed.

"Do you remember anything after you were shot?" she asked, and when I shook my head she continued. "I don't know everything, but this is what I got from Blaze." She recounted what had happened to Kal and his cronies, satisfaction coursing through me that at least Kal had been apprehended, even if some of his people had gotten away.

"And now Orion, Blaze, and Ryker are at the Council Headquarters, taking Kal in for questioning," she finished, her warm black eyes watching me carefully.

"Right." For some reason, my voice had grown tight.

But why shouldn't Ryker take Kal in? The demon-witch had been his target for months. Of course Ryker would want to see him questioned and sentenced. Plus, the Council had wanted to meet with him for weeks.

But some small, childish part of me wished he'd stayed, that he'd waited to be there when I woke up from a *bullet wound*, instead of leaving me here wounded and vulnerable in the middle of nowhere with a whole town of supernaturals I'd never met before yesterday.

Was that selfish of me?

"Are you ready to go home?" Nimue asked, a small smile playing across her features. I shook my head to clear my thoughts, then mustered up what I hoped was a smile in return.

"Can you take me back to Boston? Then, I promise, I'll be out of your hair."

Nimue rolled her eyes, shaking her head at me. "Don't even start in on the whole '*I don't want to burden you*' business."

Zara stuck her head in a few minutes later, pill bottle in hand. "New friend?"

"Sorry," Nimue said, waving her hand. "Probably should have stopped at a desk or something."

"Probably," Zara answered, a tiny bit of snark in her voice. But I'd been in her shoes before with a packed ER and not enough staff to go around. "So, since you're a doctor yourself, I'll skip all the warnings and lectures about taking it easy, no hard labor, lots of rest and fluids." She eyed me over her clip board, and I nodded. "Great. Just don't do anything stupid."

Zara handed over the pill bottle, and I twisted it to read the label. "My own blend," Zara said, sensing my hesitation.

"Part pain-killer, part witch medicine. Need to get the rest of that iron out of your body, but also you were shot, and that hurts like a bitch."

I nodded, slipping the bottle in the kangaroo pocket of Ryker's hoodie.

"Any other questions for me?" Zara asked.

I shook my head. "Thank you for everything."

She waved me off. "You're free to go, then. Take it easy, Selene. I'll check in with you tomorrow."

Zara left as quickly as she'd arrived, and Nimue held her hand out to me. "Ready?" I placed my hand in hers, she gave it a squeeze and then we flickered out.

I gripped my side, gasping for air as our feet touched down on the wood floors of my brownstone, the world spinning around me. Even with the after-affects of flickering, some of the tension eased from my shoulders at finally being *home*.

"Crap!" Nimue said, her shoulder coming under my arm as she maneuvered me to the couch just in front of us. "I wish I knew a gentler way to flicker, but it's not like I have a ton of control over it."

"It's fine," I gasped, squeezing my eyes shut against the pain raging through my chest. "I'm fine. Just… just give me a minute."

Nimue stood in front of me, her forehead creasing as she struggled to figure out what to do next.

"Would you mind grabbing me a bowl from the kitchen?" I asked her, hoping to ease her nervous energy, and also preparing for the potentiality that I'd empty whatever was left in my stomach after flickering. "Second cabinet over from the fridge."

"Yes, right. Sure. I can do that."

I didn't bother opening my eyes when the sound of the plastic bowl clattered on the floor next to me.

"What next?" Nimue asked as I focused on pulling even breaths through my nose and out through my mouth.

"Nothing," I said, patting the couch, eyes still screwed shut. "Just sit with me until Ryker gets here."

The cushions dipped as Nimue sat, lifting my head into her lap. Her fingers worked through my curls, pulling them away from my face, and I breathed deeper, knowing I wasn't alone.

"Ryker, huh?" Nimue asked, her tone full of curiosity. "Did something finally happen between you two then?"

"Kind of," I answered, a happy sigh escaping me. "Yeah."

"Do you want to talk about it?"

Her fingers worked through my hair, lulling me into a sense of security I'd so desperately missed since my mom passed, the loneliness I carried with me constantly abating for just this moment, especially as I thought about Ryker.

"He's the worst patient I've ever cared for," I answered honestly, and Nimue chuckled. I yawned, fighting the healing sleep that tugged at my consciousness. Barely above a whisper, I finally admitted, "But I think I'm falling for him, Nim."

A gentle kiss touched down on my forehead as sleep claimed me. "I'm so happy for you, Selene. You deserve happiness."

Chapter Thirty-Eight

RYKER

We touched down back in the Cove, landing in Orion's office inside Town Hall. Hoping my face wasn't as green as my eyes, I sucked air in through my nose. How was it that a dragon whose main mode of transportation was *flight* couldn't handle… whatever that was?

"Damn," Blaze said, hands on his knees as he puffed out his cheeks. "And you complain that flickering is bad."

Orion picked at the lint on his suit jacket, tugging on the cuffs, and heaved a loud exhale before stepping behind his desk and taking a seat in his leather chair.

Snapping to attention, Blaze studied Orion. "You doing okay, O? They handed your ass to you back there."

Orion's lips pursed as he scooped the papers on his desk into a neat pile, tapping them aggressively on the polished wooden desktop. "Nothing they said was unwarranted."

"Really?" Blaze scrunched his nose. "Calling you a *lackadaisical leader* seemed a bit harsh to me. Also, who says *lackadaisical?*"

"They had a point, though," Orion said as he picked up

a large stamp, glancing down at the paperwork. He scanned the document for no more than 30 seconds before he brought the stamp down aggressively, leaving a bright red *DENIED* in all capital letters on the top of the sheet.

Blaze craned his neck, trying to see what it was, then let out a high-pitched chuckle. "Sure you want to do that?"

"It's not my decision, Sabazios," Orion said, his tongue slicking across his teeth as he read through the next paper. "Like the Council pointed out, I have become too close with the townspeople of Deadlights Cove. My friendship with you is skewing my job performance. I've allowed too much to slip by in this town without enforcing the Code that clearly states how every supernatural town should operate."

"Yeah, but," Blaze looked at me, searching for support, but I had nothing to offer. While they'd offered me some leniency in their ruling today, drawing the eyes of the PRICs was never a good thing. And Orion apparently had a bullseye painted on his back. "Dev is going to lose her shit when she sees you've denied her new online sales permit."

"She knows the rules." Orion stamped the next paper with the same large *DENIED*. "I've let her get away with skirting the Code as long as possible. But that ends today."

"Your funeral," Blaze muttered as he walked by me, headed out into the hall and towards the exit. "Nice knowing you, man."

My jaw worked as I studied Orion, not sure what to say.

The stamp came down hard again, leaving another bright red reminder of the Code's requirements, and I felt somewhat sympathetic for the male.

This town was Orion's life.

Anyone who'd seen him here knew it. He followed the

letter of the law more carefully than anyone I'd ever met. As if I needed any further reason to hate the PRICs.

"Would it be the worst thing in the world if you got reassigned?" I asked, sliding my hands into my jacket pockets.

His hand faltered over the next paper before he set the stamp down, then he sat back in his chair and heaved a sigh. "Do you know how hard it is to get assigned to Earth like this? How many angels want this position?"

I could only shake my head. Even after a thousand years, I barely had a grasp on angel society.

"It took a hundred years just to get the authorization to train for it," he admitted. "For centuries, this is what I've worked and trained for, and apparently, I'm still failing at it." He pressed his eyes shut, pinching the bridge of his nose as another thought occurred to him. "And they don't even know about Petra. The shit I'd be in for that — you can't even imagine."

I sort of could, having dealt with the PRICs for several centuries, but he seemed to need this… whatever this was.

Orion sighed, hands dropping back down to his desk as he picked up the papers he'd been evaluating before, and began scribbling something on it, as if his little emotional moment had never happened. "Anything else I can help you with, Ryker?" he asked, not even bothering to lift his eyes in my direction.

I hesitated, not sure it was my business, or if I wanted to get involved, but something Errakal had said kept bothering me.

"What do you think Kal meant that Blaze was on the wrong side? Malachi mentioned their father…" I trailed off,

284

not sure where my train of thought was going with that, and Orion set down his pen.

"Do you know anything about their father?"

I shook my head. Half the demons I knew didn't even know who their fathers were.

"My guess, and that's all this is," Orion loosened his tie before pulling it over his head and undoing the top button of his shirt, "would be that Malachi thinks their father, Nergal, is the one really running this operation. Though how he'd run anything from within the Iron Keep should be impossible."

"So, Kal's threat might hold. This might not be over."

Orion's wings shifted before settling again, almost a shrug. "Unfortunately, we'll have to wait and see. But Nergal is full-demon, and ancient, so if he were able to get out or he's able to keep coordinating from behind bars, then yes, there is definitely the potential for things to get worse. I almost have to hope that Morgaine's crack-pot theory turns out to be true and species can inter-link their magic, or we might not be able to stop him at all."

Hopping down the steps two at a time from Town Hall into the square, I breathed deeply, inhaling the cool ocean air, wishing it could settle the fire raging in my veins.

Like Orion, I'd come back from Headquarters changed. Even though we'd scraped through the meeting with hardly any punishment, I could see how the pressure of this town, this responsibility, weighed on him.

But this town wasn't *my* responsibility. *My* weight.

No. *She'd* been my responsibility, and I'd failed her miserably.

"Fuck," I mumbled as I scrubbed my hands against my close-shaved head. My skin felt too tight at the memory of her laying bleeding, *dying*, in my arms. Every time I closed my eyes, it was all I could see.

With every minute I'd spent away from Selene, the more sure I was of my decision to break it off with her.

"Nimue took her down to Boston," Blaze said as he joined me, walking across the green and towards Scallywags. "She's not at your place."

I didn't bother answering even as I turned down Ocean Avenue, heading home.

It didn't matter where Selene was.

I could never see her again.

Chapter Thirty-Nine

SELENE

"You're *sure* he knows?" Nimue whispered in the kitchen, the sound pulling me back to consciousness. The sun streamed through the front windows, but low in the sky.

"Nimmie," Blaze answered, "I told him myself. If he's not here, he's not —"

"Hey Selene!" Petra shouted, eyes wide as she sat down on the coffee table facing me. "So glad to see you're awake!"

My eyes squeezed shut once more, hands lifting to cover my face. Ryker's smell of sparks and leather clung to the sleeves of his hoodie I still wore, and I inhaled, savoring the scent. "Why are you yelling?"

"Sorry," Petra said, her voice at a much more acceptable level.

"'S fine," I mumbled into the pillow now under my head. "What time is it?"

"Four," Petra answered. "You hungry? I could make… Well, I could order us something."

"Noodles." I nodded. "Some kind of noodles."

"Right," Petra said, standing and walking into the kitchen to get her phone. "I can handle that."

"Is Ryker here?" I asked, prying my eyes open to search the room. Nimue and Blaze stood shoulder to shoulder next to the fridge, eyeing each other uncomfortably. I sighed, bringing my hand down to the couch and trying to push myself upright.

"Don't even think about getting up," Mo said as she clomped down the steps behind me, blankets and pillows in hand. "You stay right where you are, Selene. I promised your mother I would take care of you like you were my own, and that's exactly what I plan to do. So lay back down right this minute."

I did as I was told, sinking back into the couch. The reminder of my mother had my eyes prickling with tears, but I pushed them down.

"Ahh, that felt good," Mo said with a smile, glancing into the kitchen where Nimue and Blaze stood. "She actually *takes* directions. I think I have a new favorite child."

"At least I'll always be your first," Blaze sighed. "No one can take that title from me."

"Sit and think about what you just said, brousin," Nimue said as she rolled her eyes, grabbed her phone off the counter and walked into the other room. Blaze cringed, and Mo shuddered.

"I'm really fine, guys," I said, attempting a smile. "I know you're all busy with your own lives. Ryker owes me after all I've done for him the last few weeks. Once he's here, you can all go home."

Mo lifted my head, swapping the throw pillow for the

one from my bed and draping a quilt over me. She stooped down, eye level with me as her hand grazed lovingly over my cheek. "No one needs that stupid dragon when you have Mama Mo here. I'll get you all fixed up and have you back taking care of all of us in no time."

I nodded, my eyes closing once more as I enjoyed the feel of her thumb rubbing lovingly across my cheek. "I'm really fine."

"I know you are, dear," Mo whispered, placing a kiss on my forehead. "The toughest girl I know."

Mo hummed a quiet tune, and my mind began to wander, but I could have sworn I heard a, *"Hush, little witchling, don't say a word, Mama Mo's gonna slay you a big black bird."*

I was faintly aware of someone scooping me against their chest and carrying me up the stairs later, but the smell of woodsmoke was slightly different than sparks — familiar, but I couldn't quite place it.

My bed sank beneath me before a warm body laid down next to me. I smiled before opening my eyes, reaching my hand across the bed to wrap my hand around his.

Smooth, silky skin met my finger tips, and my brow dipped in confusion as I peeked my eyes open. "Petra?"

My best friend smiled back at me, her red hair piled in a bun on the top of her head as she laid her head on the pillow next to me, squeezing my hand lightly. "Thought I'd watch over you for a bit."

"I'm fine." Moving slightly on the bed, I winced, my hand gripping my side. "Really."

"Good." Petra nodded, but her eyes still held the same wariness. "Then my job will be easy."

"Have we heard from Ronan? Is Corissa okay, the sea nymph girl?"

"Yes, Leenie, she's fine," Petra assured me. "She woke up a little less than twenty-four hours after the spell was reversed and magic set free again. She's still tired and resting, but she'll be fine. And just so you know, the only reason *we* know is because Dev went around hunting down anyone she could find with any ties to the sea nymphs and threatened to hex them if they wouldn't tell her how Corissa was doing because she knew you'd be worried. Eventually she got it out of Maia, the sea nymph that works at Scallywags, but you didn't hear that from me."

"Well, thank the goddess she's okay." A breath left me. "Did you eat?"

A small chuckle escaped Petra as she shook her head. "Stop worrying about everyone else. Yes. I ate. We all ate, except you." She moved to sit up. "Are you hungry now? I can go reheat your noodles for you."

I waved her off. "No, I'm really okay. I'll eat them tomorrow. I think I just need to rest a little more."

Petra laid back down, her eyes searching my face. "I'm really glad you're okay, S."

I closed my eyes, but a small smile spread across my face. "That almost feels like a declaration of love from you, P."

"I mean, you're fine, obviously."

I chuckled, reaching across the bed and holding onto her hand, glad to have my best friend here with me. "Love you, too."

The bedroom was dark the next morning as I stretched. My side still ached from the wound, but already, I felt more myself.

Petra must have left sometime in the night, probably to sleep in her own room. I rolled to the side of the bed, dropping my feet to the cold wood floors beneath me and stood.

A sharp pain radiated from my side, and I gripped it as I slowly straightened, focusing on my breathing. Once the pain ebbed, I worked my way to the bathroom, hearing only silence in the house.

The clock on the wall in the bathroom said 5:15 a.m., but since I'd slept almost the entire day yesterday, I made my way through a somewhat lazy morning routine, piling my curls onto the top of my head and quickly rinsing my body in the shower, careful to avoid the bandages on both the front and back of my right side.

Each time I saw the wound, the shot sounded in my head, ringing loudly as I fought to breathe. I'd seen my fair share of gunshot wounds from my days working in the ER, but seeing a bullet wound and *being shot* were two very different things.

Without a thought, I pulled on the black hoodie again and donned a pair of leggings, adjusting them to sit below the bandages.

I gingerly moved down the stairs into the living room, finding Mo sprawled out on the couch, snoring softly. Nimue was gone, but that wasn't surprising, since she could flicker in and out at will. I assumed Petra was in her room with Blaze, but I scanned the space, searching for a pair of over-sized boots, a leather jacket… anything to tell me Ryker had arrived in the night.

If Blaze was back from Headquarters, then their business with Kal was done, right? So he should be here by now?

Worry ate at me as I checked my phone, plugged in on the kitchen counter. I had a few missed texts from Devanna and one from Zara, the witch from the hospital in Colorado, but nothing from Ryker.

Not a phone call.

Not a text.

Nothing.

My heart beat wildly in my chest as I stared at my phone, willing *something* to appear. Panic rose as I thought through the things that could have happened to keep him from contacting me. Maybe his phone had broken during the skirmish? Or he'd been called away on more business with Kal? But, he still should have called or texted… *right?*

Needing a distraction, I pulled open the fridge, staring at the now weeks-outdated contents, and scowled. I dragged the trash can in front of the fridge and began throwing things out, one after the next, ignoring any twinges of pain in my side as I focused on my task.

Once that was done, I grabbed a spray bottle and some paper towels, proceeding to scrub the inside of the fridge. How long had it been since I'd cleaned this? Disgusted with myself, I worked, leaning into the effort as I clutched my side.

"What are you doing?" Mo's sleepy voice came from behind me.

"Sorry," I winced. "Didn't mean to wake you."

"You're fine, dear," Mo said as she rose, stretching

before padding her way into the kitchen. "Do you always clean the fridge at 5 in the morning?"

I dropped my hands down to my side, inhaling sharply through my nose. "I need to do *something.*" Turning back to the fridge, I began to scrub again.

Mo reached in, pulling my hand back, and held it lightly. "He's not here, sweetie."

"Yeah, I noticed," I bit out. "Something must have happened to keep him. It's fine. He'll be here soon."

"Selene," Mo said, gripping my hands and turning me towards her. Her eyes were sad, lips turned down. "I don't think he's coming."

I shook my head, dismissing her words instantly. "No. You don't know how much has changed between us in the last few days, Mo. He wouldn't leave me like this. He's just busy, still."

Mo nodded, but the sad look in her eyes didn't fade even when she smiled. "Can I help you clean, then?"

I handed over the spray bottle and towels, letting her take my place in front of the fridge.

As much as I wanted to believe she was wrong, her words planted a very large seed of doubt as I robotically went through the motions of making a pot of tea. He'd been so protective — *overprotective*, really — when we were in Colorado, but had all those touches been just about keeping the wolves away from me? He'd been so quick to deny I was his when West asked, but then, so had I.

Had it all been about proving his prowess to me since I'd taunted him about it?

Had I misinterpreted *everything?* Read too much into his protectiveness, his touch?

Had he ever actually *said* he wanted more? Wanted *me?*

But no. He'd opened up to me in a way I *knew* he didn't with just anyone. That had to mean something.

Ryker would be here any minute, I was sure of it.

Or at least, that was what I kept telling myself.

Chapter Forty

RYKER

I dabbed the sweat out of my eyes as I lay on my back under my 1971 Plymouth Hemi 'Cuda where I'd been trying to fix an electrical short for the past three hours. It may have been a frozen tundra outside my garage, but dragons always ran warm. Did this need to be fixed? Not necessarily, but after two and a half weeks unable to do jack shit for myself, I needed to do something productive, and my vehicles could always use a tune up to be at their best.

My phone buzzed in my pocket, and for a second my breath caught as I wondered if it might be…

But it didn't matter, even if it was. And it wouldn't be her anyway. She had too much self-respect to beg me to come back to her.

Not that we'd ever even been a *thing*.

The stupid thing buzzed again, and I wished my hands weren't covered in grease so I could silence it. Probably one of Selene's friends to yell at me, or any one of these nosy locals coming to me to fix their problems for them again.

I'd had enough. Of them, of this, of helping other people. It was easier to be on my own.

I liked it better this way.

A minute later, there was a crash, then a yelp, and I cursed under my breath.

"Fuck do you want, Blaze. Don't break my shit." I couldn't see him from under the car, but I'd known the demon for over a century. I didn't need to see to know it was him.

More fool me, because next thing I knew, there was another glass-shattering crash as his demon instincts urged him to disobey me, and I cursed again.

"Sorry. I didn't want to do that one, but, you know." Blaze's voice drifted down to me from the edge of the car. "Came to see if you want to get a drink at the bar tonight."

I scoffed. "Pass."

I felt a boot nudging my toe, and jerked my foot away from him. Fucking demons.

"C'mon, you know you want to."

"I don't."

"You've been cooped up here for three days. Do you even have any food left?"

I gave an aggravated sigh, and rolled out from under the car to level a glare at him. Grabbing a rag, I wiped off my hands and got to my feet. "What, you're all spying on me now?"

Blaze grinned and pointed out the garage doors. "The guys have had the coffee van parked on the cliff-edge of your driveway. They say this spot gets the best sunrise and they wanted the light for some new portraits they were taking. Then they just wanted to see how long it would take you to notice them."

"Fucking Hel," I grumbled, glaring out the doors, but I couldn't see them from here. I wanted to tell myself they wouldn't be nude portraits, but then I'd be a liar. I turned my eyes back on Blaze and narrowed them. "Mo send you to check up on me or something?"

The grin dropped off his face as his brows rose, his expression turning more serious than usual. "At the moment, Mo wants nothing to do with you." He gave me a pointed look.

My chest tightened. Even if he was being annoying about it, it still made me feel like shit. Mo was like a second mother to Selene, after all. I should have assumed. Of course she wouldn't give a damn about me right now.

Still, knowing Blaze like I did, he probably wouldn't leave me alone until I agreed. And gods knew I could do with a drink, even if it cost me social interaction. He was right, anyway. I was out of food and vodka up here.

I chucked the rag down and sighed. "Fine. I'll be down in a bit."

Blaze smirked at me like he'd won something and clapped me on the shoulder before flickering out, and I rolled my eyes. I'd never tell him, but the fact that he wasn't holding my asshole actions against me maybe meant something to me.

Scallywags was packed when I got there a few hours later, and I considered turning on my heel right then. Except

Blaze had already spotted me and patted a spot at the bar, indicating a chilled glass of vodka already set out for me.

Didn't he already have a friend? What was his deal?

I forced myself over to the bar and slipped onto the stool, taking a sip of my drink.

"Oh look, it's alive," a voice came from beside me as someone took the next stool. Devanna's purse clattered to the bartop before she tapped her black nails on its surface to get Blaze's attention.

"Don't sound so disappointed," I murmured, barely taking the glass away from my lips.

"But I am," she snapped as Blaze set her drink down. She took a sip and then tilted her head musingly. "Then again, maybe not. This way, I could still kill you myself."

I eyed her in the mirror behind the bar, glaring daggers at me, and shook my head.

"Give it your best shot, witch."

She scowled, but let it go, and we both sipped in silence. It was a pity she'd probably hate me forever now, since she was one of the few tolerable beings left in this world.

"You know what your problem is?" Dev blurted abruptly some time later.

I looked up from my glass, startled. I'd thought we'd been enjoying a nice silence together, but apparently she'd been stewing on something.

"You're just *selfish*, like all dragons."

My brow lowered as I turned slightly to face her, huffing a breath through my nose that would've been smoke in my dragon form and choosing to ignore the tiny detail that she'd probably never *met* another dragon. "Selfish?" I growled. "How do you figure that?"

"If you cared about anyone but yourself, you wouldn't have just up and ghosted Selene. She didn't deserve that, and you know it. You were just too chicken-shit to face her yourself."

I felt my eyes flick to dragon for a minute at her insinuation. If there was one thing I was *not*, it was a coward. "I was letting her down easy. We were never a thing anyway."

"Sure," she snorted, rolling her eyes. "Keep telling yourself that."

My voice lowered as my irritation rose. I wasn't even sure why I was explaining myself to her. I didn't owe Dev anything. "Selene would've realized sooner or later that I'm no good for her. I was only saving her the trouble."

"You really are an idiot, then, if that's what you think."

I tossed my drink back before slamming the glass down on the table. "What the Hel is that supposed to mean?"

"You know what? No. You don't deserve my help."

"Oh, this is you *helping*, is it?"

She waved a hand like she was done speaking to me, and I gave Blaze a nod for another pour.

"Selene was good for you, I thought." The new voice came from my other side, and with a start I realized Orion had been sitting there. I really was out of it if I hadn't even noticed when he'd sat down.

Dev made a disgusted noise in the back of her throat, but whether that was at the comment itself or the angel who'd said it was unclear.

"She wouldn't take me back now, so it doesn't matter

anyway. You're all wasting your breath." Whatever these meddling fools thought, I knew I was right. Even if I wanted to go talk to Selene about any of this, she wouldn't want to talk to me, to see me. Selene knew her own worth, knew she deserved better than what I'd done by just walking away. That was part of what I was counting on. A fail-safe, in case I was ever weak enough to try to see her again.

"Right," Dev laughed, the sound sharp as an axe drop. "Because everything about you *screams* that you understand women." She sipped at her whiskey, her eyes practically rolling back into her head, and I heaved a sigh.

I was done with this shit. Grabbing my jacket, I slipped my arms back into the sleeves, then tossed a twenty onto the bartop.

They hadn't seen Selene crumple to the ground with a bullet hole in her side because I'd failed to protect her. They hadn't seen the way her eyes closed as pain pulled her from consciousness. They hadn't seen the way her back arched off the ground when I'd fucking *poisoned* her. Never had I felt so helpless, so broken. I couldn't —

"Ryker," Orion called from behind me and I paused with my hand on the door, the winter air just outside the bar cool on my face. My dragon didn't want to answer his call, though, clawing at me to shift, to take to the skies and distance myself from this pain. This town. These people.

"Just wait," Orion said, closing the distance between us and stepping up to my side. Something in me snapped, and I shoved hard on the door, sending it flying open and creaking on its hinges as I exited the bar.

"I'm done," I growled, sounding more dragon than human, and hopped down the stairs to the street.

"She's okay," Orion called, and I skidded to a halt, back ramrod straight. "In case no one has mentioned it in their guilt trip, Selene has been up and walking for the last few days. She'll make a full recovery."

I nodded, but said nothing, still staring out at the ocean waves in the distance.

"Don't be like me, Ryker," Orion said from closer behind me than before. His words caught me off-guard, and I turned a quizzical look at the mayor. His hands were stuffed into his pockets, wings tight behind him as he surveyed the town that was his pride and joy. "Don't put yourself so dead last that you never actually live life."

"I've lived over a thousand years, Orion. I've done enough living for several lifetimes."

Orion tilted his head, turning towards me. "Have you, though?"

My jaw worked, but I didn't answer him. What was I supposed to say to that?

Without my permission, my mind traveled back over the last five months. First, the Halloween party and the night after with Selene. She made me feel more alive than ever that night, as passionate and wrapped up in the moment as I was.

Then my injury. What I'd thought was just sexual chemistry between us grew to a begrudging respect, maybe even… friendship.

And then Colorado. The Jeep. The hunt. The way I couldn't seem to keep my hands off her in front of the wolf pack, my dragon demanding I make it known that she was *mine*.

The sight of her unconscious and bloody surfaced as it

had done so many times this week, and I shook my head to free myself from the image. My throat tightened, my chest ached, my eyes burned.

"I can't lose her again, Orion."

His hand rested on my shoulder, squeezing lightly and then dropping back to his side. "You're going to lose her forever if you don't go after her. Which is worse? Having her for only a short time, or not at all?"

I didn't have an answer for him, and he didn't wait for one before turning and heading back inside.

The cold ocean air bit at my skin, chilling even with the fire roiling in my veins. But neither the warmth of my dragon nor the freezing air compared to the way my heart raced in my chest, as if it were cracking in two.

Should I go after her?

Was I making a mistake?

Hel, would she even open the door for me? I'd left her, injured and alone. Abandoned her with strangers, and ran. After all she'd done and sacrificed for me, I'd repaid her in the *worst* way. Even if I wanted to go after her, just to see for myself that she was okay, I hadn't the slightest idea how to get her to speak to me again.

Laughter floated through the air from the bar, and I turned, looking through the window. Blaze stood behind the counter, pouring Orion another IPA while Dev reached across the bar, grabbing the whiskey by the neck and topping off her glass.

I stared at the familiar scene, indecision warring so intensely, I couldn't seem to make myself move.

What kind of life could I offer Selene? Would she travel with me when I was gone for months at a time on jobs all over the world? Unlikely, knowing how much she liked the comfort of her own space, her own things.

Would she want to leave everything and live here with me? Doubtful, knowing how hard she'd worked on her practice in Boston.

Would she want *me?*

But Orion, Blaze, and Dev didn't seem to think I should give up so easily. As much as I'd come to know Selene in the last few weeks, Dev had been one of her best friends her whole life, and Blaze was with Selene's roommate.

My hands clenched into fists at my side as I warred with myself, finally deciding what to do. I spun on my heel, ripped the door back open, and stomped back to the bar. After practically throwing myself onto the stool I'd abandoned, I pushed my empty glass across the counter towards Blaze, tapping the wood bartop for another, and sighed.

"Tell me how to fix this."

Dev's stool slowly rotated towards me, squeaking loudly as if to emphasize the moment. A slow smirk lifted the right side of her mouth, mirroring her raised brow. "Say please."

Chapter Forty-One

RYKER

"Flowers," Blaze said before I could take a sip of my vodka.

"Too cliche," Orion answered, shaking his head.

"*You're* cliche," Dev nearly growled, and my head snapped back and forth like I was watching a tennis match. "Depends on the female. For me, I'd much rather have jewelry, or maybe a new ceremonial knife. But for Selene? Yes. Flowers. Hibiscus flowers, to be exact."

I hadn't the slightest clue where I'd go about finding hibiscus flowers in February in Maine, but I'd track them down.

"What you need to do is make a grand gesture," Orion went on, and I turned to the male, confusion creasing my brow. In the hundred years I'd known the angel, had I *ever* seen him in a relationship?

Dev threw down her glass, turning to speak directly to Orion. I leaned back on my stool, avoiding her dagger eyes. "Did you take that straight from *The Notebook*?" Her eyes snapped to me, and I fought not to sit a little straighter. "All you need to do is give her a heart-felt apology, tell her what a lousy sack of shit you are, and grovel like I'm holding my newly gifted ceremonial knife to your balls, ready to castrate you. Because that's what I'll do if you don't fix this."

"Grovel." My eyes narrowed at her, but she only nodded and raised her eyebrows in a *That's what it will take* sort of way.

I was a *dragon*. Dragons didn't grovel for shit. Dragons took what we wanted and hoarded it in our lairs. We torched anyone and anything that stood in our way.

But Selene wasn't some *thing* to be coveted and locked away, even if she was a treasure. Maybe the most important one I'd ever sought. And if I couldn't just snatch her away, then I had to earn her. Deserve her.

Grovel.

Heaving a deep sigh, I took a long sip of my drink as Dev hummed a knowing sound by my side that sounded a little too much like, "You know I'm right."

When I'd finally had enough of Dev and Orion's conflicting advice, I walked home, the frigid breeze scraping my skin as it came in off the ocean. My house loomed before me, empty and lonely as I made for the black front door. Still wary of using my magic, I pressed in my passcode, listening as the lock turned over, then pushed it open. The stairwell to my left led upstairs, but my feet had a mind of their own, moving instead towards the frosted glass doors in front of me. Setting my hand on the screen, red lights flashed, then slid open, revealing my cars.

I'd sold the Lamborghini earlier this week, and an empty

space now sat open in the slips. But I didn't stop at the other cars, heading straight for my truck, and pulled open the door. Without a further thought, I pulled myself up into the driver's seat, flicked on the engine, and opened the garage door.

It was time for a drive.

Hours ticked by, headlights flashing in my vision as I drove in silence, the coastline to my left. No destination in mind, I let myself enjoy the feel of the steering wheel under my hands, the loud bass line pumping through the speakers drowning out any further thoughts.

Snowy pines gave way to towns as I drove, noticing the bright lights and haze of the city ahead. Rush hour traffic was over, but cars still flooded the highway as I entered Boston, heart beating wildly in my chest.

This plan was half-assed at best, as I didn't even know where specifically Selene lived in the city. So even if I wanted to find her, I couldn't. Maybe that was how it should be.

My phone vibrated on the center console, followed by the screen of my truck lighting up with a text message. It was from Orion, and contained only an address. A *Boston* address.

A slow smile spread over my face as I slapped my hand down on the steering wheel, and entered it into my GPS.

Chapter Forty-Two

SELENE

My stomach rumbled as I lay sprawled on the couch, Petra in the chair to my right. I had been home from Colorado for four days now, and I was finally feeling almost normal. As glad as I was to have Petra here, to have someone take care of *me* for once, I was growing tired of the way she watched me with sad eyes.

"Quit staring," I said, my tone harsher than I'd meant it to be, instantly flooded with regret. "Sorry."

"Don't be." Petra shrugged. "I *was* staring."

I chuckled, shutting my eyes as I rubbed at my temple. This last week since returning home had been hell. Even though I was in great physical shape and took excellent care of myself, I'd been shot with an iron bullet, then nearly overdosed on *ferrouscide*. Even magical healing wasn't enough to cure all that immediately.

Mo had left earlier that morning after taking care of my every need in a way I desperately needed, but never would have vocalized. Anger still roiled in my veins every time I thought of that stupid dragon and the way he'd ghosted me, but I used it to power me through each day. I refused to even *think* his name, even if my heart felt like it was splitting in two.

But I'd survived the death of my mother when I was eighteen. I'd survived college and medical school on my own. I'd survived grueling hours as I worked my way through internships, fellowships, and opening my own practice. I'd survive this heartbreak, too.

"I ordered us Chinese," Petra said as she checked her phone for the millionth time that day, texting Blaze probably. She was madly in love with him and they were starting a new life together. I couldn't blame her for it, and yet, a deep resentment, one I both hated and couldn't eradicate, sat heavy in my gut every time I thought about my happily coupled-up friends.

When would it be *my* turn?

Would it *ever* be my turn? Or was I destined to die alone?

A knock at the door had my eyes snapping open and up to the door as I shifted forward on the couch, dropping my feet down.

"Probably the food," Petra said, standing.

"I'll get it." I waved her off, tugging at the black oversized hoodie I kept torturing myself with by wearing daily. It hung almost down to my knees over my pink leggings, swimming on my small frame, but I couldn't seem to let go of it. Each day that passed it smelled a little less like him, and maybe that was for the best.

Of all of the injuries I'd suffered, the one to my heart hurt the worst.

Heavy footsteps sounded away from the front steps outside, but it wasn't unusual for deliveries to be left on our doorstep. I paused, pulling my hair up into a ponytail, before I unlocked the door and opened it.

I read the doormat at my feet, *Be Our Guest! But Leave by 9*, but there wasn't a bag of Chinese food waiting there. Confusion set in as my eyes roved the stoop for packages before I looked up, and the air sucked from my lungs as I took in the large man standing at the foot of my steps, holding a bouquet of bright red hibiscus flowers.

After several seconds of silence ticked by, I managed to find my voice. "What are you doing here?"

Ryker's head turned to the side, glancing down the street and I flicked my eyes to the side, following his gaze. A long row of brownstones lined the street, lights on overhead dotting the darkness. A chill breeze blew up the street, and I crossed my arms, hands lost in the sleeves as I huddled against the cold.

I clenched my teeth, hurt changing to anger at the fact that he showed up here, and *still* had nothing to say for himself.

Rather than say anything, I turned back to the house, stepped inside, and put my hand on the door.

"Flores, wait." His voice rumbled as he leapt up the steps two at a time, his tattooed hand shooting out, catching the door before it closed. "Just, please wait."

"For what, Ryker?" I seethed, because anger was better than tears. "*What* am I waiting for? For your guilt to assuage? For you to leave again and never say a word? None of this meant anything, right?"

Ryker's free hand rose, running across his short hair, growing back in blond once again now that his magic was back. His fingers flexed on his scalp when his head tipped forward, as if he could pull on the strands that used to hang there.

"It meant *everything,*" he growled, and my heart stuttered. "And I hate that you could dismiss everything that happened between us so easily."

"That *I* could dismiss it so easily? You're the one who —"

"— But I only have myself to blame for that," he cut in. "And I've never been more sorry."

Tears welled in my eyes, ones I'd held back for days once I realized he really wasn't coming.

"You left, Ryker."

His head dropped, chin resting on his chest as he sighed. "I know. And if I were you, I'd never forgive me. You deserve so much better than me."

I sniffed, wiping the tears that spilled down my cheek as I took in this immense, strong male crumbling at my feet.

"I just need you to wait," Ryker said, his voice sounding choked, but still he didn't look up at me, flowers hanging at his side. "Wait for me."

I shook my head, not understanding his meaning, but his head rose, hand dropping to his side before he tugged on his hoodie I was wearing, and pulled me towards him.

"Wait for me," he said again, his forehead dropping down to mine, eyes closed. "I've never been more sorry for anything in my life than I am that I left you. Never regretted anything as much as walking away from you when you needed me most. I *hate* myself for it, and I promise never to do it again. And now I'm here, standing at your door, begging you to wait for me." His fingers tightened on my hips as he drew in a breath. "Before you, I never even wanted to try something like this, something *more* than a one-night stand or a friends-with-benefits thing. I've lived a long time," his voice grew hoarser the more he spoke, the honesty seeming to tear out of him. "And it became easier, over the years, not to get too attached to anyone. When I saw you shot, bleeding out — I was terrified I was about to lose you too. And then I made it all worse by poisoning you, and I'll admit I ran away. I never wanted to be able to hurt you again.

"I'm still terrified, Selene. But for you — I'm going to learn how to do this. It won't be perfect, it won't happen right away, but I'll learn how to be the male you deserve. To be everything you need. But I've been on my own a long time, and I might need some help, and I'll definitely need your patience. Let me love you, Flores." His voice dropped to a whisper. "Fall for me, Selene."

Tears pooled in my eyes as I lifted my hands, still swimming in his sweatshirt, to his jaw. My voice was choked, clogged with emotions, as I said, "Look at me, Ryker."

His green eyes opened, landing on mine, searching my face, and the pieces of my broken heart began to mend with the depth of emotion I saw swimming there.

"I already have," I whispered, tears dripping down my cheeks as I let a smile spread across my face. "I already have fallen for you, Ryker."

A shuddered breath left him as he dropped the flowers on the stoop and shifted his hands on my hips, lifting me up into the air. Air whooshed out of me as I threw my arms around his neck, feet dangling above the ground, but I didn't have even a moment to recover as his lips slammed down on mine.

Fire singed through every nerve in my body in a delicious passion, heating me from within as he stepped into the house. I lifted my legs, wrapping them around his waist as he walked, closing the door behind us.

"Hey —" The sound of Blaze's voice snapped me back to the present as I pulled away from Ryker, glancing over my shoulder into the living room behind me.

Petra stood at the edge of the kitchen beyond, Blaze next to her as she tugged on his arm. "Sorry. We were just leaving."

"Yeah," Blaze said, a mischievous smile spreading across his face as he looked at Ryker and then me. "I can see why you said you needed immediate transport, Petey. Time to go."

With a wink, Blaze seized Petra's hand, and they flickered away.

Ryker barely even acknowledged they'd been there and were now gone, his focus completely on me, his lips ghosting down from my ear to the crook of my shoulder as he walked us further into the apartment.

"Are you fully healed?" came his voice near my ear, the sound rumbling through his chest and sending delicious shivers down my spine.

"I've been healed since I left Colorado. Just been resting up here."

"Good."

His lips found mine as he started up the stairs, still carrying me.

"My room is —"

"Yeah, I know which one is your room. I can scent you a mile away, Flores."

I swatted his chest, not totally sure that was a compliment, as together we banged open the door to my room. Setting me down on the bed — he was still being gentle with me, despite the fact I'd said I was healed — I felt something underneath me on the bed and paused.

"What the —"

Pulling out a small magenta stuffed bear, I laughed as Ryker grumbled under his breath. I inspected the tag and read out the name of the Beanie Baby. "Valentina. Blaze's idea of playing Cupid, I guess?"

"Blaze's idea of a death wish, more like."

"You know," I played with the bear's ears as Ryker crawled up over the bed, looming over me and forcing me to lie back. "Now that we're *together*, you should probably tell me what the deal is with all the Beanie Babies."

He pulled away enough to meet my eyes, his own flicking to dragon for a moment as he considered me.

"If I tell you that, you'd practically be bonded to me for life, Flores. There are two souls in this world who know my deepest secret, and they guard it with their lives. Are you sure you want to become the third?"

The way he asked it, I knew this was about much more than this secret, whatever it was. He was making a point. He was asking, in a roundabout way, if I was sure about *us*. About giving him another chance, forgiving him, and moving forward.

A smile tilted up the corner of my lips as I tossed the Beanie Baby to the side and pressed a hand to his chest instead.

"Call it doctor-patient confidentiality. Your secret's safe with me."

THE END

There's more to come in our little paranormal universe! Join Aimee's newsletter at aimeevancebooks.com to be the first to know!

Deadlights Cove

Smoke Show

Deja Brew

A Very Merry Christmoose (Novella)

Wing and a Miss

Pier Pressure

Karma is a Witch

Foxing Day (Novella)

Timber Creek

Wild Wild Wolf

Love Bites

ALSO BY AIMEE VANCE

Mayhem Hockey Club

Moms of Mayhem

Call of the Norns: A Viking Time Travel Fantasy Trilogy

Fates Illuminated

Fates Promised

Fates Defied

Acknowledgments

When we started writing *Smoke Show*, the idea was to create a chaotic supernatural town where everyone could fit in. Along the way, we have truly fallen in love with this world and these characters.

To everyone who has ever picked up one of our books, thank you for reading and diving into this universe we've made. It's been so fun to share it with you! We have so many more stories to tell, and we hope you'll stick around!

To our DC Team — Amy, Brit, and Elle: thank you for being our most eager readers, catching our typos, and offering feedback. We're lucky to have you by our side!

From B: To J, thank you for finding consistency errors and your encouragement and support of our imaginary world.

From Aimee: To Chris and the girls, your excitement and support makes all of this hard work worth it. I love you!

About B. Perkins

B. Perkins has been making up stories about magic since she learned how to write words on paper. When not immersed in fictional worlds, she enjoys spending time in nature with her boyfriend and two dogs. (The cat is never invited, because it would be terrified). She has several degrees in various things, and if all they're good for is to provide background in creating fantasy worlds and systems, then maybe they were worth it.

Smoke Show is her debut novel and the first in the series, Deadlights Cove.

About Aimee Vance

Fueled by peach tea and chaos, Aimee Vance writes heartwarming and laugh-out-loud romance stories. She holds a B.S. in Public Relations from Texas Christian University and has always been an avid fantasy reader.

Residing in Texas with her husband, two young daughters, and Labrador Retriever, Aimee loves to transport readers to worlds hidden between the pages where magic and love intertwine. She prefers sassy heroines, grumpy heroes, and enough humor to keep you chuckling with every page.

facebook.com/aimeevancebooks

instagram.com/aimeevancebooks

goodreads.com/aimeevancebooks

amazon.com/author/aimeevancebooks

bookbub.com/authors/aimee-vance